*the
further
adventures of*

SHERLOCK HOLMES

THE TITANIC TRAGEDY

AVAILABLE NOW FROM TITAN BOOKS
THE FURTHER ADVENTURES OF SHERLOCK HOLMES SERIES:

THE ECTOPLASMIC MAN
Daniel Stashower

THE WAR OF THE WORLDS
Manley Wade Wellman & Wade Wellman

THE SCROLL OF THE DEAD
David Stuart Davies

THE STALWART COMPANIONS
H. Paul Jeffers

THE VEILED DETECTIVE
David Stuart Davies

THE MAN FROM HELL
Barrie Roberts

SÉANCE FOR A VAMPIRE
Fred Saberhagen

THE SEVENTH BULLET
Daniel D. Victor

THE WHITECHAPEL HORRORS
Edward B. Hanna

DR. JEKYLL AND MR. HOLMES
Loren D. Estleman

THE GIANT RAT OF SUMATRA
Richard L. Boyer

THE ANGEL OF THE OPERA
Sam Siciliano

THE PEERLESS PEER
Philip José Farmer

THE STAR OF INDIA
Carole Buggé

THE WEB WEAVER
Sam Siciliano

the further adventures of

SHERLOCK HOLMES

THE TITANIC TRAGEDY

WILLIAM SEIL

TITAN BOOKS

THE FURTHER ADVENTURES OF SHERLOCK HOLMES
THE TITANIC TRAGEDY
Print edition ISBN: 9780857687104
E-book edition ISBN: 9780857687128

Published by
Titan Books
A division of Titan Publishing Group Ltd
144 Southwark St
London
SE1 0UP

First edition: March 2012
10 9 8 7 6 5 4 3 2 1

Names, places and incidents are either products of the author's
imagination or used fictitiously. Any resemblance to actual persons, living
or dead (except for dramatic purposes), is entirely coincidental.

Visit our website: **www.titanbooks.com**

What did you think of this book? We love to hear from our
readers. Please email us at: readerfeedback@titanemail.com,
or write to Reader Feedback at the above address. To receive
advance information, news, competitions, and exclusive offers
online, please sign up for the Titan newsletter on our website:
www.titanbooks.com

A CIP catalogue record for this title is available from the British Library.

Printed in the USA.

This book is dedicated to my mother
Marguerite Seil

and the memory of my father
Emery Seil

Chapter One

THE EVENING OF TUESDAY 9 APRIL 1912

In the spring of 1912, at the age of sixty, I was leading a solitary life in rooms in Piccadilly. While continuing to see a few regular patients, I had, for the most part, ended my medical practice. My working time was now devoted almost entirely to writing historical novels. This turn in my writing career had come as quite a surprise – and I must say, disappointment – to my publisher, who would have preferred that I did nothing but record past adventures of my friend, Mr Sherlock Holmes. As a favour to him, and many loyal readers, I occasionally sifted through old notes on Holmes's cases and produced a new manuscript. But I also was respectful of Holmes's desire for solitude and anonymity.

Holmes had long since retired from his illustrious career as a detective and was now living on a smallholding on the South Downs. He rarely came to the city, but several times a year I would travel to his country retreat and inform him of whatever news I had heard about recent criminal investigations. I often called at Scotland Yard to see young Inspector Wiggins, who provided me with detailed accounts of current cases. There were times too when Wiggins, baffled by a particularly complex case, would travel to Sussex to consult his old mentor.

My visits to Holmes seldom involved talking over old times. He had little patience with nostalgia. Whenever my conversation wandered to decades-old memories of past cases, he would rise from his chair and draw me over to one of the many scientific projects that were in progress in and around his home. I was always reluctant to visit the beehives he kept in his orchard, even when I was fully covered by protective clothing. But I was fascinated by his promising work in the scientific analysis of crime evidence. I recall one day in particular when we travelled to a local inn to purchase drinking mugs – that is, unwashed drinking mugs, taken right off the bar. After giving the landlord a generous payment, Holmes gathered up the mugs with a gloved hand and packed them into a box. At home, he applied various dry chemical mixtures to the glass, hoping to develop a method of bringing out detail in smudged fingerprints.

I thought about Holmes as I sat at my dining room table late one night, researching the early battles of the Boer War. Outside, the wind howled and heavy rains rattled against the windows. I had just put another log on the fire, and it was engulfed in crackling flames. I welcomed these sounds. My rooms had been much too quiet since the death of my wife six months earlier. I thought back to other stormy nights at Baker Street, when there would be a knock on the door, and a rain-soaked stranger, speaking to us in frightened, confused or demanding tones, would ask our help in solving a problem. But those days were gone, like all the history that lined my bookshelves.

As my mind wandered, I decided that it was time to abandon my research for the evening. Leaving my books on the table, I walked to the window and looked at the street below. In the glow of the street lamps, I watched as the rain poured on to the cobbled street and rushed along the gutters. Except for the fury of Mother Nature, the streets were quiet. The only sign of life was a small pack of neighbourhood dogs conducting their nightly prowl of the area. I was about to leave the window and retire to my bedroom when I noticed the flash of headlamps approaching up the street. A large, black motorcar came to a stop directly in front of my rooms. The headlamps blinked off and, for several minutes, it appeared that no one was going to leave the car. But then a man stepped out of the driver's seat and rushed to the back to open the door for a passenger. The man in the back seat, wearing a dark hat and raincoat, climbed out of the car and immediately looked up to the window where I was standing. We watched each other for a few moments, before he lowered his head and walked in the direction of my door.

I heard his knock, just as I reached the foot of the stairs. I tightened the collar of my dressing gown round my neck, slid back the bolt and opened the door. The gust of cold, wet wind penetrated my body, and I began to shiver. But the stranger stood calmly, as though this were a casual visit on a sunny afternoon.

'Doctor Watson?'

'Yes.'

'My name is Sidney Reilly. May I come in?'

'It's very late. Unless this is a medical emergency, I must ask you to come back in the morning.'

'Doctor,' he said with a half-smile. 'I have an important message for you from Mr Sherlock Holmes. And by tomorrow morning, I suspect you'll be on a ship bound for America.'

I froze for a moment, not knowing whether I should believe this extraordinary statement. But then, the appearance of this stranger at night was worthy of Holmes's sense of drama. Ten years earlier in Baker Street, I would not have been so fearful of admitting a mysterious late-night caller. But then, ten years ago I would probably have remembered to slip my service revolver into my dressing gown before opening the door.

I pulled the door back and asked Reilly to follow me upstairs. As we entered the drawing room, I took his rain-soaked hat and coat. Reilly was a dark, trim man in his late thirties. When he spoke he had a trace of an accent, or mixture of accents. He had calm, piercing eyes that seemed to gaze over every feature of the room as he walked towards the fire.

'Doctor, I have been told that you are aware of the high position Mr Holmes's brother, Mycroft, holds in our intelligence service. I too work for the government, and when Mycroft Holmes picks you up in the morning to take you to the railway station, he will verify that. He would have accompanied me this evening, only he had to make some last-minute arrangements for his brother.'

'Forgive me if I am sceptical, Mr Reilly. But let us assume for the moment that what you are saying is true. Why would you expect me to be boarding a ship for America in the morning? Is this something Holmes wishes me to do?'

Reilly reached into his pocket and handed me a small envelope. It was addressed to me in Holmes's handwriting. 'I haven't read it, but I believe that note will answer at least some of your questions,' he said.

I tore open the envelope and read the note, which had been dated that same day:

My dear Watson,
I realize that this request comes at a particularly sad time for you, but once again, I am in need of your help. In the morning I will board a ship for America, and will not be seeing you again for some time. The government has asked me to conduct a secret investigation and, after some encouragement from persistent senior officials, I have accepted. I

would appreciate it if you could find your way clear to join me on this voyage. My investigation does not begin until I reach America, so the voyage will be relaxing and uneventful. The trip would do you good and I would greatly enjoy seeing you at the start of this adventure. However, after we reach New York, I fear that my mission will lead to our separation, so come at once if convenient—if inconvenient, come all the same. Mr Reilly will provide you with a ticket.

Very sincerely yours,
Sherlock Holmes.

'I am convinced, Mr Reilly. I will have my cases packed and be ready to travel in the morning.'

'Very good, Doctor. That concludes our business. You understand, of course, that everything you see and hear – including our meeting tonight – must be treated in the strictest of confidence. Your friend, Mr Holmes, is undertaking a mission that could prove to be a turning point in the nation's security.'

'During my long association with Holmes and his clients, I have never betrayed a confidence. You can rely on me, completely. Now, can you tell me with what I am getting involved?'

'I regret that I am unable to oblige. Mr Holmes will tell you as much as he can, once you get on board the ship. But I can tell you that your friend is a hard man to bring out of retirement. I'm sure you're familiar with Winston Churchill, the First Lord of the Admiralty. Well, he and I first visited Holmes's retreat about a week ago to ask for his help. He listened to us, but wasted no time in turning us down. It was only after we made a return visit with the Prime Minister and Foreign Minister that he agreed to carry out the investigation.'

I chuckled. Retirement had done little to change Holmes. He remained as independent as ever. Even as Holmes approached his sixties, he could not resist a challenge to his remarkable talents.

Reilly began strolling around the room, first examining the mantelpiece, then the bookshelves. After perusing everything with a quick sweep of his eyes, he turned to me with a look of disappointment.

'Forgive me, Doctor,' he said. 'I've read every article you've written about your adventures with Mr Holmes. I was expecting to see a few keepsakes from 221B Baker Street... Maybe some of Holmes's scrapbooks, or a Persian slipper full of tobacco hanging from the fireplace. But there's nothing here, and I saw very few mementoes at Mr Holmes's country estate. If you will forgive my curiosity, what happened to it all?'

I took Reilly by surprise with a hearty laugh. 'Do you believe in time travel, Mr Reilly?' I motioned to a closed door next to the sideboard. 'If you'll step through that doorway with me, I will take you on a journey into the past that would make H G Wells envious.'

I struck a match on the mantelpiece and opened the door. Light from the electric lamp over my dining table stretched across the fading twenty-year-old carpet in the adjoining room. 'This is the one room in the house where I don't allow electric lights.' The first match had burned to my fingertips, so I struck a second one and lit two oil lamps that were fixed to the walls.

'Mr Reilly, welcome to 221B Baker Street. If you look around, I'm sure that you'll find more than enough mementoes to satisfy your curiosity.'

Until now Reilly had been emotionless to a fault. But suddenly, upon seeing this room, his eyes lit up and he began a whirlwind examination of its furnishings. 'This is wonderful, Doctor. I can't believe it. It's just as you described your Baker Street rooms in the articles.'

'Well, I confess that I never expected to become a museum curator; nor that my past life would end up as an historical display. But when Holmes moved out of 221B, I just couldn't accept seeing all those memories of happier times being scattered about. So Holmes generously gave everything to me, and bought new furnishings for his country home. Of course, there were a few pieces that he could not part with. For example, if you'll look over at that side table next to the settee, you'll see a violin. I had to purchase that at a second-hand shop. Holmes took his with him. But most of the furnishings are original.'

'Back there, in the corner, is that where Holmes conducted his experiments?'

'Yes, smelly old things they were, too. I used to welcome the aroma of Holmes's tobacco smoke, because it would cover up the smell of sulphur. Here, let me give you a tour.'

Reilly sat in Holmes's velvet armchair and, after asking permission, tried on the deerstalker cap that was hanging on the wall rack. He chuckled at the stack of letters that were fixed to the mantel with a jack-knife.

'Tell me, Doctor. The letters VR that are perforated in the wall. Did you reproduce them with a revolver, as Holmes did, or did you use a quieter, more conventional approach?'

'I used a hammer and a spike. I am not as precise a marks-man as Holmes, and the London police these days are less tolerant of the sound of gunshots than they used to be.'

'Mr Holmes was a remarkable man.'

'He still is. Just a little less active.'

Reilly froze for a moment, his eyes fixed on the floor. When he looked at me again, the cold, commanding gaze had returned to his eyes.

'Doctor, I am concerned about the safety of your friend, and the success of his mission. It is important that when you see Mr Holmes on the ship, you bring certain facts to his attention.'

'And what might those facts be, Mr Reilly?'

'Simply, Doctor, that times have changed. And so has the world in which Mr Holmes will be carrying out his mission. Mr Holmes has confronted opponents who were both cunning and dangerous. Still, most of them had certain standards by which they played the game. I don't quite know how to define it. You might call it a Victorian ethic...something in their upbringing that tempered their lawlessness. Doctor, believe me when I tell you, that that is not the case in modern espionage. Mr Holmes will be dealing with individuals who care nothing about human life. He will be in grave danger. And unless he is willing to become as cold and ruthless as his opponents, I suspect he will not survive.'

I did not know how to react to this extraordinary statement. At first, I was offended that this upstart should be so disrespectful of Holmes's experience and abilities. Still, there was something in his manner that told me that he knew his business, and he did not give idle warnings.

'Mr Reilly, I assure you that Mr Holmes is quite capable of taking care of himself. He may not be as young as he used to be, but his mind is as sharp as ever. And as for cunning opponents, if you've read my articles, you must be aware of his confrontation with the late Professor Moriarty. As you may recall, Holmes had laid a trap from which the professor knew he and his cohorts could not escape. When Holmes refused to back away, Moriarty on several occasions sent henchmen to kill him. Holmes and Moriarty had their final confrontation at Reichenbach Falls, where they struggled and Moriarty fell to his death. I could scarcely imagine a villain as dangerous as the professor.'

'As I recall, Doctor, at Reichenbach Falls – before the struggle – didn't Professor Moriarty allow Mr Holmes a few moments to write a note to you, explaining what was about to take place? I seem to recall from your work that you found such a note under Holmes's cigarette case when you returned to the Falls.'

'Yes, the professor waited whilst Holmes wrote a brief note. It was a simple courtesy and posed no added danger to the professor.'

'My point, Doctor, is that a professional agent would not have confronted Holmes face-to-face—let alone allow him the time to write a note. He would have killed Holmes quietly, at the first sign of trouble, with a knife in the back or a garrotte around the throat. That's the type of opponent Holmes will be facing. I'm alive and speaking to you today, only because I have been willing to play as rough as my opponents.'

'I remain as confident as ever in Holmes's abilities,' I said quietly. 'But I will do as you say and pass on that word of warning.'

'I hope so, Doctor. I hope so. I am a great admirer of Mr Holmes. I would hate to live with the memory that I had sent him on his final adventure.'

I handed Reilly his hat and coat as he stood at the top of the stairs, preparing to step back out into the pouring rain. Before buttoning his coat, he reached into an inside pocket and pulled out an envelope. 'Thank you again for the journey back in time, Doctor. Here's your ticket for tomorrow. I hope you enjoy the voyage, and please remember what I said.'

'I will, and thank you again, Mr Reilly.'

I walked down the stairs with Reilly and opened the front door for him. He stepped out to his motorcar, as the driver opened the door to the back seat.

After bolting the front door, I walked back upstairs and warmed myself by the fireplace. I took a clean butter-knife from the sideboard and opened the envelope Reilly had given me. I was pleased to see that it contained a first-class ticket, since I had long made a habit of treating myself to comfortable travel accommodation. Not only that, but the ship itself would make this a rare treat. I would be travelling on the maiden voyage of the biggest, most luxurious ship ever built. Its name was written on my ticket in proud, bold letters – RMS *Titanic*.

Chapter Two

 ❧

THE MORNING OF WEDNESDAY 10 APRIL 1912

M ycroft's motorcar pulled up at Waterloo Station well in advance of the *Titanic* Special Service's departure at a quarter to ten. I had packed a large suitcase in haste for the journey, hoping to purchase whatever else I might need on board the ship, or in New York. Mycroft was trimmer and more energetic than he had been when I last saw him, some three months earlier. It appeared that my lectures on his poor dietary and exercise habits had had their desired effect. He confided to me that members of the Diogenes Club, who had known him for decades, were astonished to find him taking morning walks.

'Have a good time, Watson,' said Mycroft, as we stood by the kerb, waiting for the driver to give my bag to the porter. 'And please suggest to my brother that he might find a holiday beneficial.'

A newspaper photographer stepped out of the crowd and pointed his camera in our direction. Mycroft immediately moved towards his car, turning his back on the enterprising photographer who, after a few moments, gave up and went in search of a less bashful subject.

'The departure of the *Titanic* appears to be quite a significant event,' Mycroft said. 'That's understandable, of course. When it was launched last year, more than 100,000 people came to watch. I had the opportunity to go on board for a short time during its sea trials. It is a beautiful ship – the biggest there is. Inside, it is like a city, carrying up to 3,300 passengers and crew, with every diversion for a sea voyage that one could wish for – squash courts, a swimming pool and even lifts to carry you from deck to deck.'

'I would expect to see Fleet Street represented at the departure of the ship itself, but why here at the boat train?'

'A fascination with the rich and famous, I suppose. This Special carries only first-class passengers. Second and third class took another train a couple of hours ago. You will be meeting a few celebrities, I have no doubt.'

'At the moment, I'm more interested in how I will locate Holmes on board that huge ship. Do you know his cabin number?'

'It is close to your own and he will find you. He has a talent for that kind of thing, you know. And remember, he'll be travelling under an assumed name. It would not be wise to tell others he is on board. Only you and the captain will be aware of his presence – and, of course, Miss Christine Norton.'

'Perhaps I'm getting a little confused in my old age, Mycroft. But why tell the captain that Sherlock Holmes is among the passengers? And who is Miss Norton?'

'Oh, have I not mentioned Miss Norton? She is a courier for the Ministry. Very young, but intelligent and resourceful. Her mission is to take some secret military papers to the United States and I have asked Sherlock to look after her. The captain has been alerted that the three of you are on a secret mission and was asked to provide you with any assistance you may require.'

I am and always have been an even-tempered man. But I do not like being deceived, especially by a friend. I paused for a moment to contain my anger, then replied to Mycroft's extraordinary statement in calm, but firm tones.

'Do you mean to say that I have been roped into some kind of spy mission? I understood that I was to go on a quiet ocean voyage with an old friend. Now, it appears, I'm in the middle of some sort of intrigue.'

'You do indeed appear to have changed, Watson. I remember you as a man with a sense of adventure.'

Mycroft's face broke into a broad smile, one that caused me to become even more annoyed by his deception. But I began to wonder at that point whether I had over-reacted. After all, the train was still at the station. There was still time to back out.

'It is merely an exchange of documents. I will admit, the papers in question are of a highly delicate nature. It would be critical if certain foreign powers obtained them. But no one knows they are on board. You might like to remind yourselves of them now and then in between games of squash and shuffle-board.'

'I will take your word for it, Mycroft. But I would have appreciated an earlier indication of the true nature of my task. Now, how will I recognize this lady of the name of Miss Norton?'

'You do not know her. But I believe you have met her mother.'

'You don't mean...! Is Holmes aware that he will be working with Mrs Irene Norton's daughter?'

'Not yet. For security reasons, he has not been told the lady's name; only that she will contact him in his cabin. You might like to tell him the rest after the ship departs. It should be a pleasant surprise for him. I don't believe that he has ever met the young woman.'

'Mycroft, I do believe you are becoming as deceitful as Professor Moriarty himself. But I do thank you for this opportunity to see Holmes before he begins his mission in the United States. Your Mr Reilly tells me there is some danger.'

Mycroft started, then peered into the distance as if lost in thought.

'It is a dangerous world, Watson. A very dangerous world. But my brother has encountered danger many times in the past. I am confident that he'll make it through this ordeal. Meanwhile, you have a train to catch. I will not detain you any longer. Tell Sherlock that I will dine with him at the Diogenes Club when he returns.'

We shook hands and I walked quickly into the station, which had a clean, modern look, following its recent renovation. The boat train was not difficult to locate. It was the centre of attention, surrounded by well-dressed passengers, with their friends and relatives who were seeing them off. Porters and servants were moving quickly to load the train. I hurried to my compartment in one of the chocolate-brown coaches.

It was a relaxing eighty-mile journey, passing through Surbiton, Woking, Basingstoke, Winchester and Eastleigh, on its way to the White Star berth at Southampton docks. Shortly after the train left Winchester, I decided to walk down to the dining car for some tea and biscuits. There was little of interest in the morning paper and, growing tired of my private compartment, I was in the mood for some conversation with other passengers – perhaps some of the 'rich and famous' Mycroft had mentioned. But as I entered the dining car, I found that all of the tables were occupied. This turned out to be a blessing, in disguise. An uncommonly attractive young woman – perhaps thirty years old – was sitting alone. I approached her and asked if I might join her. She readily acquiesced.

'Thank you. I was afraid, for a moment, that I would have to order tea in my compartment. This is much more pleasant. My name is Watson, Doctor John Watson.'

She stared at me for a moment and then asked tentatively, 'Might I inquire if you are the Doctor Watson who wrote about Sherlock Holmes?'

I confessed that I was.

'This is indeed fortuitous. I read one of your adventures in an old *Strand Magazine* only a few weeks ago. My name is Miss Holly Storm-Fleming.'

There was something about the lady's appearance and manner that was almost contradictory. This was clearly a lady of taste and breeding. She wore a silken, light blue dress with white lace trimming. When she spoke, her voice was clear and expressive, with a slight American accent. Her light brown hair was perfectly in place, falling softly about her shoulders. Yet, she was not at all reserved. Miss Storm-Fleming possessed an unrestrained vitality that brightened her every word and move.

'It is my pleasure, Miss Storm-Fleming – or should I say Mrs?'

'My husband passed away two years ago. Fortunately, his estate was large enough to enable me to live comfortably and go back to the United States whenever I like...'

'Are you from America?'

'Yes, I was born and raised in Chicago. I moved to New York when I was twenty-one. That is where I met my husband, Gerald. He was there as part of a British trade delegation, and I had a small part in a Broadway production. The members of the delegation attended one of our performances and afterwards they were invited to a reception to meet the cast. We started talking and, the first thing I knew, I was heading back to London with him.'

'And now you're returning to New York. Do you go there to visit friends, or is this just an opportunity to travel on the *Titanic*?'

'Oh, a little of both, I suppose. I still have good friends in the theatre, and I will be getting together with them. But on this occasion, I have to confess, the *Titanic* was a big part of it. And how about you, Doctor? Why are you taking this voyage?'

'I find that I am getting on in years and I discovered that – although I've travelled extensively on several continents – I have never been to

America. This seemed like an excellent opportunity.'

'Will Mr Holmes be on board? I'd love to meet him.'

I was not in the habit of lying. I especially did not want to be dishonest with someone as kind and charming as Miss Storm-Fleming. But national security and Holmes's own safety were at stake. It was indeed important that I was discreet.

'Unfortunately Holmes will not be travelling with us. He is retired now, but still very involved in several research projects. I am afraid he has little interest in being idle on board a ship.'

The remainder of the journey passed by quickly. It was not long before the train arrived at Southampton and we were approaching the docks. We arrived at half past eleven, precisely on time. The boat train wound its way along the water-front before slowly turning on to a side track flanking the White Star dock at Berth 44.

Miss Storm-Fleming and I parted company in the dining car, so that we could return to our respective compartments to gather up our belongings.

'I look forward to meeting you again on board ship, Miss Storm-Fleming. Allow me to ask you to join me for dinner one evening.'

'I will be looking forward to it, Doctor... Imagine, meeting the famous Doctor Watson. This voyage will be more exciting than I expected.'

Chapter Three

ᘒ

NOON ON WEDNESDAY 10 APRIL 1912

The *Titanic* was indeed a magnificent sight. It was, of course, a huge ship. But beyond its size, it had a grace and stature reminiscent of the stately wooden sailing vessels that had excited me so in my youth. But with modern engineering, crossing the Atlantic was no longer a hardship. It was more like spending a week in a fine hotel.

The ship's superstructure shone in the midday sun. The thin gold line at the hull's upper edge clearly and proudly identified the new vessel as part of the White Star Line. The *Titanic*'s four huge funnels towered against the blue sky. The air was crisp, and there was a smell of burning coal in the air. As I moved with the crowd, the excitement of the approaching journey began to affect me.

Before stepping onto the gangway, I moved to the side and examined my ticket. My cabin was on C Deck, on the port side. I was eager to see the *Titanic*'s accommodation. The advertisements I had read had promised unparalleled luxury.

When I reached the deck, one of the stewards also examined my ticket and led me across the wooden decks through a doorway to the interior of the ship. The steward, an efficient young man with little time to spare, marched quickly through the corridors until we came to the door marked C28.

I was most favourably impressed by my quarters. They were small, but much more homelike than other ships' cabins I had seen. There was a large green sofa, a wardrobe and a dressing table. I was especially pleased to see the comfortable-looking bed, rather than a fixed berth.

'The gent's lavatory is down the hall and to the right,' said the steward, pointing aft of the ship.

'I understood that there were private baths on this deck.'

'There are, sir. One cabin in three has one. The cabins are arranged in groups of three that can be let together, or separately. There are connecting doors, but do not be concerned. They are all locked here in this section.'

'And since my cabin opens to the main corridor, I won't have a view of the water. I was hoping to have a window.'

'Oh no, sir. All first-class cabins have a view. Over there in the corner there's a little passage to your porthole.'

'Very good. And my bag?'

'It will be up soon, sir. If you need any assistance in the future, just press the button and someone will be along to help.'

'Thank you, young man. Any suggestions on what I should see first?'

'There's much to see and do throughout the first class, sir. Just two things to look out for. Stay away from the professional gamblers, and know where the doctors are, in case you get seasick. Beyond that, this is a luxury ship, sir, and we hope you enjoy your voyage.'

The steward accepted my tip with a quick salute and rushed back to the gangway to assist other passengers.

The ship was due to depart at noon, just minutes away. I left my cabin to witness this colourful event and to attempt to locate Holmes. I walked down the hallway and, instead of climbing the stairs to B Deck, decided to make use of the ship's most modern convenience. One of the three lifts was already open, so I stepped inside the dark mahogany cage, which was occupied by several passengers and crew. Overhead, the large winding gear that moved the cage up and down was visible through a glass ceiling.

'Most impressive,' I told the lift operator, as he looked outside to check for other passengers.

'Yes, sir, quite a new idea for liners.'

As he began to close the collapsible gate, I noticed a tall man in a naval uniform running towards us. I put out my hand to hold the gate back to let him in.

'Thank you, friend,' said the navy man, who seemed to smile and eye me suspiciously at the same time. He had an easy air of authority, which was suggested, perhaps, by his brisk Scottish accent. His hair, including his well-trimmed beard, was fully grey. As the lift ascended, he glanced at each of the passengers over the rim of his glasses. All seemed eager to leave as the gate opened on B Deck.

I climbed the stairs to the boat deck and saw that the rail was already lined with passengers, waving to friends and family on the dock below. Suddenly, the air vibrated from the booming sound of the ship's huge whistles. The crowd on deck cried out with excitement and waved final farewells to their relatives and friends. The *Titanic* was preparing to depart.

'It's just about time,' said a raspy voice to my left. 'I see that they have singled up and we'll be leaving in a minute or two.'

I turned and saw the naval officer standing next to me. His hands were folded behind him, with his head tilted back. Ignoring the crowd, he focused his attention on the layout of the ship and the crew's preparations for departure.

'It's a very exciting moment, is it not?' I replied. 'That is...being on this grand ship as it begins its first voyage.'

'Oh, I've headed out on more ships than I care to remember – Navy ships mostly. If you take away the fanfare and hoopla, one trip's pretty much the same as the next.'

'You've been at sea for a long time, then.'

'All my life. Been on just about every type of ship – some in battle. I believe I know the sea as well as the next man.'

'By the way, my name is Watson. Doctor John Watson. And you are...?'

'Commodore Giles Winter of the Royal Navy. Pleased to meet you, Doctor.'

'I cannot understand, for the life of me, why a Navy man would want to spend his holiday on a cruise. Or is this perhaps a business trip?'

'Business. Just doing a routine evaluation of the vessel. I did the same thing on board the *Titanic*'s sister ship, *Olympic*. White Star has a third ship planned of the same design. In the event of war, we like to know the capabilities of all ships that are available. This ship, for example, could be useful as a troop carrier or hospital ship.'

'That makes sense. But I must say, I'd just as soon not think of prospects like that on a day like this.'

'And that, Doctor, is precisely my remit – to ensure that civilians like you can go about your lives without worrying about war.'

'I assure you, Commodore, I have seen battle. In fact, while serving as an army surgeon in Afghanistan, I was seriously wounded at the Battle of Maiwand.'

'Afghanistan, yes, that was a bad one, all right. But land wars just do not compare to sea battles, if you will forgive me saying so. There is nothing worse than having a ship sink under you. Your only hope is that your enemy will be generous enough to pull you out of the water.'

'You know, you are as stubborn as a friend of mine. You may have heard of him, a detective of the name of Mr Sherlock Holmes.'

'Holmes... So, you're *that* Doctor Watson. I have read a few of those stories. He must be an extraordinary fellow, that Mr Holmes.'

'Oh, I suppose so. But I have to confess, I exaggerated his talents a little, to create a better story, you understand.'

The commodore paused for a moment, considering this revelation. 'Are you saying this Holmes was not the great detective you made him out to be?'

'Oh, I'd say he was certainly a great detective but he had some flaws. For example, at times he was prone to exhibit over-confidence. And you know how I referred to him as a master of disguise? Well, he was not always in top form.'

'What do you mean?' he asked, narrowing his eyes to a cold stare.

'Take that disguise you are wearing now. Did you really think that a beard, some hair dye and a disguised voice would fool an old friend?'

The commodore's features remained the same. But there was something familiar in his laugh that confirmed that I was once again in the company of my friend, Mr Sherlock Holmes.

At that moment, the ship's whistles, mounted on the two forward funnels, sounded the three traditional salutes of departure. The crowd cheered in excitement as the engines grew louder and steam billowed into the air. Our journey had begun.

'My dear Watson! And for just how long did I manage to deceive you?'

'Certainly in the lift. But it did not take long for me to doubt the naval officer after we started chatting on deck.'

'It is a simple disguise, I grant you. But I do believe that no one on board has met me before. It should be good enough. And thank you for coming, Watson. Did Mycroft explain our little mission?'

'In general terms,' I said, wondering how I was going to break the news of Mrs Norton's daughter. 'He said we were to look after a young woman on board who is carrying some secret government documents.'

'Indeed. She will be contacting me in my cabin after departure. In fact, we should go there now and await her arrival.'

Holmes had been given cabin C30, which was in the same block of rooms as my own. There was a connecting door that opened to the porthole passage in my cabin. I was not surprised to find that the furnishings in our two cabins were similar.

'Holmes, I fear I have a question to ask of you: how long has it been since you have heard from Irene Norton?'

The question startled Holmes, but he answered without hesitation.

'As you know, Watson, we have been corresponding for some time. The last letter I received was about six months ago. But why do you ask that?'

My readers may recall Holmes's relationship with Irene Adler from the adventure I called *A Scandal in Bohemia*. Holmes had long admired her as the one woman who had ever bettered him in a case. Several years after she married Godfrey Norton and left London, Holmes received a letter from her. It said how much she had enjoyed their little contest and hoped that there were no ill feelings. Holmes replied with a short note, assuring her that he too had found their adventure an interesting challenge, and wished her well. After a time, they began a regular, though not frequent correspondence.

'Well, during my brief conversation with Mycroft before boarding the ship, he told me the name of the agent we will be expecting. The agent is Irene Norton's daughter, Christine.'

Holmes stared at me for a moment, then responded in casual tones. 'That is a surprise. I would have thought she is too young for field work. She is in her early twenties, I believe. Well, her mother has a first-rate

27

mind. If she inherited that, she will serve Mycroft and His Majesty's government very well.'

It was another quarter of an hour before we heard a knock on the door, and Holmes admitted Miss Christine Norton. She was an attractive young woman, dressed very properly in a brown dress and hat. On seeing Holmes, her eyes widened, as if meeting a member of the royal family on the streets of London.

'Mr... Commodore Winter. We have never met, but...'

'Won't you come in, Miss Norton. You have your mother's eyes and ears. Ears are generally quite distinctive among individuals, and often a family trait.' He motioned for her to enter, and closed the door behind her.

'Yes, you're certainly Mr Holmes,' she said, smiling and appearing more relaxed. 'You are just as Mother described you...beneath that disguise, that is. And, of course, I feel I know you from reading Doctor Watson's adventures.'

'Allow me to introduce you to the author himself. Miss Norton, this is Doctor John Watson.'

'Miss Norton, I am very pleased to meet you. Will you not sit down? I'll call the steward and order something cold to drink. Will lemonade be suitable?'

'Yes, yes, Watson,' Holmes interrupted. 'Lemonade will be just fine. Tell me, Miss Norton, what are the particulars of this little assignment my brother Mycroft has given you? He is a very secretive fellow and, I'm afraid, he has told me very little.'

'Of course. But before I begin, I must remind both you and Doctor Watson that what you are about to hear is a matter of the highest national importance. I am providing you with full details of the mission, only because your brother knows your methods, and understands that you will only accept cases in which you are in full possession of the facts.'

'Neither Doctor Watson nor I would repeat a word of this, Miss Norton. Please proceed.'

'You are no doubt aware of the growing tensions that exist between His Majesty's government and Germany.'

'They would be difficult to ignore,' I said. 'Stories of German spies and infiltrators have been in all the newspapers recently.'

'Those stories may be exciting to the public, but not altogether accurate. Nevertheless, they do tend to contribute to already strained relations between our two countries. The threat of war is very real.'

As Miss Norton spoke, I sensed a change in the ship's motion and heard some shouting through the porthole. I was tempted to remark on this extraordinary event, but Holmes, after glancing about for just a moment, continued to question Miss Norton.

'We are familiar with international affairs, Miss Norton,' Holmes said, leaning forward in his chair. 'Please tell us about the documents you are taking to America.'

'Yes, of course. The plans are for a new, prototype submarine called the *Nautilus*. As I am sure you know, our Navy is the best in the world. But there are some in the Admiralty who fear that we are falling behind in submarine engineering and building. There are fears that German advances in submarines could one day pose a serious threat to our fleet. Our submarines tend to be small vessels designed to protect the coast. The *Nautilus* would be 240 feet long, double-hulled and have a range of around 5,000 nautical miles. The future of large submarines in the British Navy may very well depend on this venture.'

'I see. But you have not yet explained why you are carrying the plans to the United States. Are the Americans involved in the development of this vessel?'

'Indirectly. The plans are nearly complete, but our engineers are having some difficulties with the engine design. We have to adapt certain German engineering methods, and we are hoping the Americans can offer some fresh ideas.'

Holmes smiled, then rubbed his eyes with the thumb and forefinger of his right hand. 'Miss Norton, please explain why German design appears in British submarine plans. I suspect that there is something you are not telling us.'

'You're asking very difficult questions, Mr Holmes. I must decline to answer further.'

'My dear Miss Norton, my brother told you to provide me with all the facts in this case. I cannot possibly protect these plans unless I am fully conversant with all details, and any potential threat to their safety.'

'Very well. We have, for some time, had an agent in Russia who is providing us with German ship designs. You see, the Russians have begun to build a vast number of ships to replace vessels lost during the Russian–Japanese war. Germany has arrangements to build many of those vessels. Our man in St Petersburg has infiltrated the Russian ship-building industry at a very high level. This has given him the opportunity to request German designs, and pass them to us. Some of the ideas used in the *Nautilus* have come to us from this agent.

'Yes, I thought I detected a trace of a Russian accent during my discussions with Mr Reilly,' said Holmes, tapping his fingers together, then turning to glance at me.

Miss Norton's eyes widened for a moment. Then, with a sigh, she settled back in her chair and offered a word of caution.

'This agent, who is one of our best, would be in great danger if his identity were ever revealed.'

'Whoever he is, his secret is safe with Doctor Watson and me. Now then, Miss Norton, do you have any reason to believe that any foreign power or potential adversary is aware of these plans, or the fact that you are carrying secret documents on this ship?'

'None at all, Mr Holmes. But plans that have existed as long as those of the *Nautilus* are difficult to keep secret. And while I am fairly new to the secret service, it is always possible that someone could be tracking my whereabouts. We must remain cautious.'

'I agree,' said Holmes. 'And if I am not mistaken, that knock at the door is the steward bringing our lemonade.'

I opened the door and a steward walked in, holding a jug and glasses on a serving tray. He was an older, more relaxed man than the one who had shown me to my cabin.

'The ship seems to have come to a stop, steward. Is there any trouble?'

'Looks like you missed all the excitement, sir,' the steward said, as he arranged the glasses on a table. 'As we moved out, another liner that was docked nearby, the *New York*, started bobbing up and down. The *Titanic* must have quite a wake. Anyway, the *New York* broke free of its moorings, swung out and almost hit us. But the captain ordered full astern and a tugboat got a line on the other ship. Everything is quite in order now, but we will be delayed for a while.'

After the steward left, Holmes handed glasses to Miss Norton and me, then held his own glass high. 'My friends, here's to a pleasant, successful voyage.'

The cabin was warm, and I drank half my drink in one swallow.

'And now, Watson, Miss Norton, I suggest that we take our glasses on deck to see what all the commotion is about. This may be the last excitement we see on this trip.'

As we walked to the stairway, Miss Norton stopped suddenly and turned to Holmes. 'The plans,' she said, containing her excitement in a whisper. 'Someone could have used all the activity on deck as a diversion to break into my cabin.'

Holmes put his hand on her shoulder before she had a chance to hurry back through the hallway.

'Steady, Miss Norton,' he said with a reassuring smile. 'Let us all walk back slowly, as though you were returning to fetch your shawl. We do not want to attract the attention of any of our fellow passengers. And besides, I doubt that the mishap with the *New York* was planned or foreseen by any foreign agents who may be on board.'

Miss Norton took her cabin key from her bag and heeded Holmes's advice. She walked calmly to cabin C26, directly opposite Holmes's quarters, and opened the door. Her movements had been most casual. But once inside, she quickly placed a chair beside the porthole and climbed on top of it. With her keys, she prised away a small section of wooden moulding. Behind it was a keyhole, into which she placed a charm from her bracelet. This allowed her to swing back a metal door, revealing the interior of a small, shallow safe. A folded packet of papers came tumbling out.

'Captain Smith arranged this personally before the voyage,' Miss Norton noted, after stepping down to retrieve the plans. 'My superiors thought it would be less obvious, and more secure, than storing them in the ship's safe.'

'Let us hope they are correct,' said Holmes, who was now standing on top of the chair, inspecting the safe's hinges and lock. 'Incidentally, Miss Norton, I am sure you know the story of how I once tricked your mother into revealing the location of a photograph, just by creating the illusion that the building was on fire. Your mother ran directly to the photograph and pinpointed its location for me.'

'As you may recall, Mrs Norton recovered very nicely from that mistake,' I said with a chuckle. 'She turned the tables in the end.'

'She certainly did,' Holmes said, suddenly lost in distant memories. 'But the point I want to make is that the plans will only be safe if we remain cautious of our moves at all times. Do we understand each other, Miss Norton?'

'Fully, Mr Holmes.'

'Good. Now, this door over here – where does it lead?'

'It communicates with the next cabin. It is occupied by a rich dowager, Mrs Applegate, who travels frequently on the White Star Line. Captain Smith booked her there, knowing she was no threat to the security of the plans.'

'Very well,' said Holmes.

'Fine,' Miss Norton said, looking to each of us with a wry smile. 'Now, why should we not put these plans away so that you gentlemen might take me on a tour of the ship?'

On deck, the spectacle was nearly over. The *New York*, now under the control of the tugs, was being manoeuvred towards the quayside. After more than an hour's delay, the *Titanic* again moved towards the head of the ocean channel. Passengers who had stayed on deck to witness the near-collision and its aftermath were beginning to move below.

Our self-guided tour of the ship whetted my appetite for the journey ahead. There were so many things to do, and comforts to enjoy. And, at every turn, I was awestruck by the fine construction of this elegant ship.

Public rooms available to us first-class passengers included the dining saloon, reception room, restaurant, lounge, reading and writing room, smoking room, and the verandah cafés and palm courts. For recreation, travellers could exercise in the gymnasium, compete on the squash-racket court, go for a swim or relax in the Turkish and electric baths. Further services for passengers were provided by a large gentleman's hairdresser's, a darkroom for photographers, a laundry, a lending library and a telephone system.

I was most impressed by the grand staircase in the forward section. More than sixty feet high and sixteen feet wide, it extended up to the boat deck, with large entrance halls at each level. It featured Louis XIV wrought-iron scroll work relieved by occasional touches of bronze. The oak panelling of the stairwell was illuminated by sunlight, entering through a large dome of iron and glass. On the uppermost landing there was a huge carved panel, with a clock at its centre. The female figures on the clock, I was told, depicted Honour and Glory, crowning Time.

As Holmes, Miss Norton and I gazed up at this impressive sight, my attention was diverted by something of even greater beauty. A figure in light blue was descending the staircase. It was Miss Holly Storm-Fleming, the lady I had met on the train. She smiled warmly in my direction, as she managed each stair with the utmost care.

'Doctor Watson! I was hoping I might meet you this afternoon. Is not this the most magnificent ship you have ever seen? As many times as I have crossed the Atlantic, I am still looking around as though it were my first time on an ocean liner.'

'Indeed it is, Miss Storm-Fleming. And may I add, the surroundings suit you very well.' I found myself speechless for a moment, until Miss Norton broke the silence by clearing her throat.

'Forgive me, Miss Storm-Fleming, this is Miss Norton. I met Miss Norton on board a short time ago. Her parents are close friends of mine.' I turned to Miss Norton. 'Miss Storm-Fleming and I met on the boat train, and had a very pleasant conversation.' The two women smiled and nodded to each other.

'And this is Commodore Giles Winter of the Royal Navy. We met this afternoon in the lift.'

'I am always pleased to meet a Navy man,' Miss Storm-Fleming said, extending her hand. 'If I have any technical questions about the ship, I will know who to see.'

'Cruise ships are a little out of my field, but I will certainly oblige if I can. Pleased to meet you, madam.'

'Well, Doctor. I was just going down to my cabin to change for dinner.'

'My friends and I were planning an early dinner in the restaurant.

Would you care to join us?'

'I would be delighted.'

'Would five o'clock be suitable?'

'I will meet you there at five. Until then, I hope you enjoy your tour of the ship.'

Holmes watched Miss Storm-Fleming disappear down the stairway, and then turned to me with an amused expression. 'Well, Watson, I see that yet another lady has fallen prey to your charms.'

'Really, Holmes, I have only just met her. She is alone on board and looking for company.'

'And I'm sure she will be a very charming dinner companion, old fellow. But be cautious, just in case her inquisitiveness strays in undesirable directions.'

Chapter Four

THE EVENING OF WEDNESDAY 10 APRIL 1912

The restaurant offered first-class passengers smaller, more intimate surroundings than the dining saloon. Its fawn-coloured walnut panelling and rose carpet created an atmosphere that was most tasteful and relaxing.

Its main attraction was convenience. The dining saloon had fixed hours for each meal – 8.30 to 10.30 for breakfast, 1 to 2.30 for luncheon and 6 to 7.30 for dinner. The restaurant remained open daily from 8 am to 11 pm. When travelling with Mr Sherlock Holmes, one could never count on eating regular meals at regular times.

Miss Storm-Fleming looked most fetching in her evening gown, although its bright red colour attracted the attention of diners at nearby tables. Or perhaps it was the gleam of her gold necklace and cameo. Miss Norton wore a soft gown of rich blue. Both Holmes and I, of course, had dressed in formal attire for dinner.

Dinner conversation was largely introductory, with each of us providing a little personal history, and our reasons for taking the voyage. I was both impressed and amused by Holmes's totally fictitious account of Commodore Winter's naval career. I made a mental note to suggest to Holmes that he take time from his beekeeping to try his hand at writing sea stories.

Miss Norton too showed some creativity in avoiding the subjects of her government job and the prominent role her mother had once played in one of Holmes's adventures. Instead, she spoke of her education, and her plans to find adventure in life before settling down. I was able to remain truthful on most counts, except for my reasons for being on board.

'Tell me, Doctor Watson, are you writing any more stories about your friend, Mr Holmes? I believe I've read nearly all of them, and look forward to future adventures.'

'In answer to your question, Miss Storm-Fleming, since Holmes retired, I have done little writing about his adventures. From time to time I dig out my notes to a past case and prepare a manuscript. But these days, my time is mostly occupied in writing historical novels.'

'Historical novels. How interesting,' Miss Storm-Fleming said. 'In what period?'

'My latest effort takes place during the Boer War.'

'I would like to read it when it is finished.'

'I will send you a copy. Meanwhile, please remind me to give you one of my more recent works before we leave the ship.'

'That would be most appreciated. And you will inscribe it, of course.'

'If you wish.'

She smiled, confirming her request, and turned her attention to Holmes. 'Tell me, Commodore, have you read any of Doctor Watson's work?'

'Oh, I do quite a lot of reading when I am out at sea. I know I have read that one about the *Beast of the Baskervilles*. Some of the shorter stories too.'

'What did you think of them?'

'Well-written little yarns. Quite up to the mark.'

'As a navy man, there were a couple of stories, I imagine, that were especially interesting to you. Let me think...' Miss Storm-Fleming put her hand to her forehead. 'You may have to help me Doctor Watson... There was *The Naval Treaty*, about a stolen government document, and just a few years ago there was *The Bruce-Partington Plans*, about some stolen submarine drawings. Did you read either of those?'

'I cannot admit that I did. But I must ensure that I do before I make my next voyage.'

Miss Storm-Fleming's eyes were fixed on Holmes. Fortunately, he had the makings of a great poker player. The mention of submarine plans did not cause him to change his expression. I wondered whether Miss Norton and I had displayed a similar lack of interest.

When the dessert tray came by, Miss Norton and I pointed our selections out to the waiter. Holmes and Miss Storm-Fleming declined the offer of sweets and ordered coffee. We continued our conversation as the *Titanic* slowly made its way to Cherbourg, France, where it was due to pick up 200 to 300 additional passengers. After we had finished our dessert, Holmes pushed his chair back from the table and looked at his watch. 'It is half past six. We appear to be dropping anchor. Would anyone care to go on deck and take a look? It is too dark to get much of a view of the coast, but we will be able to see the lights of the city.'

As we rose, Miss Storm-Fleming pulled her watch from her handbag and double-checked the time. She then excused herself, saying she would prefer to go back to her cabin and rest.

'It has been a wonderful evening,' Miss Storm-Fleming said. 'I have enjoyed meeting all of you... I expect we will meet later, Doctor Watson. And please do not forget that book you promised me.'

We wished her a pleasant evening and made our way to the boat deck. This afforded us a high vantage point for watching the arrival of new passengers.

The sun had set and the faint afterglow of daylight was fading. The *Titanic* was fully illuminated with electric lights, and must have made an impressive sight from shore.

Cherbourg was a deep-water port protected by a long sea-wall. One of its most charming features was a walkway that jutted out into the harbour, leading to a small lighthouse. Unfortunately, the harbour did not have docking facilities to handle ships as large as the *Titanic*. Instead, two tenders were used to shuttle passengers to the ship. *Nomadic*, the larger of the two vessels, carried first- and second-class passengers. Third-class passengers were transported on the *Traffic*.

'An interesting lady, your friend Miss Storm-Fleming,' Holmes said, as we stood at the rail. 'I hope that she does not turn out to be an agent of a foreign power.'

In my mind, I knew that Holmes was right to raise the question. But in my heart, I resented his suggestion that Miss Storm-Fleming might be guilty of such a crime. 'I will have to admit, that reference to submarine plans was a bit suspicious. But it could simply have been a casual comment. We were discussing your adventures.'

'Remember,' Miss Norton said, 'that it was Miss Storm-Fleming who brought up the subject of your articles to begin with.'

'She was simply asking me about my work. That is a perfectly reasonable topic for conversation, especially since she is obviously familiar with my writings on Holmes's adventures.'

'Her voice is clearly American,' Holmes said. 'I pride myself in identifying speech mannerisms. While she has an urbane quality – no doubt from her extensive travels – I found no strain of German or any other foreign tongue. She could, of course, be in the pay of some foreign power...'

'All I'm suggesting, Holmes, is that we be cautious, but give the lady a chance. After all, there is no evidence as yet.'

'And then there's the matter of her watch,' Holmes continued.

'What about her watch?'

'Everything she wears − her dress, her jewelry − suggests elegance. That is, except for her watch. It is of a simple design—it is not even a lady's watch. It is, however, the product of a Swiss company that is known for making highly accurate timepieces. Now, why should a lady of leisure choose such a watch?'

'Perhaps it belonged to her late husband,' I suggested.

'That's entirely possible. Or perhaps she has a fear of missing trains. In any case, it is unusual and therefore well worth noting.'

We looked below as passengers began to leave the *Nomadic* and make their way up the ramp to board the *Titanic*. After having been delayed by the *Titanic*'s late arrival, the new passengers appeared as though they might be tired, hungry and a little bit impatient.

'Stay here and make sure that every bit of my baggage makes its way to my quarters,' requested one middle-aged woman, as she led an entourage of servants across the ramp.

'It appears that it will be some time before her porter gets his dinner,' I told Holmes, with a sympathetic chuckle.

Holmes did not reply. His eyes were fixed on the deck of the *Nomadic*. 'Watson, the man in black on the deck of the tender...do you recognize him?'

I looked into the yellow glow of the *Nomadic*'s deck and, after a short time, was able to pick out the man Holmes had described. 'I am unable to see him at all well. Do you know who he is?'

Holmes remained silent until the man made his way on to the ramp. 'Do you see him now, Watson? Do you not recognize him? It's Moriarty!'

For a moment I was concerned that my dear friend, Holmes, might be losing his mind. Miss Norton, also amazed by what she had heard, nearly dropped her bag over the side.

'Holmes, Professor Moriarty has been dead for more than twenty years!' I exclaimed. 'What in heaven's name are you talking about?'

'Not Professor James Moriarty, Watson. The man coming on board is Colonel James Moriarty – the late professor's brother.'

I took another look at the figure in black. He assumed an erect military posture as he walked across the ramp with the rest of the crowd. From time to time, his head shifted up and down, and from side to side, as he examined the ship and his fellow passengers.

'I do believe you are right, Holmes. It is indeed the colonel. What the devil is he doing here?'

'Two brothers named James?' Miss Norton asked, in somewhat sceptical tones.

'Yes,' said Holmes. 'It shows a sad lack of imagination on the part of their parents. I never was able to deduce how the professor turned out to be so brilliant.'

'Holmes, do you suppose he still blames you for his brother's death. I recall the letters he wrote to the press after the Reichenbach Falls affair. They were a distortion of the facts.'

'I do not know, Watson. As far as I have been able to determine, forgiveness has never been a Moriarty family trait. In any case, it appears that my modest disguise is about to be put to the test.'

Chapter Five

THE LATE EVENING OF WEDNESDAY
10 APRIL 1912

The *Titanic* had left Cherbourg shortly after eight o'clock. Its next stop would be Queenstown, in southern Ireland, late the next morning. After that, our trans-Atlantic crossing would begin.

Miss Norton returned to her cabin, while Holmes and I walked down to the smoking room on promenade deck A. It was a pleasant room in which to end the evening. The walls were panelled in mahogany, with mother-of-pearl inlay. There were stained-glass windows along most of the outer wall, and a large, open fireplace, with a painting hanging over the mantel. A cloud of smoke filled the room, mingling the aroma of various fine blends of tobacco. While women were not strictly forbidden from entering the smoking room, it was respected by the ladies as a retreat for gentlemen.

The room was crowded with men, still in evening attire, sipping drinks and engaged in casual conversation. Some were not so casual, as they sat around tables, intently looking at the playing cards that were fanned out in their hands. At least one of the games appeared to be for high stakes.

I had read the notice about professional gamblers, which had been circulated with the passenger list. Card-sharps were common on trans-Atlantic liners. Passengers with a lot of money and little to do could easily be lured into a game. The steamship companies discouraged these high-stake games, but did not prohibit them. They did not want to get involved in policing gambling on their ships.

Holmes and I stood beside one of the tables for a few moments, watching the four men play their hands. The centre of the table was filled with chips, indicating that the hand was well under way. Holmes tapped me on the shoulder and motioned to a tall man with a thin moustache. As we walked away from the table, my friend said quietly, 'That man is cheating.'

I looked back in astonishment. 'What! How do you know? I saw nothing unusual.'

'He clearly has more cards in his sleeve than he does in his hands.' Indeed, the man, who later that evening was identified to me as Hugo Brandon, appeared to be winning handsomely.

'Holmes, we must report this at once!'

'No, Watson. There is more at stake on this voyage than the gambling losses of a few men. We dare not draw attention to ourselves. However, I will alert Captain Smith to the situation when we meet him tomorrow.'

'We'll be meeting the captain?'

'Yes, more of a courtesy than anything else. He's been more than helpful in assisting Miss Norton. And as captain, he is responsible for the safety of this ship. He would like to be kept informed on what is happening and who is involved. Mycroft has assured me that the captain is a man of the highest character and can be trusted.'

We walked to the fireplace, where a group of men, some seated and some standing, were involved in a conversation. The fire was crackling, causing the brandy glasses resting on the centre of the table to sparkle. From this closer vantage point, I was able to read the inscription on the painting, *Plymouth Harbour*.

A young man with a boyish face and an old man with a fluffy white beard were the centre of attention. They were engaged in a lively debate, and the contrast in their styles was striking. The younger man was somewhat formal – forceful in making his point, but careful not to offend. The bearded man was stronger, and much more colourful in his language. By questioning the passenger next to me, I learned that the young man was Thomas Andrews, managing director of Harland & Wolff, the giant ship-building company. Andrews was one of the main designers of the *Titanic*. He was debating with a very formidable opponent – William Thomas Stead, a journalist and editor, who was travelling to America to address a peace conference at the request of President William Howard Taft.

I was familiar with Stead's illustrious career. For many years, he had been a crusader for various causes. Perhaps my memory was jogged by our ocean voyage, but I particularly remembered a story he had written about a fictional voyage to the Chicago World's Fair of 1893. It took place during a trans-Atlantic crossing on the White Star liner *Majestic*. In it, a clairvoyant passenger had visions of survivors from the wreck of another vessel, which had foundered after striking an iceberg. It concluded with the *Majestic* rescuing the survivors. Stead had a reputation for investigating psychic phenomena and consulting mediums.

'Twenty-five years ago – twenty-five years ago, Mr Andrews – I was warning the public about the shortage of lifeboats on these liners,' Stead said, waving his arms for emphasis. 'If anything, the problem has become worse, not better. The ships have grown larger and larger, but the number of lifeboats has remained the same. What do you have to say to that?'

Andrews leaned forward and chose his words with deliberation. 'I would say, Mr Stead, that you have overlooked the enormous progress that has been made in the engineering of large ships, and the important safety features that have been incorporated into the newer vessels, like the *Titanic.*'

'Are you saying it is unsinkable, then? I have read about all the boasting that has been going on.'

'No, of course not. No ship is unsinkable. But I'd go so far as to say that this ship is as close to being unsinkable as any vessel can be.' Andrews looked at the passengers who were gathered around, wondering perhaps whether they were being shaken by this discussion. Their expressions ranged from interest to outright amusement.

Andrews continued. 'Let me explain. This ship has sixteen watertight compartments down below – all with doors that can be closed from the bridge. It can remain afloat with any two of the compartments flooded, or any three of the first five flooded. Even in the unlikely event we had a head-on collision and flooded the first four compartments, we still would not sink.'

'But you did not answer my question,' said Stead, his voice filled with challenge and impatience. 'What if one of these big liners does go down, and there are not enough lifeboats for everyone on board. What do you do then?'

'Well, to begin with, all our liners have a sufficient number of lifeboats to meet Board of Trade...'

'Board of Trade! Those regulations are archaic. Besides, the Board of Trade is in the pocket of the ship owners.'

'And even if a serious accident did happen, a modern ship could remain afloat for many hours – perhaps even days – before it went down. In these busy shipping lanes, that is plenty of time to signal another vessel and ferry the passengers over in lifeboats.'

This seemed to reassure the passengers who were listening to the debate, but not Stead.

'Competition,' Stead said. 'That is all it is, competition between the lines. You do not want to take up room on deck with lifeboats, when you can fill it with walkways and amusements for passengers. All you people care about is packing these things with paying customers.'

Andrews rose from his chair, showing anger for the first time. Still, he retained his composure as he spoke.

'Mr Stead, let me assure you that safety is – and always has been – the first concern of Harland & Wolff. If I were not fully convinced of that, I would not be working for them. Now you may think what you like, but I must ask you not to spread unnecessary fears among the passengers. Wait until you are ashore, then you can write whatever you like in the newspapers. But please do not spend this entire voyage disturbing our guests with your stories.'

Stead took a deep breath and turned away. Andrews, realizing that he would not be getting a reply, wished the others good night and departed.

Stead chuckled and looked to the men who remained gathered around the fire. Some appeared as though they were about to make a graceful exit. 'You know, I've always enjoyed a good argument,' Stead said. 'But I keep forgetting that some people do not. I hope he did not take it personally. Well, I will make sure I buy him a friendly drink before we reach New York...unless, of course, the ship sinks first.'

Everyone laughed and was put back at ease. Stead went on to tell a most fascinating fable about an Egyptian mummy, which carried a curse that brought sickness, death and destruction to anyone who possessed it. The Egyptian, Stead postulated, must have suffered greatly before his death, because his image on the sarcophagus carried a look of fear and anguish. The curse continued to this day, despite efforts over the years to exorcize the evil spirit lingering in the Egyptian's remains.

There was a short silence after Stead finished his story. It was broken by lighthearted comments. Some suggested relatives or business competitors to whom they would like to send the mummy.

Holmes was standing quietly, staring into the fire. I nudged him with my elbow and said, 'A remarkable story, do you not agree?'

'Yes, Watson, very enjoyable... Well, my old friend, may I buy you a brandy? We could sit back and discuss old times.'

'Holmes, you've never shown an interest in reminiscing before.'

'Then, perhaps, it is time that I did. What do you say?'

Holmes was in a rare mood. I could not recall the last time I had seen him so sombre. He was not the type to take ghost stories seriously.

'I would be delighted. Lead the way, Commodore.'

We sat there for some time and had a most enjoyable conversation – one that brought back many happy memories.

Chapter Six

THE MORNING OF THURSDAY
11 APRIL 1912

Captain Edward John Smith was affectionately referred to as 'E J' by regulars on White Star's trans-Atlantic runs. He was a big man with a grey beard and a firm, autocratic disposition. While strict with his crew, he was considered fair and was well liked. In addition to being an experienced seaman, he was a good host. His hospitality and congenial, soft-spoken manner had drawn a loyal following of regular passengers over the years.

'The uniform suits you, Mr Holmes,' said the captain, as the two shook hands. 'Were you actually in the Navy at one time?'

'No. Doctor Watson, here, has all the military experience.'

'Yes, of course, Doctor Watson. I am very pleased to meet you.'

'I believe you have already met Miss Norton.'

We had called on Smith, by appointment, in the private sitting room adjoining his cabin. It was comfortable, spacious and a good location to discuss our mission without fear of being overheard.

'Mr Holmes, your brother Mycroft assured me that this mission the three of you have undertaken will in no way endanger the passengers on this ship, or disrupt the crossing. Do I have your word on that as well?'

'I can provide no absolute guarantee, but thus far the journey has been a peaceful one. I must ask you, Captain, have you noticed anyone among the passengers and crew who might be of concern to us?'

Captain Smith stood quietly as he lit a cigar he had pulled from a case on the table. A blue cloud of smoke encircled his head as he puffed away. He took a deep breath and savoured the aroma before answering Holmes's question.

'I have met a fair number of passengers, but not a fraction of the more than 1,200 on board. As for crew, there are a lot of new faces – people I have not sailed with before. That happens when you get a new ship.'

'How many people are on board in all?' I asked.

'Well, we should pick up another 100 or so in Queenstown. That would bring the total up to around 2,200.'

Holmes crossed his arms and casually stroked his beard. 'Captain, I have long taken pride in my devotion to facts. But a man in your position, with your long experience, develops strong instincts over the years. Has anything happened thus far that makes you feel uncomfortable about any of the passengers or crew?'

'Well...there is one man who may require some discipline – one of my lower-ranking officers, Fred Bishop. I caught him in my cabin the other day. He claimed he was looking for me. But when I asked him why, he brought up a small navigational question that could well have waited until later.'

'Can you tell me anything else about him? Are you familiar with his service record? Is there anything unusual about his mannerisms, habits...?'

'There is one thing, Mr Holmes. I do not like to bring it up, with all this nonsense about German espionage rings circulating the country. But Bishop does have a trace of a German accent. When I mentioned it to him, he said he had spent a number of years living in Germany and working with German crews. In fact, that had been in his service record and I had forgotten about it. His last assignment was on board a German liner. But I am sure you will agree, Mr Holmes, that is hardly a reason to brand someone as a spy.'

'I agree, but let us keep an eye on him in any case.'

Miss Norton, noticing the memorabilia on the wall shelves, began to make her way across the room.

'Young lady,' the captain said firmly, 'I must ask you to stand quietly while I am smoking. Your movement is disturbing my smoke!'

After a momentary pause, Miss Norton apologized and returned to her previous position. The captain took several quick puffs from his cigar and the cloud of blue smoke once again encircled his head.

'There is one other point I'd like to make,' said Smith. 'The owner of the line, Mr J Bruce Ismay, is on board this ship. He is staying in a suite of cabins on B Deck. So far, there has been no need to alert him to your activities. But if the situation ever warrants it, I may have to inform him – at least about the particulars that affect this ship. Do I make myself understood?'

Indeed you do, Captain,' Miss Norton replied. 'But in that event, I must ask you to inform him that this is a matter of national importance, requiring the strictest secrecy.'

'Most certainly,' said Smith. 'Is there anything else we need to discuss?'

I turned to glance out of the porthole. The skies were clear and the sun danced on the tall waves below. We would be reaching Queenstown later in the morning, and then leaving for open sea.

'Captain, we will need to use your wireless equipment as a priority.' Holmes's directness did not seem to offend the captain. 'Also, would you ensure that your wireless operators fully understand the urgent nature of any messages we send?'

'We can take care of that straight away, Mr Holmes. Would you all care to follow me?'

Captain Smith led us outside for a brief stroll around the boat deck to the wireless room on the port side. The crisp sea air was a refreshing change from the captain's heavy cloud of cigar smoke. As we passed the gymnasium and climbed several steps to a raised section of deck, the captain pointed up to two parallel wires running from mast to mast, down the length of the ship.

'That is the aerial for sending and receiving messages. As you will see, a connecting wire leads into the wireless room. We have the most advanced Marconi equipment available. I will let the operators explain the details to you.'

The wireless room was a small area located just forward of the elevator gear. As we entered, we saw two young men in their early twenties. One was in uniform, seated behind the Marconi equipment, and the other was lying on a small bed, comfortably attired in a shirt and trousers. On noticing the captain, the man on the bed jumped to his feet. The man at the equipment continued to tap away at the telegraphy key. I was impressed by the tall stack of papers on the table next to him, presumably messages that were being sent by passengers.

'I beg your pardon, Phillips,' said the captain. 'I did not mean to disturb you during your rest.'

'No trouble at all, sir. I was just resting my eyes.'

The young man at the telegraphy key completed the message he was sending, and rose from his chair.

'Bride, please pause for a moment,' said the captain. 'I want you both to meet three distinguished guests. Commodore Winter, Doctor Watson and Miss Norton, this is Jack Phillips, our senior wireless operator. The young man who was just demonstrating his dexterity at the telegraphy key is our junior operator, Harold Bride.'

Hands were shaken all around. The young men greeted Miss Norton with particular congeniality and enthusiasm.

'The commodore is here on official business,' the captain continued. 'In part, he is here to evaluate the ship's capabilities in the event of war. But he and Miss Norton also have another more confidential government mission. You are both under orders to give their messages the highest priority, second only to those dealing with the safety and smooth operation of this ship. Also, you must keep their work, or any messages they send, in the strictest confidence. Understood?'

The two young men looked perplexed, but agreed without hesitation.

'Doctor Watson, here, while not directly involved in their mission, should be shown the same courtesies.'

'Yes, sir,' said Phillips.

'And now, if you do not mind, gentlemen, Miss Norton, I have a ship to attend to. If you do not have any plans for dinner, you are most welcome to join me at my table tonight. Meanwhile, Mr Phillips will explain the capabilities of our Marconi equipment.'

After the captain had left, the two men became more relaxed. Bride went back to his equipment and Phillips began a most interesting description of his work. I guessed that this was not the first time he had been asked by a captain to put on a show for special guests.

'Wireless equipment has been in general use on commercial liners for about three years now. The Marconi apparatus we have here is the most powerful on any merchant vessel. Mr Bride and I, in fact, are employed by Marconi International Marine Communications Company, and we work on this ship under an arrangement with the White Star Line. The two of us work in shifts and are pretty much able to provide round-the-clock service. Some ships have only one wireless operator, and consequently offer communications on a more limited basis.

As you can see, there are two complete sets of apparatus – one for transmitting and one for receiving messages. They are powered by a five-kilowatt motor generator, fed at 100 volts dc from the ship's lighting circuit.'

'What happens if you lose power in an emergency?' I asked.

'We have standby power. There's an oil engine generator on the top deck, as well as a battery of accumulators... Now, when a signal comes in on the aerial, it feeds into this tuning coil...'

'What about range?' asked Holmes.

'We have a guaranteed working range of 250 miles under any atmospheric conditions. But we generally maintain a range of up to 400 miles. At night, I have sent and received at a distance of up to 2,000 miles. We can reach Clifden Station on the west coast of Ireland. Then, as we approach North America, there is Glace Bay Station in Nova Scotia and Cape Race in Newfoundland. And, of course, there is also ship-to-ship.'

'Very good,' said Holmes. 'Your information has been most interesting and helpful.'

'Glad to be of service, Commodore. If you'd like to come back again during the trip, I can give you a more detailed description of how it all works... You too, Miss Norton, Doctor.'

'We may indeed do that,' said Holmes. And as the captain said, we may need your assistance in the future.'

'We will be delighted to oblige.'

Phillips opened the door and ushered Miss Norton out onto the deck. 'I hope your work does not keep you so busy that you do not have the time to enjoy the voyage. She really is a beautiful ship.'

'She is, indeed,' said Miss Norton. 'And do they let you leave your equipment from time to time to obtain some fresh air?'

'It is mostly working and sleeping, but I do have a little spare time.'

There was another round of hand-shaking, and the three of us departed. We walked forward along the officers' promenade, past a row of lifeboats. The deck came to an end at the wheelhouse, and we stopped at the rail, looking down at the forecastle deck, and the froth produced by waves curling off *Titanic*'s bow. While the sea was choppy, the skies ahead were clear. It promised to be another enjoyable day for strolling the decks and taking advantage of all the pleasures this giant liner had to offer.

As we stood quietly, admiring the majesty of the sea, a full Atlantic swell hit our port side. Moments later, a cool mist floated across the deck. Yet, if it had not been for our clear view of the horizon, we would hardly have noticed the ship's rolling, back and forth motion. The mighty *Titanic* quietly absorbed the impact, cradling its passengers from the forces of nature. How far we had come from the days of the frail wooden sailing vessels.

'It is a trifle chilly here,' said Miss Norton. 'Would you mind if we sheltered from the wind?'

'Not at all,' I agreed, feeling somewhat cold myself. 'Besides, this promenade is strictly reserved for officers. We should go before someone asks us to leave.'

Miss Norton laughed. 'We may be trapped up here. I am unsure as to whether the captain left the gate unlocked.'

But we passed back easily onto the first-class promenade. As we did, we were approached somewhat abruptly by a man and woman who had been standing by the rail.

'Doctor Watson! Excuse me, Doctor Watson! You are Doctor Watson, aren't you? One of the ship's officers told me he had seen you heading in this direction with the captain. I hope I am not disturbing you.'

'No trouble at all, Mr...'

'Futrelle, Jacques Futrelle. I have been hoping to meet you ever since

I heard you were on this ship. And this is my wife, Mrs May Futrelle.'

'Mr Futrelle, I am glad that you sought me out. I have enjoyed your detective fiction greatly. In fact, Holmes once told me that he admired the way you emphasized deductive reasoning in your stories. I especially enjoyed that short story, *The Problem of Cell 13*. Oh, allow me to introduce you to my two companions – Commodore Giles Winter and Miss Christine Norton.'

As Futrelle shook hands with Holmes, the excited smile disappeared suddenly from his face. For a moment, his eyes were fixed on Holmes's hand. Then he seemed to study the commodore's bearded face.

'Have we not met before, Commodore? Your face seems familiar.'

'I do not recall an occasion but I have indeed heard of you and read some of your stories. It is a pleasure, sir.'

'Excuse me,' Miss Norton said. 'Your name sounds French, and I have always assumed you were from France. But your accent seems to be American.'

'Born and raised in Pike County, Georgia, Miss Norton. But do not be embarrassed. You are not the first person to come to that conclusion.'

Futrelle was an energetic, full-faced man in his mid-thirties. His attractive wife stood by quietly as we conversed. She too was a writer of some repute.

'May and I were just about to go for a swim when we caught up with you. But I would greatly like to continue our conversation – perhaps this evening?'

'I would be delighted,' I said. 'An after-dinner drink would be most enjoyable. Perhaps you will tell me about the next adventure of Professor Van Dusen, The Thinking Machine.'

'I am afraid I am at a dead end in plotting the professor's next story. I would appreciate any suggestions you could offer.'

'It would be a pleasure. Until this evening, then.'

The Futrelles turned and waved once more as they walked down the deck hand in hand.

'Holmes, I think Futrelle may have recognized you!' I exclaimed.

'Perhaps. My photograph has been published before. But if he does suspect, he was not sure enough to say anything. Either that or he was simply respecting my effort to conceal my identity.'

'We may have to bring him into our confidence before he shares his suspicions with others,' Miss Norton said. 'We do not have to give him any details – just let him know you are working on a confidential case.'

'We may have to consider that. But first let us try to determine just how strongly he suspects, and how good he is at keeping a secret.'

Chapter Seven

By late morning the outside air had warmed considerably, and I decided to return to the boat deck to do some reading. Appropriate to the occasion, I had packed one of William Clark Russell's fine sea stories, *The Wreck of the Grosvenor*.

Holmes, in the guise of Commodore Giles Winter, was exploring areas of the ship that were out of bounds to passengers. Miss Norton was resting in her cabin. After a particularly eventful first day on board ship, I welcomed this opportunity to blend in with the other passengers and to enjoy the comforts of this luxurious liner.

I selected a reclining deck chair on the starboard side. It was not long before a boy came by, laden with blankets. I accepted one gratefully and spread it over my legs.

I found it difficult to concentrate on my reading. My attention was drawn to the activities of my fellow passengers. They seemed so at peace with their idleness. Couples, both young and old, strolled hand in hand. I thought back to how I had buried myself in my work for so many months. Then my mind wandered to past travels and the delightful holidays I had taken with my wife. I had forgotten how travel could dissipate anxieties and rejuvenate the soul. For years, I had prescribed holidays for my patients. Unfortunately, it had never occurred to me to prescribe one for myself.

'Why, Doctor Watson, what a pleasant surprise!'

Miss Storm-Fleming appeared by my side.

'Perhaps you would care to join me,' I suggested, indicating the reclining deck chair next to me. 'Would you care for my blanket? I will request another from the boy when he returns.'

'Oh, no, thank you. I came up to get some sun... How are you enjoying your voyage so far? And where are your friends? I was beginning to think of you as the Three Musketeers.'

'I suppose we have been spending a lot of time together,' I said, smiling at the comparison. 'But even musketeers need to have their own adventures from time to time.'

'Exactly! And perhaps, after this voyage, you will forget Sherlock Holmes, and go on to write *The Adventures of Doctor Watson*. Of course, I would be a little offended if I was not included as your faithful companion.'

'I doubt that the adventures of a retired doctor would draw much interest from the reading public. But, in any event, I would still appreciate the company of such a delightful fellow traveller.'

Miss Storm-Fleming spoke softly. 'Doctor Watson, you appeared very preoccupied just now, before I came over. Your book did not seem to be holding your attention.'

'I was reflecting on how much my wife would have enjoyed a cruise on a ship like this. I suppose I feel somewhat guilty about enjoying myself.'

'We live in a world filled with exciting possibilities, Doctor Watson. But none of us has the time on this Earth to experience all of them. Your wife was married to someone who cared a great deal for her. Can you not be thankful for the happiness you gave her, and leave it at that? You are an author; it is time to write the next chapter in your life.'

'Your husband was a most fortunate man,' I said. 'Have you been able to write the next chapter in your life?'

'I have begun,' Miss Storm-Fleming smiled at me, then stared out into the rolling waves of the Atlantic. 'I do not know how it is going to turn out yet, but that is what makes life interesting. Do you not agree?'

Before I could answer, we were interrupted by a stocky, well-dressed man whom I judged to be in his late forties. His dark, receding hair was combed straight back. Our visitor's long sideburns came within an inch or two of his full, grey moustache. He showed no signs of discomfort over disturbing our conversation. On the contrary, his firm, impatient manner made it very clear that he expected our immediate attention.

'Herr Watson! I was told that you are Doctor John Watson. Is this correct?' While his English was fluent, his accent was decidedly German.

'Yes, I am Doctor Watson. And who am I addressing?'

'Good. My name is Hans Von Stern. I wish to consult you on a professional matter. It concerns my wife, Elisabeth.'

'Is she ill?'

'No, no, you misunderstand. You have worked for many years with the detective Sherlock Holmes. Correct?'

'He is a friend of mine, yes. But I am afraid I do not understand you.'

'Well then, my wife has received a threatening note. I would like you to investigate the matter.'

I laughed quietly to myself and Miss Storm-Fleming, after hesitating for a moment, joined in. I was not surprised to find that Von Stern neither understood nor appreciated my sense of humour.

'Mr Von Stern, Mr Holmes is the detective. I am simply a doctor. While I have accompanied Holmes on many of his investigations, I have none of his skills.'

'You underestimate yourself, Doctor. I have read your accounts of

Herr Holmes's adventures. You are a man of great insight and have learned much from your association with your friend.' Von Stern studied Miss Storm-Fleming for a moment, then shifted his attention back to me. 'So, will you help me?'

Still amused by the situation, Miss Storm-Fleming ventured, 'This could be the first *Adventure of Doctor Watson*. It looks like an opportunity to be your associate has come more quickly than I expected.'

'Young lady, I do not believe that I have had the pleasure...'

'Mr Von Stern, this is my friend, Miss Storm-Fleming.' I added, with a smile, 'You may speak as freely before her as you would to me.'

'Very well, then. Here is the note Elisabeth received this morning. It was slipped under our cabin door during the night.'

Von Stern pulled a folded piece of paper from his jacket pocket. It contained words of various sizes that had been clipped from the headlines of magazines. Only her name had been printed by hand, in pencil.

'Baroness Von Stern – Your past is known. You will be contacted. Pay or be exposed.'

'You must show this to the captain at once,' I said. 'This is a most serious matter.'

'No! I will not expose my wife to an official inquiry. Besides, it may be no more than a cruel joke.'

'Are you a baron?' asked Miss Storm-Fleming.

'Yes, that is my title. Now then, Doctor Watson, will you help?'

Von Stern was impatient for answers. I wished that I could introduce him to Holmes. But I knew that would not be possible. 'Baron Von Stern, do you have any idea what this is all about?'

'None, Doctor. My wife has no secrets.'

'Has she received any blackmail notes in the past?'

'This is the first.'

'Do you suspect anyone on this ship?'

'So far, I have recognized no one on board, or on the passenger list... You will help, then?'

'Baron Von Stern, I do not think that I will be of much assistance, but I will at least give the matter more thought. Where can I reach you?'

'We are in cabin B10 on the port side of the ship.'

'Very well, then, I may want to speak to your wife later. Do you mind if I keep this note for a while?'

'If it will be of any help.'

The baron departed, at least partly satisfied with the limited assistance I had offered. Miss Storm-Fleming watched the baron as he walked away, then turned to me with a gleam of excitement in her eyes.

'What intrigue!' she said. 'Would it not be amazing if we were able to capture a blackmailer and turn him over to the captain? Do they have brigs here on these big ocean liners?'

'Miss Storm-Fleming, I would not expect too much from this. As the baron said, it could simply be a prank.'

My words of caution did not seem to quell her enthusiasm.

'I suppose so. But it *is* an adventure, Doctor Watson. I think that is just what this trip needed – an adventure!'

I laughed. 'All right, then. I will attempt to provide you with one. But please do not be too disappointed if I am unsuccessful.'

Miss Storm-Fleming and I continued our conversation and had a most enjoyable morning. We hardly noticed as the *Titanic* entered St George's Channel on its way to Queenstown. But soon the great ship made a wide port turn, slowed and came to a complete stop near another vessel.

'Why are we stopping?' Miss Storm-Fleming asked. 'We have not yet reached Queenstown.'

'I believe we are just picking up the pilot to guide us into Cobh Harbour.'

We continued to travel through the harbour until the ship stopped, once again, and lowered its anchor about two miles from shore.

'One of the crew told me that this stop is likely to take a couple of hours,' I said. 'Those two tenders approaching are the *America* and the *Ireland.* They're bringing a hundred or so second- and third-class passengers on board, along with the mail.'

Miss Storm-Fleming and I moved to the rail when the tenders came alongside. There were a few passengers who were making ready to leave the ship. They had experienced the thrill of *Titanic*'s maiden voyage, without paying the full trans-Atlantic fare. One of the departing passengers was a young man loaded down with photography equipment. I wondered whether he was acting in a professional capacity, or was simply an amateur.

The boarding process was more leisurely than it had been at Cherbourg. There were fewer passengers arriving in the tenders, and the crew had little difficulty directing them to their quarters. And since there were so few, if any, first-class passengers boarding at this stop, there was far less baggage for each individual.

One of the newcomers, carrying his Irish pipes, made his way quickly to the aft of the ship. Soon we heard the sound of lively Irish airs.

'Look!' cried Miss Storm-Fleming, suddenly. She was not gazing at the tenders, but at the skies behind the ship. Other passengers also looked excitedly in that direction.

A man had climbed to the top of the aft funnel from the inside, and was now staring over the rim. His face, blackened from soot, peered out to the Irish coast. Then, after resting his chest against the rim, he gazed down upon the passenger decks.

'Looks like one of the stokers,' said a junior officer, who had been standing by the rail, taking notes on the loading operations. 'Probably some Irishman wanting to look at the Emerald Isle.'

'How did he get up there?' Miss Storm-Fleming asked. 'Won't he suffocate?'

'That fourth funnel's a dummy. There is a ladder inside that leads up from the engine room. It is a long climb, but I suppose it is worth it for a breath of fresh Irish air.'

Miss Storm-Fleming and I laughed, as did the other passengers who had gathered round. That is, all but one. An old woman with a dark shawl wrapped around her shoulders continued to stare upwards in silence. Slowly, she made the sign of the cross across her chest.

'Don't worry, madam,' said the officer. 'He is perfectly safe. Some of the men who work below can climb better than chimpanzees.'

The woman, suddenly conscious of the attention she was receiving, nodded with a faint smile and walked away.

We returned to the rail and watched, as sacks of mail were loaded on to one of the tenders. Soon, the anchor was raised and the engines were fired up. The *Titanic* was ready to head for open sea.

'I am afraid I must ask you to excuse me,' I said. 'I told Commodore Winter that I would meet him for lunch.'

'Back to the musketeers? Well, just remember, I will be looking for opportunities to steal you away!'

'I will look forward to seeing you again,' I responded.

I walked down the stairway and found Holmes waiting on the promenade near the restaurant. He was pacing back and forth with his hands clasped behind his back.

'Ah, Watson, good, you made it! Let us get a table. There is much I would like to accomplish this afternoon.'

'Good afternoon, Holmes. And how have you been spending your time on board this beautiful ship?'

'It is a wonderful vessel indeed, Watson. I was just down in one of the boiler rooms. Do you know, with a little experimentation I believe I could develop a method to identify where a sample of coal was mined, simply by running a chemical test on its ash. You see, while all coal ash may look the same, there are certain trace elements...'

I rather boldly interrupted my friend. 'I need to tell you about a most interesting conversation I just had with a Baron Hans Von Stern. It seems his wife just received a blackmail note, and he asked me to look into the matter.' I handed Holmes the note. 'I declined at first, but he was very insistent. I told him I would give it some thought. Do you make anything of it?'

'It is difficult to tell, but I would judge by the individual printing of the baroness's name that the writer was a woman.' Holmes removed a jack-knife from his pocket and carefully removed the word 'Pay' from the note. 'And if I am not mistaken, the reverse side of this scrap of paper shows a portion of the cover of the most recent *Strand Magazine*. I believe an article of yours ran in that issue.'

'It does appear to come from the *Strand*... Do you think the baroness is in any danger?'

'It is curious that the baron and his wife should receive a blackmail note after they have just boarded a ship bound for America. Why not deliver it while they are in their home country, near a bank where they keep their money. Still, it could be a genuine blackmail attempt. In any case, there is little we can do at present. Speak to the baroness and keep me informed of any new developments, and it might be wise to suggest to the baron that he contact the captain.'

'I already have, and he declined. As far as I know, he has only told Miss Storm-Fleming and me.'

Holmes smiled. 'I am glad to see that you are enjoying this trip so much, old friend. Well, Watson, it appears that we have made a number of other new friends on this cruise. It only seems proper that we invite them to dinner. The conversation could be very revealing. I think I will have a word with the captain about issuing some invitations. Perhaps we should meet Colonel Moriarty and Mr Bishop as well.'

'Holmes?'

'Six o'clock, Watson. And it will be black tie.'

Chapter Eight

ↄ

The Evening of Thursday
11 April 1912

The ship's bugler sounded a cheerful notice that only one hour remained to dress for dinner. First-class passengers began scurrying to their cabins. Those without personal maids or valets recruited stewardesses or stewards to help them through the ritual of formal dress. I had come prepared with formal attire and was just adjusting my waistcoat when Holmes knocked at my cabin door. Upon opening it, I saw Miss Norton, looking most delightful in her black evening dress, standing next to Holmes. True to form as Commodore Giles Winter, Holmes was in full dress naval uniform. Standing with calm, naval poise, he was a far cry from the energetic, often impatient master of detection I had known for so many years. But I knew that beneath the beard and uniform, the Holmes I knew was still eager to attack a new puzzle.

'Remember, both of you, this dinner will afford us an excellent opportunity to observe our guests and any exchanges that may occur between them,' Holmes said. 'We must place ourselves around the table to see and hear as much as possible. The captain has sent personal invitations to each of the people on our list, and all have accepted.'

'What should we be looking for?' asked Miss Norton.

'Anything and everything,' Holmes replied. 'Every detail, no matter how insignificant it may seem. We have witnessed some odd behaviour on board this ship. None of it may relate to the safety of the plans but we must take it all into account.'

We made our way to the grand staircase and descended one deck to the dining room. At the foot of the stairs we entered the reception room, where a number of passengers were clustered in small groups. The reception room was a place of simple, dignified beauty. It was decorated in Jacobean style, with white, carved panelling. On the wall directly ahead of us, a large French tapestry was displayed prominently above a sea of rich, dark carpet. Most of the passengers were standing, although a few took advantage of the comfortable cane chairs. Others gathered around the grand piano in the far left corner to listen to a medley of classical works.

Captain Smith was standing to the right, showing passengers a large, impressively detailed model of the *Titanic*. The three of us made our way over to him, hoping for an opportunity to exchange a few private words.

'I wish we were able to display this model outside the glass case,' Smith told the half-dozen or so passengers who had gathered around. 'It is really quite a beautiful thing – one of several used by the designers when the ship was built. If I had a key to the case with me, I would remove some of the pull-away sections and show you the interior of the ship. You would be amazed by the detail. Unfortunately, they tell me that it won't float. And that must be my ultimate test of a good ship – whether it is waterproof.'

The crowd laughed, and a few moved in for a closer look.

Captain Smith broke away and guided the three of us to a quiet corner. 'The dinner party is all arranged. We'll be sitting at the large oval table in the centre of the dining room. I cannot say I like the idea of young Bishop being there, though. It is somewhat of an honour for an officer to be invited to the captain's table. There are others under my command who are more deserving than Bishop.'

'Indeed, Captain, I appreciate the difficult position this puts you in. But I can assure you that this exercise is of great value to the safety of the plans.'

'I understand, Mr Holmes. And now, if Miss Norton would care to join me, I suggest that we all go in for dinner.'

Miss Norton took the captain's arm, and the two of them led the way into the main dining area. Other passengers, noting the departure of the captain, also moved towards the dining-room doors.

The dining room was a magnificent sight. Its design was similar to that of the reception room but it was larger – much larger. The leaded glass windows that lined the walls on either side made me feel that I had just entered the dining hall of a great mansion. Despite the size of the room, a sense of intimacy was created by the columns that supported the white plastered ceiling. In addition, recessed bays along the walls created a number of private dining areas. Throughout this great hall, fine oak furniture stood on tastefully designed linoleum tiles. But the true elegance and magic of this room was brought to life by cleverly arranged lighting, and the sight of passengers in formal dress at dinner.

Captain Smith sat down at the head of the table, after showing Miss Norton to the seat next to him. I walked around the table, looking at the cards that had been put at each place setting. Mrs Futrelle sat to the left of the captain, followed by her husband, then Miss Storm-Fleming, then me. Hugo Brandon, the gambler, was seated next to Miss Norton. Mr Bishop, the young ship's officer, was already seated in the next chair down.

Holmes was seated at the far end of the table, opposite Captain

Smith. As I passed, I paid my respects to the baron and baroness, who were seated to Holmes's left.

'Doctor Watson, allow me to introduce you to my wife, Elisabeth.'

Baroness Von Stern, in her early forties, appeared strong and healthy. Her solid grip as we shook hands demonstrated that physical exercise was part of her daily life.

'Good evening, Herr Doctor. My husband said that you have been most kind by offering to help with our little problem.'

'I am not a detective, but I will do what I can. Aside from this unfortunate incident, have you been having a pleasant cruise?'

'Oh, yes. The facilities on this ship are most satisfactory. My husband and I have enjoyed the squash-racket court. Do you play?'

'From time to time, but not well, I'm afraid.'

'Then you must join us some time. It is simply a matter of practice and determination.'

'Thank you, I would be delighted.'

I took my seat, and looked at the place setting between Holmes and me. The card read 'Colonel James Moriarty.'

Within ten minutes, the remaining seats at the table were filled. Miss Storm-Fleming looked charming in her green evening dress. As she took her seat, I felt her silk glove in my hand.

'So here we are, Doctor Watson. I hope you brought your dancing shoes for later in the evening. I hear the band will be playing.'

'I am afraid my dancing shoes are somewhere at home in my attic, but I can improvise.'

I observed Colonel Moriarty to the extent I could without appearing to stare. I could not detect any signs that he recognized his brother's old rival. In fact, he and Holmes, as Commodore Winter, were engaged in pleasantries about their respective naval and military backgrounds. The true test was about to come.

'Colonel Moriarty, I want you to meet Doctor John Watson from London. We met each other as we left Southampton, and we have been engaged in several interesting conversations since.'

Moriarty appeared startled for a moment, then smiled and reached out to shake my hand.

'Excuse me, but are you not the Doctor Watson who chronicles the adventures of Mr Sherlock Holmes?'

I confessed that I was.

'Then we have something in common. My brother was Professor James Moriarty. He died at the hands of your friend many years ago.'

'It did seem to be a fair fight, I hope you will not be offended but...'

'Precisely, no offence taken. My brother pursued Mr Holmes and confronted him at Reichenbach Falls. I can hardly blame your friend for surviving the struggle. After all, my brother had one or two sins for which he had to account. If he had not died at Reichenbach, I am sure a hangman's noose would eventually have caught up with him.'

'I am most glad to hear that you no longer hold any ill will towards Holmes.'

'I would like to meet him some day and tell him that face to face.'

'I am sure he would appreciate your lack of ill will.'

Moriarty and I continued our conversation. I discovered that he had read nearly all of my stories of Holmes's adventures. I had just begun to discuss my historical novels when Miss Storm-Fleming broke in.

'Please forgive me, Miss Storm-Fleming, for my lack of attention. But Colonel Moriarty and I have been discussing...'

'I am pleased to meet you, Colonel Moriarty. My name is Holly Storm-Fleming.'

'Doctor Watson, if I have taken you from the company of this charming young lady, then I am the one who needs forgiving.' He turned to Holmes, who was engaged in a conversation with the baron and baroness. 'Perhaps the commodore would introduce me to his friends.'

'I would be delighted. Colonel Moriarty. This is Baron Hans Von Stern and his wife, the Baroness.'

They exchanged greetings.

'Baron, if I may ask, why are you and your wife taking this voyage?'

'Books, Doctor Watson. I am a dealer in rare books. In fact, when we reach America, I plan to spend several weeks buying and selling. I have brought a trunk of fine old volumes with me, including some rare editions of the Bible.'

'Then you are no doubt aware of the valuable book that is being transported to America on the *Titanic*,' said Holmes.

'And what book is that, Commodore?'

'Why, the jewelled copy of the *Rubaiyat of Omar Khayyam*, of course. Surely you have heard about it?'

'Oh yes, certainly, I believe I have read about it. A beautiful volume, but a little out of my price range, I'm afraid.'

'Where in Germany are you from?' Miss Storm-Fleming asked.

'Munich – a beautiful city with wonderful people. Elisabeth and I entertain constantly. Have you visited our city?'

'I regret to say that I have not. Is this your first trip to the United States?'

'Yes, it is. We are very excited about it. When we arrive in New York, we are particularly looking forward to American theatre. I have heard that many of the productions are most lavish, filled with powerful arrangements of dance and song.'

'There's a great variety of theatre in New York,' said Miss Storm-Fleming. 'Everything from the large musical productions you have just described to quieter, more restrained plays – powerful in their own way.'

'Perhaps we will have the time to sample several performances. You apparently have spent a good deal of time in New York theatres.'

'Before I was married, I lived in New York and worked as an actress.'

'Excellent! We would appreciate your guidance in selecting theatrical productions...'

We were interrupted by a team of waiters bringing the main course. I had just finished an excellent salad, consisting of cucumber, strips of salmon and a fine dressing. For my entrée, I selected lamb with mint sauce, accompanied by green peas and new potatoes. One of the waiters poured the bottle of Bordeaux I had ordered for Miss Storm-Fleming and myself.

I had been so involved in our dinner conversation that I failed fully to appreciate the magic of my surroundings. Diners, after several glasses of wine, were engaged in lively, demonstrative conversations. It had all the colour and elegance of one of London's finest restaurants, combined with the adventure of a trans-Atlantic crossing.

In a recessed bay across the room, Mr J Bruce Ismay, owner of the White Star Line, sat at the head of a small table. He seemed to be enjoying himself – and why not? The *Titanic*'s first voyage was cause for great pride and celebration.

At the far end of our table, Miss Norton was charming Bishop – and with great success, I might add. The shy young officer was becoming quite talkative. I looked forward to Miss Norton's account of their conversation later in the evening.

Brandon and the baron too had been having an involved conversation. The baron spoke with firm hand gestures, while Brandon sat with his forearm on the table, speaking in calm tones.

'Your understanding of Germany needs improving, Mr Brandon,' said the baron. 'The lower classes have an excellent standard of living. While I hate to disagree with a fellow countryman, Marx's philosophy is filled with flaws and is completely undeserving of all the attention it has received.'

Brandon's face reddened. He pointed a finger at the baron and began to reply. But upon noting that he had become the centre of attention, he sat back quietly in his chair. 'No great matter,' he said with a smile. 'I hope you will excuse my playing devil's advocate, but I really enjoy a good debate. No offence taken, I hope.'

The baron paused and eyed Brandon suspiciously. He looked back at the baroness, who had put her hand on his shoulder. 'No, Mr Brandon. Of course not. I too enjoy a good argument – sometimes to the point of getting carried away. I hope, as well, that I have not offended you.'

'No harm done at all, except that our dinner is getting cold. Shall we begin?'

'I agree. Lively conversation excites the appetite.' The baron held up his wine glass, as if proposing a toast, and turned his attention to his meal.

Holmes and I exchanged glances. We had indeed assembled an interesting group of dining companions.

Our dinner party concluded without further incident. In fact, as everyone followed Captain Smith's lead and rose from their chairs, there was a spirited exchange of smiles and handshakes. After so much food and wine, I yawned and thought for a moment about retiring to my cabin. But this was the RMS *Titanic*, and the night was still young.

Chapter Nine

THE LATE EVENING OF THURSDAY
11 APRIL 1912

Holmes puffed on his pipe as his mind sifted through the day's events. I relaxed with a brandy, feeling more confident than Holmes that the situation on board was well under control. Indeed, we had encountered a surprising collection of passengers. Yet our inquiries thus far remained precautionary. There was no reason to believe that the plans were in danger.

Holmes and I had conversed a little with our dining companions before retiring to the smoking room. Miss Norton elected to remain on the dance floor for a while longer. Before we left – while young men waited patiently for an opportunity to dance with her – she told us of her conversation with Bishop. It seems that the young officer previously served aboard a German liner, the *Deutschland*. He claimed that he had relied on his early language training in English schools for a working knowledge of German. Yet, when Miss Norton asked him a question in German, his reply, also in German, seemed fluent.

'I say, Holmes, Miss Norton was quite the focus of attention out on the dance floor tonight, don't you think?'

Holmes, after a moment's pause, looked away from the cloud of pipe smoke above his head.

'What was that, Watson?'

'I asked whether you noticed Miss Norton's popularity on the dance floor?'

'Oh, yes indeed. In fact, I was honoured – with all those young men around – that she danced the first dance with me.'

'After all these years, Holmes, I did not know you could dance.'

'A detective travelling incognito must know many things, Watson.'

Holmes puffed on his pipe once more, then turned to me and murmured, 'In fact, I noticed that you too have not lost your touch.'

'Yes, Miss Storm- Fleming is a good partner. It was a shame that she had to return to her cabin so early. I did not notice her drinking that much wine but apparently it made her very sleepy.'

'Just as well, Watson. There's work to be done. Did you notice that Brandon and the baron have rather strong, opposing political views. And do you not find it surprising that a man who spends his time gambling with wealthy passengers is also a devoted reader of Karl Marx. Perhaps he sees himself as a present-day Robin Hood, stealing from the rich, and so on...although somehow I doubt that his proceeds go to the poor.'

'I say, Moriarty seems very pleasant. Not at all what I expected.'

'He certainly is on his best behaviour – especially after the things he said about his brother's death. Perhaps he's turned over a new leaf.'

'And the Futrelles? They seem harmless enough.'

'Yes, Watson. But do not forget, Futrelle has a keen mind, and he is very observant. His curiosity could pose a threat to our work at some stage of the game.'

'I have read his crime stories. They are certainly imaginative, but I have always considered them to be a trifle fanciful.'

'Agreed, but he has a good eye for detail. Did you notice...'

All eyes in the smoking room had turned to the entrance, where Miss Norton stood. She was looking excitedly from table to table. Finally, she found Holmes and me seated at the far side of the room. Lifting the hem of her dress, she hurried across this male bastion, bumping into chairs as she moved towards our table.

'My dear Miss Norton, what can be the matter?' I said, as I pulled out a chair and invited her to sit.

'My room, it has been entered! Everything is scattered about. And you will not believe this, but on the wall, in large red letters, someone has written the word *Rache*.

Holmes and I exchanged glances, but said nothing.

'And the plans...?' said Holmes. 'Are they safe?'

'Oh, yes, I checked them immediately. They're still behind the panelling where I hid them. But someone clearly knows that I have them.'

Holmes did not appear to be fully satisfied with Miss Norton's assurance that all was well.

'Are you certain that you were alone in the cabin when you checked the plans?'

'Absolutely certain. It is a small cabin. There is no place to hide.'

'And the door...was it ajar?'

'No, it was closed... Mr Holmes, why are you concerned? Are you saying the break-in was a trick to get me to reveal the location of the plans? You seem to be dwelling on that ruse you played on my mother long ago. I assure you, there was no one peeking through the porthole.'

'We must consider all possibilities, Miss Norton. In any case, there is only one way to find out.' Holmes rose from his chair. 'And if the plans are still there, I suggest that we immediately move them to a safer place – one of the ship's safes, for example.'

We followed Holmes's lead in maintaining a brisk pace to Miss

Norton's cabin on C Deck. When we arrived at her door, she took the key from her bag and placed it in the lock. She started when she turned the key and it moved freely, without making a sound.

'I'm sure I locked it,' she said anxiously.

The door opened when she turned the knob. Inside, the cabin was in disarray, as she had described it. Clothing had been tossed out of the wardrobe and Miss Norton's trunk. And, as she had said, the word *Rache* was written on the wall in large red letters. But there were some differences from the description she had given us on our way to the cabin. The door adjoining the cabin, which had been locked throughout the voyage, was now open. And high on the wall above the porthole, the loose section of moulding had been prised away, and the door to the small safe was ajar. Holmes placed a chair quickly below the opening and stepped up for a clear view of the interior.

'Gone!' he said. 'The plans have been taken!'

'This does not make sense... The door was closed and locked...' Holmes jumped off the chair and darted into the next room. 'I checked it before I left. The keyhole was covered. There is no way anyone could have seen me when I checked the plans.'

As she spoke, Miss Norton and I followed Holmes into the adjoining cabin. Inside, we found the dowager, bound and gagged in her bed. The old woman seemed frightened when I removed the scarf that had been tied over her eyes. But she began to relax as I assured her that we were there to help. Holmes untied her hands and feet.

'It was terrible! Are they still here...could they still be around?'

'No, madam. You are quite safe,' Holmes said in a gentle and reassuring voice. 'The door was open and we found you here.'

'Are you hurt?' I asked. I poured some brandy from my flask, and pressed the glass to her lips.

'No, no, I am not hurt. Just a trifle shaken. Who were those people?'

'We do not yet know,' said Holmes. 'You say "they". How many of them were there?'

'I am not really sure. There might have been only one. But I had the impression there were two. I was asleep, when suddenly I felt a man's hand over my eyes and a cloth – that cloth – being stuffed into my mouth. They tied me up. There is little I can tell you beyond that.'

'Did they speak? Could you tell us anything about their voices, or what they said?'

'No, not really. Just a few simple phrases. Shortly after I was bound, I heard the words "got it". Then, a few minutes later I heard someone say "sawdust". I suppose that is how I gained the impression that there were two of them. The voices sounded different. But they did not sound at all familiar.'

'"Sawdust"? What do you make of that?'

Holmes closed the door to Miss Norton's cabin, revealing a small telescope-like device attached to the wood, about half-way down the door. The intruders, in their haste, had forgotten to take it with them.

'A clever optical device.' Holmes put his eye to the metallic object, then motioned for me to do the same. 'You'll notice, Watson, that the optical system allows you to see most of Miss Norton's cabin. The opening on the other side of the door is so small, there is little likelihood that she could have spotted it.'

Holmes returned to the dowager, who was being comforted by Miss Norton. 'Madam, I must ask you again, did you see or hear anything else that might help us to identify the intruders? This is of the utmost importance.'

The dowager put her shaking fingertips to her forehead, considering the question. At this moment, Holmes's eyes widened and he reached forward to draw her hand towards him.

'Look at this, Watson. Blood, around her fingers...and a strand of black hair caught on her fingernail... Madam, did you by any chance scratch the man who took hold of you?'

She reached out for a moment, as if re-enacting the ordeal, and then exclaimed, 'Yes, yes I did! I scratched his face...right around the eyes! And I remember something else. He had a beard...maybe a moustache too.'

'Excellent!' Holmes said. 'Madam, you have been a great help.'

'This narrows it down considerably,' I said. 'How many black-haired, bearded men are there on board with a scratched face? Of course, it is a huge ship. We cannot very well examine the face of every bearded man on board. And what if he shaves off his beard?'

'It's not as bad as you think, old fellow. Did you notice the black smudges on the carpet? There were some in Miss Norton's cabin too. That's coal dust. I suggest we begin our work in the area of the engine room.'

'Yes, Commodore, I believe you are right,' I said. 'But do you have any thoughts as to who the second man may be? And what about the word *Rache* written on the wall? This is very singular.'

'Yes, very singular indeed.'

Holmes and I walked into Miss Norton's cabin while Miss Norton stayed with the old woman. Holmes pulled his glass from his pocket and took a closer look at the large red lettering.

'Interesting that they should use this word. What do you make of it, Watson? Do you suppose someone on board is aware of my identity?'

'I think it is highly likely. Why else would they use a word with such a clear attachment to one of your cases?'

My readers may remember the case I called *A Study in Scarlet*. In it, the word *Rache* was written on a wall in blood. *Rache* is the German word for 'revenge'.

'Revenge?' said Holmes. 'Revenge against whom? Against Miss Norton? Against the British government? Against me?'

'Moriarty!' I exclaimed. 'Perhaps Colonel Moriarty is seeking revenge for the death of his brother.'

'That is certainly a possibility. It is also possible that someone is trying to convince us that Moriarty stole the plans. After all, what kind of thief chooses to advertise his identity by leaving such a clue?'

'When we find the man with a scratched face, perhaps we will obtain some answers.'

'Well, we must find him soon, Watson. The *Titanic* docks in New York in six days. After that, our suspects will leave the ship and all will be lost.'

Chapter Ten

The Morning of Friday 12 April 1912

'Gentlemen, Miss Norton, I recognize the importance of these plans and the limited time you have to recover them. But please understand that I cannot have the passengers on this ship disturbed. You must conduct your investigation quietly, and involve as few people as possible.'

The captain, after many years in authority, had developed the ability to give orders in a diplomatic way. At sea, business leaders, government officials – any passenger on the ship – fell under his command. Yet, despite his tactful approach, he left no doubt that his orders must be obeyed.

'But of course, Captain,' said Holmes. 'Rest assured, I have handled cases of far greater delicacy. Your passengers will not be disturbed.'

The four of us were walking casually along the boat deck towards the wireless room. Miss Norton had not yet sent a message to her superiors, announcing the loss of the plans. Despite the sunshine and the fresh, crisp sea air, she looked pale. This, her first major assignment, appeared to be heading towards a disastrous conclusion.

In the wireless room, both Phillips and Bride were hard at work –

Phillips clicking away at the wireless key and Bride taking down messages.

'Phillips, when you've finished that message, Miss Norton has an important message that must go out immediately,' said the captain.

Phillips half nodded as he transmitted the final words printed on the sheet before him. Then he turned his chair and looked up at Miss Norton with a smile.

'Miss Norton, what can I do for you?' Phillips seemed disappointed when Miss Norton did not return his smile. In fact, she was most business-like.

'I have a message to be delivered to a Mr Holmes at the Diogenes Club in London. I have written down the particulars.' She handed Phillips a wireless form, on which she had written a brief message in pencil. Phillips looked at the message, glanced at the captain, and then returned his attention to Miss Norton.

'Yes, madam. Right away.'

Phillips was about to send the message, but he was interrupted by the imposing voice of the commodore. 'One moment, Mr Phillips. Do you mind if I ask you a question?'

'Go ahead, sir.'

'Since last night, have you been asked to transmit any messages that you would judge to be unusual?'

Phillips chuckled. 'Funny that you should ask that, sir. Bride and I had a laugh over this one. It came in early this morning.'

Phillips flipped through sent messages he had spiked, and ripped one from the centre.

'Here it is.' Phillips, a gregarious young man, clearly enjoyed this opportunity to entertain visitors. 'Listen to this, it doesn't make any sense: "Have met the Hot Russian Honey Bear and am ready to talk business. If I am detained, meet me on board by the pipe organ in the smoking room".'

'Pipe organ in the smoking room! That's nonsense!' said the captain. 'There's no pipe organ on this ship. There is no organ of any kind in any of the smoking rooms.'

'Pray, may I see that message?' said Holmes.

Holmes examined the wireless form carefully, first reading it in detail, then observing the paper more closely through his glass.

'There is little I can tell from this,' he said. 'No handwriting, all typed. Good firm key strokes... possibly a man, but I am not sure. The addressee is a Mr Basil, for pick-up at the Marconi office in New York.'

'And the sender?' I asked.

'Listed as a Mr Robert Smith. That's undoubtedly a fictitious name, but we should check it against passenger and crew lists. Captain, would you make arrangements for that?'

'Of course. Do you suspect that this has something to do with the theft?'

'It is very possible...' Holmes took a blank piece of paper from Phillips's desk and scribbled out a brief message. 'Now, Mr Phillips, would you add these words to Miss Norton's message and send it immediately?'

Phillips seemed puzzled that his humorous story was taken so seriously. But he followed the commodore's instructions.

'I hope you don't mind my adding a postscript to your message, Miss Norton, but I suspect our friend in London would want to know about this latest development.'

'No, of course not. Now, if you'll excuse me, Commodore, gentlemen, I'm going to the message desk to see if I can get a description of our Mr Smith.'

'Good. And with your permission, Captain, I have one more message to send.' Holmes dashed out a brief note and handed it to Mr Phillips. 'It is to an associate of my brother in the United States Navy. Perhaps he can help us to identify our Mr Basil.'

'Very good, Commodore,' said the captain. 'I must leave you now for I have a ship to run... Incidentally, you wanted to accompany me on my daily inspection of the ship. We meet at 10 am on the bridge. Be there in full dress uniform. Oh, and Doctor Watson, you are invited too... Come as you are.' An hour later, Holmes and I were on the bridge with Captain Smith. There were others there as well – the chief engineer, the purser, the assistant purser, the ship's surgeon and the chief steward. All were in full dress uniform. The captain, wearing two medals on his dark coat, was an impressive figure, indeed.

Holmes had come well prepared for his role as Commodore Winter. He was wearing his Royal Navy dress uniform with no less than four medals – all borrowed, of course. I must admit, I felt a bit out of place in my brown tweed suit. If only I had thought to bring my old army uniform... Well, perhaps not such a good idea after all.

We moved into the captain's quarters, where each of the officers present delivered a report, based on their inspections of their own areas an hour earlier.

At 10.30 am sharp, we began our inspection of the ship. It was a fascinating journey, taking us through corridors and facilities in first, second and third class. We walked through dining rooms, kitchens and pantries, examining them for cleanliness and, in general, they met the high standards of the White Star Line. We passed through gentlemen's hairdressers, bakeries and lounges. Except for a few minor infractions, all was 'shipshape'.

My assignment during this tour was to chat with doctors in each of the ship's hospitals, asking whether anyone had come in with scratches about the face. While word of the attack on the dowager had been kept from the passengers and most of the crew, Holmes and I had the captain's permission to conduct a discreet inquiry. Much to our disappointment, we learned nothing from the medical staff.

The inspection moved downwards into the lower decks, where we entered the great storage rooms and cargo holds. The central half of lower deck G was taken up by boiler casings and coal bunkers. This day the captain had elected not to inspect the forward end of the deck, which housed the ship's post office, third-class berths and quarters for some of the crew. Instead, we descended into the aft section. There were a few second- and third-class cabins in this area, but our tour was limited to the complex network of storage rooms for food and kitchen supplies. The dark solitude of these dimly lit corridors was broken only by the vibrations of the engines below, and the sound of our shoes clanking against the metal floor. And it was cold, very cold, due to the remarkable efficiency of the ship's refrigeration equipment.

We conducted a random inspection of several storerooms, each isolating a specific type of food. Behind one door we found eggs by the thousand, all in neatly stacked crates. Another nearby room was filled with vegetables, and just along the hall we found bacon, ham and cheese. Two of the larger rooms contained beef, with fish and poultry separated in a smaller chamber. I thought back to our elegantly served meals the previous night, and marvelled at the work of the kitchen staff in serving so many guests.

As I stood by the captain, I expressed my surprise at this incredible volume of food. He nodded, then handed me a sheet of paper from the library of material he carried on the ship. It was a manifest of the ship's food stores: 75,000 pounds of meat, 11,000 pounds of fish, 1,750 quarts of ice cream, 2,200 pounds of coffee, 36,000 oranges, 6,000 pounds of butter, 1,120 pounds of jams and marmalade...the list went on and on. The passengers on the *Titanic* were a hungry lot, indeed. In fact, they were also a thirsty lot: 20,000 bottles of beer and stout, 1,500 bottles of wine, 15,000 bottles of mineral water and 850 bottles of spirits.

We walked down yet another stairway onto the orlop deck,

where we found even larger refrigerated sections. This was for the huge volume of frozen cargo the *Titanic* was transporting across the Atlantic. Here, no food was visible, just stack after stack of wooden packing crates.

At this point, the captain dismissed most of his entourage. He invited us to continue, as he and Chief Engineer Joseph Bell inspected the ship's electrical equipment and engine rooms. As the four of us walked down a narrow corridor, the sound of the ship's electrical and propulsion equipment became much louder. When the chief engineer opened a watertight door at the far end of the hall, the sound was absolutely thunderous.

The captain drew Holmes and me closer and, in a raised voice, described our surroundings. 'This is our central electrical station. It is all contained in this watertight compartment, which is sixty-three feet long and twenty-four feet high. We are, as you can see, standing on the upper level. The equipment along this wall is our feeder switchboard. Electricity comes up from the main dynamo through insulated cables below this platform and into the twenty-five black polished slate panels. They contain the fuses, automatic cut-outs and ammeters for controlling the ship's electrical system.'

I strained to hear the captain's every word, above the roar of the engines. Holmes, much to my embarrassment, was standing at the side, flicking through the pages of the small notebook he carried in his pocket.

The captain continued, 'As you know, Doctor, this ship uses a tremendous amount of electrical power. Electric lighting is just part of it. We also use electricity to power deck cranes, engine room winches, passenger lifts, fans, watertight doors, and equipment for kitchens, gymnasiums and workshops.'

The captain, Chief Engineer Bell and I moved over to the rail, which overlooked the huge apparatus on the deck below. Holmes looked up from his notebook, noted our new location and, with a quiet smile, came over to join us.

'Mr Bell, if you'll do the honours...' said the captain, looking at the chief engineer, then nodding in the direction of the lower deck.

'Yes, sir. Commodore, Doctor Watson, these are our four 400-kilowatt engines and dynamos. They have a combined output of 16,000 amperes at 100 volts.' The veteran seaman emphasized the next point, with a touch of pride. 'That exceeds in current the capacity of many central stations in large cities.'

'Most impressive,' I said. And it truly was. It was a magnificent engineering achievement.

Holmes nodded in agreement. 'Yes, most impressive, indeed,' he said. But I could detect in his voice a note of impatience. After all, this technical presentation was contributing nothing to the recovery of the plans.

'Captain,' said Holmes, interrupting the chief engineer as he was about to continue. 'I must thank you and Mr Bell for this very interesting tour. But, as you know, Doctor Watson and I have a luncheon engagement. Before we leave, however, I am most anxious to see the turbine and reciprocating engines that drive the ship, as well as the boiler rooms.'

'Forgive me, Commodore, but you won't find much of interest in those boiler rooms,' said Bell, restraining his amusement at the commodore's request. 'They are quite typical and, I might add, typically dirty. But if you'd like to see the engines...

'The boiler rooms, too, if you do not object,' Holmes insisted. 'In fact, it would be most helpful to my knowledge of the ship's operations to speak to some of your stokers.'

'Stokers!' Bell exclaimed. 'Those boys only know one thing – how to feed coal into a furnace.' The chief engineer was clearly insulted. 'Now, if you want to know about the engines, I know every nut and bolt...'

'Mr Bell...' The chief engineer stopped short at the sound of the captain's voice. 'Please lead the way to the turbine engine room.'

'Yes, sir. This way, gentlemen.'

Holding tightly onto the handrail, I followed Bell down a flight of metal steps onto the lower deck of the electrical station. We passed two of the four electrical engines, and then stepped through yet another watertight door. The roar of the dynamos was nothing when compared to the almost deafening sound we encountered in the next room. There, we found the ship's huge turbine engine, tirelessly turning the shaft that rotated the ship's centre propeller. A crew member stood next to it, squirting oil through an open panel.

'As you know, the *Titanic* is a triple-screw steamer,' said Bell. 'The central propeller is driven by this Parsons low-pressure turbine. Both of the two wing propellers are driven by a set of reciprocating engines, which are in the next compartment down. This combination of engines is relatively new, first used on the *Laurentic*. It allows us to take steam from the reciprocating engines and gain additional power by running it through the low-pressure turbine.'

'It is enormous!' I said.

'Yes, indeed, Doctor Watson,' Bell replied. 'The entire turbine unit weighs no less than 420 tons. The rotor is twelve feet in diameter and more than thirteen feet long...'

Holmes took his watch from his coat pocket and checked the time. The captain took this as a signal.

'Thank you, Mr Bell. Now let us move along to the reciprocating engine room... Gentlemen, I think you will find our next destination even more interesting. It is the heart of the ship's propulsion system. And there is no one better qualified to describe it than my chief engineer.'

Bell, smiling at this vote of confidence from the captain, again took the lead, and opened the door to the next compartment. And, without fail, the progression of louder and louder whirring and rumblings of machinery continued. It is difficult to imagine how the upper decks remained so quiet and peaceful. We were now in the rough underside of this floating palace – an area that few passengers were invited to see.

'Here they are, gentlemen, the reciprocating engines,' Bell continued. As you can see, there are four of them – two on each side. They are designed to take steam at 215 pounds per square inch – much, much greater than the turbine you just saw. Each cylinder is ninety-seven inches in diameter, and the heaviest cylinder, with liner, weighs fifty tons.'

Three crewmen passed through on their way to the turbine engine room. One had a beard, but it was light brown.

'Any questions, Commodore, Doctor Watson?' asked the captain.

Holmes shook his head. His arms were folded in front of him and he was glancing about the room impatiently. I decided that this was not the time to expand my knowledge of nautical engineering.

'Very well,' said the captain. 'Mr Bell, proceed to the Number 1 boiler room.'

The boiler room was much as I had envisaged it. Stokers were lined up shovelling coal from a bin into the fiery open doors of the furnaces. It was hot, sweaty, grimy work. The stokers, covered in coal dust, did their jobs mechanically, perhaps thinking of home, or looking forward to an evening drink with their shipmates before retiring to their bunks. A few, on noticing the captain and chief engineer, firmed up their posture and shovelled more vigorously.

'This is one of six boiler rooms on the ship,' Bell said. 'Together, they contain twenty-four double-ended boilers and five single-ended boilers, designed for a working pressure of 215 pounds. Smoke from the boilers is released through three of the ship's four funnels. The aftermost funnel is used strictly for ventilating purposes and releasing chimney smoke from the ship's galleys. Now, the coal that fires the engines is stored on each side of the ship and fed into cross bunkers that extend across each of the boiler rooms...'

'Mr Bell, as I mentioned earlier, I would like to talk to some of your stokers,' said Holmes. 'Might we proceed into the next boiler room...'

'What is wrong with the men right here, Commodore? Take old Fred, down there at the end. He has been stoking for White Star Lines now for...'

'I am sure they are all fine men, but I have a particular type of individual in mind,' Holmes said, once again leaving the perplexed engineer with an expression of total frustration. 'Captain, would you mind if Doctor Watson and I continued on alone. I do not want to encroach on any more of your valuable time, or Mr Bell's.'

'Very good, Commodore. In fact, it is time that Mr Bell and I rejoined my senior officers and concluded our inspection of the ship. But please take care – I do not have to remind you of the safety hazards below deck.'

'We will be careful, Captain, and our thanks to you and Mr Bell for this fine tour.'

Captain Smith and Bell departed through the reciprocating engine room, while Holmes and I continued into the No. 2 boiler room. While none of the stokers in the first boiler room had black beards, our luck changed in the second. Two of the men who were shovelling coal had jet-black beards. Holmes and I approached the tallest, most muscular of the two, who appeared to be in his mid-forties.

'That looks like mighty thirsty work. Can I offer you a sip of brandy?' Holmes took a flask from his coat pocket and, after removing the cap and taking a swallow, handed it to the tired crewman.

'Don't mind if I do, Admiral. Not a bit.' The stoker took the silver flask in his big, calloused hand and poured a generous portion down his throat. 'This coal dust, it just coats your mouth and teeth all day. I don't mind firin' my own furnace a little, if you know what I mean.'

'I do indeed. I am Commodore Giles Winter and this is Doctor Watson. I am doing a little research on the *Titanic* for the Navy. How do you like working on her, Mr...?'

'Hardwood, Edwin Hardwood. Pleased to meet you... Well, I like the *Titanic* just fine, just fine. The boiler room's a little less confined, and a whole lot cleaner than on some other ships. But I tell you, the thing I really like is the crew's quarters. The food's good and they give you some livin' space. And the skipper's good too, real decent sort... Does he know you're roamin' around down here? I wouldn't want you two gettin' in any trouble.'

'Oh, no problem at all,' said Holmes, noticing that the other black-bearded stoker had put down his shovel, and was looking in our direction while mopping his brow. 'In fact, we just left the captain next door in the aft boiler room. He was giving us a tour and let us continue ahead on our own.' The stoker smiled and nodded, while taking another drink of brandy. 'By the way,' said Holmes, 'that is quite a handsome beard you have. I was talking to one of your fellow stokers earlier. He had a black beard too and said it took him twenty minutes each day just to wash the coal dust out. Maybe you know him? I do not recall his name but he had fresh scratches on his face...'

Hardwood laughed and took another drink of brandy. 'That sounds like young Strickley. He said he got them scratches when he fell on a pile of metal scraps. I think he maybe got a little too friendly with one of them girls in steerage he's always sneakin' over to see.'

'I would like to talk to him again. You say his name is Strickley?'

'Yah, Ed Strickley. He's workin' today. Number 4 boiler room, I think.'

'Well, Mr Hardwood, it has been a pleasure meeting you. Before the Doctor and I leave, why don't you have another sip of that brandy. Very good, is it not?'

Hardwood took another generous swallow from the flask and returned it to Holmes. 'Indeed it is, Commodore. Life to a tired working man. Much appreciated.'

After receiving hearty handshakes from Mr Hardwood, Holmes and I moved on two compartments to No. 4 boiler room. It did not take us long to find our man.

'Mr Strickley?' said Holmes. 'I am Commodore Winter and this is Doctor Watson. The chief engineer was giving us a tour of the engine rooms, and he asked Doctor Watson to take a look at those scratches of yours. He is afraid they might become infected.'

Strickley was a big man, about six feet, six inches tall, with broad shoulders and muscular arms. His hands clenched the handle of his shovel, which he held level with his waist.

'What you talkin' about? I ain't been near Bell since before I got these scratches early this morning.'

'One of your fellow shipmates told him about them,' I interjected. 'Apparently he was quite concerned about your health.'

'Well, I don't need a doctor. I cleaned it up myself. I get cuts like this all the time, and none of them killed me yet. Just fell into some metal, that's all.'

'You know, there was an elderly woman in first class who said she scratched an intruder in her cabin last night, someone with a beard like yours,' Holmes said, glaring into the man's frightened eyes. I kept my eyes on the shovel, ready to fend off any attack against Holmes or myself.

'Well, I wasn't nowhere near first class, and old ladies cannot see in the dark!'

'Who said anything about it being dark?' said Holmes.

'If you want to make any charges, go take it up with your friend,

Bell! Meanwhile, stay out of my way!' With that, Strickley stormed through a doorway towards the forward end of the ship.

Holmes and I were the centre of attention, as we stood among the stokers, who had lost all interest in shovelling coal. 'Well, Holmes,' I said quietly, 'it appears that Mr Strickley is a very likely suspect.'

'Yes, I think I will ask the captain to arrange a meeting with our excitable stoker under more friendly conditions. Unless he is prepared to jump ship, there is nowhere he can hide.'

Chapter Eleven

'Most satisfactory, Miss Norton, most satisfactory.'

These words of support from Holmes did a world of good for our young companion. For the first time since the plans were stolen, I saw her smile. The colour was returning to her face, and her enthusiasm for finding our adversaries, and the plans, was renewed.

The three of us were sitting in the restaurant enjoying a splendid lunch. Or, should I say, I was enjoying this fine meal. I had finished my grilled mutton chops and was encouraging the last of my peas on to my fork. Holmes, during the entire meal, had been sitting back in his chair, listening intently to Miss Norton. Neither of them had touched their food.

The restaurant was not even half full. It was a little late for lunch, and most of the passengers had already finished their meals and gone on to other leisurely pursuits. Several tables away, Mr and Mrs Futrelle were having a quiet lunch together.

'I'm very glad that you found my report useful, Mr Holmes.' She cut into her meat for the first time. 'But you and Doctor Watson deserve the prize for the most progress. When will we have the opportunity to speak to Mr Strickley?'

'I have informed the captain of our encounter this morning, and he will notify us when our secretive stoker is available for questioning. But do not underrate the information you have gathered. Strickley is just a pawn in this game. You have supplied some interesting new pieces to the puzzle.'

Miss Norton had spent the morning casually chatting with our dinner companions from Thursday night. She was able to draw from each of them some explanation of their whereabouts at the time of the theft.

The baron and baroness said they had returned to their cabin early. Moriarty was in the first-class smoking room, having a drink with friends. Bishop, who was off duty, said he went to his cabin to read, after taking a walk on the deck. Mr and Mrs Futrelle spent the evening in the reception room, off the first-class dining room, listening to the ship's band. Brandon said he was having a private card game in his cabin, but would not reveal the names of the other players. Miss Storm-Fleming reported that, after a brief rest in her cabin, she attended a party in the Café Parisien on B Deck. The party, Miss Norton noted, was hosted by none other than John Jacob Astor, the wealthy American property magnate, and his young wife, Madeleine.

'But Holmes, we were in the first-class smoking room last night. I did not see Moriarty.'

'I did. He was sitting near the far wall, opposite the fireplace from where we sat. He was talking to two men, neither of whom I could identify.'

'Then Moriarty has an alibi.'

'A most convenient alibi. No, Watson, if Colonel Moriarty is anything like his late brother, he would commit the crime through his henchmen, while leaving himself in the clear. Let us not dismiss him just yet.'

'It appears that all the rest of our dinner guests were alone for at least part of the evening, except for the Futrelles – and Brandon, who would not provide the names of his companions,' I noted. 'I suppose even Miss Storm-Fleming could have done it, since she left the party early and returned to her cabin. But remember, Mrs Applegate heard two male voices in her room.'

'She heard only a few words,' Miss Norton said gently. 'Just like Moriarty, Doctor Watson, Miss Storm-Fleming may not have been in the cabin, but she could have been involved behind the scenes.'

'I am afraid the only members of our dinner party who are in the clear are the Futrelles,' said Holmes, pulling a piece of paper from his coat pocket. 'After we returned from our tour of the ship, I received this wireless message from Mycroft. It is marked "confidential", so Mr Phillips had it delivered to me immediately.'

My dear Commodore,

Am conducting the inquiries you requested. Mr and Mrs F have solid reputations. In fact, Americans say F has assisted them previously. All others have unknown or suspicious pasts... In response to your second message, no success in tracking down Mr Basil. Will continue inquiries into both matters.

Regards,
Mycroft.

'My brother has never been as energetic as me, but he has investigative talents that I have long envied. Still, I have never considered accepting his invitations to work for the government. As you know, Watson, I prefer...'

'Good afternoon, Commodore.' Jacques Futrelle, appearing somewhat nervous, was standing next to our table. His wife remained seated across the room. 'Doctor Watson, Miss Norton, I hope I am not disturbing you.'

'Not at all,' I replied. 'Please, do be seated. Would your wife care to join us?'

'I wonder if you would be so good as to allow me a few private words for a moment?' Futrelle paused, choosing his next words very carefully. 'I have a matter of a personal nature to discuss. Miss Norton, perhaps you would care to join my wife for a moment.'

'Mr Futrelle, I can assure you that Miss Norton will hold whatever you have to say in complete confidence. Please, tell us what is on your mind.'

'Very well... Commodore, I have noticed some things since we met and I have come to some conclusions as a result of those observations. I wondered if I might discuss these with you.'

'Please proceed.' Holmes's eyes were fixed solidly on Futrelle's.

'First of all, I must mention that I have never met Doctor Watson's friend, Sherlock Holmes. But I have long admired him, and have looked on him as a model for my own amateur interest in detective work. But to get to the point, Commodore, I have noticed that you too have strong observational and analytical skills.'

'Thank you,' said Holmes. My friend's expression did not change. But there was perhaps just a hint of a smile.

'I've also noticed that you, like Mr Holmes, must be a bee enthusiast. I see the marks of no less than fourteen bee stings on your hands.'

'Go on, Mr Futrelle.'

Futrelle's look of discomfort became even more apparent. He looked at Miss Norton and me, perhaps hoping that one of us would say something. Neither of us did.

'Well, Doctor, you and the commodore appear to be firm friends. That is also very interesting, since you told me earlier that the two of you met for the first time on this cruise.'

'You've stated your observations,' said Holmes. 'Pray tell us what conclusions you have drawn.'

Futrelle leaned forward in his chair, looking squarely into Holmes's eyes. 'My conclusion is that Commodore Giles Winter does not exist, or is a borrowed identity. I believe that you are, in reality, none other than Mr Sherlock Holmes, the noted detective.'

Holmes studied Futrelle for a moment, and then let loose a hearty laugh. 'Mr Futrelle,' he said, reaching out to shake the writer's hand, 'my congratulations. You have indeed lived up to the reputation of your fictional creation, Professor Van Dusen. Sherlock Holmes, at your service.'

Futrelle displayed both surprise and relief at the detective's reaction. 'Mr Holmes, I apologize if I have intruded on your privacy. Either you are working on a case that requires this disguise, or perhaps you are using anonymity to allow a quiet holiday at sea. In either case...'

'No trouble at all. Although I am a little disappointed that this disguise was not more successful. Doctor Watson saw through it immediately – but now, a perfect stranger.'

'If I may be so bold, Mr Holmes, why are you in disguise? Are you working on a case? Of course, you understand, I'm not asking for details. It is not any of my business, really...'

Holmes was sitting back in his chair, with his fingers raised to his lips. He turned his attention from Futrelle and looked at Miss Norton, and then at me, with a questioning gaze. After a moment's contemplation, he leaned forward and put his hand on Mr Futrelle's forearm.

'Mr Futrelle, I need your assurance that you will treat this entire matter, including my own identity, in the strictest of confidence.'

'Of course. I have only spoken to my wife of my observations and I will ask her to keep them to herself.'

'Very good,' said Holmes. My friend glanced about the room and continued to speak in a low voice. 'Now, you asked whether I was working on a case. In fact, Miss Norton, Doctor Watson and I are engaged in a matter of some importance and delicacy. It concerns certain documents that were stolen from Miss Norton's cabin last night.'

'May I ask, what is the nature of these documents?'

Holmes paused. We had every indication that Futrelle could be trusted. And given how little time we had left to recover the plans, his assistance could be valuable. But still, confiding in him would involve some risk.

'Miss Norton works for the British government,' Holmes said. 'She was acting as a courier to deliver the documents to representatives of the American government. I can say nothing beyond that, except that it is vital that we recover the papers.'

'I see... Well, I appreciate your trust and you have my word that none of this will go any further.' Futrelle began to rise, but then, on second thoughts, he sat back down on his chair and spoke slowly, searching for just the right words. 'Mr Holmes, I am only a writer, but my experience as a journalist has led me to develop some skills of detection over the years. If you find you need assistance during the remainder of this cruise, please let me know. I would consider it an honour and a pleasure to work with you.'

Holmes smiled. 'The thought had occurred to me too. I understand that you once did some work for the American government of a similar nature.'

Futrelle was clearly taken aback by this statement.

'However did you know that? I have never told a soul about that assignment.'

'I have a small confession to make,' said Holmes, taking pleasure in this opportunity to turn the tables on Futrelle. 'I took advantage of the ship's excellent wireless facilities to contact Miss Norton's employers and check the backgrounds of several people on board – yourself included. They, in turn, contacted the Americans, who mentioned this little detail.'

Futrelle chuckled heartily. 'For a moment I thought you were going to say you deduced that fact simply by observing mud splashed on my trousers or callouses on my hands.'

'Perhaps I should have withheld the explanation and allowed you to maintain your high estimation of my abilities.'

We all laughed, relieving the tension that had developed since Futrelle came over to join us. This seemed like a good time to satisfy my curiosity.

'Futrelle, could you tell us specifically what your involvement was with the American government?'

'I am afraid, Doctor, that that was another case where I pledged myself to secrecy. I can only reveal that I was asked to help with one case only, and that involved locating a missing person.'

'And did you find him?' asked Miss Norton.

'It was a woman, and yes, we did.'

'This has proved to be a useful conversation for all of us,' said Holmes. 'Mr Futrelle, if we find that we need the assistance of an observant pair of eyes, we will be in touch. Meanwhile, we would appreciate your discretion.'

'You shall have it, Mr Holmes... Oh, excuse me, Commodore.'

'Thank you.'

'Now, I am afraid I must leave you. My wife just glanced at her watch, which means she is anxious to begin our walk around the deck. Please would you excuse me?'

'We look forward to seeing you later,' said Holmes, rising and shaking the writer's hand. Futrelle said goodbye to Miss Norton and me, and rejoined his wife. After exchanging a few words, they left the restaurant, Futrelle waving to us as he passed through the door.

'Well, Holmes, it appears that we have some unexpected assistance in our investigation.'

'Yes, I would have preferred to retain my anonymity but perhaps this will work out for the best.'

'Do you really plan to include him in our investigation?' Miss Norton asked.

'He has a keen mind, and we do have more suspects than the three of us can keep an eye on at any one time. It is at times like this that I wish I had Wiggins and my Baker Street Irregulars available.' He smiled. 'Terribly inconsiderate of them all to grow into manhood.'

'Well, with just the three of us at the moment, how should we proceed?' Holmes, who had just begun to poke at his mutton chops, replied to my question by issuing instructions.

'Watson, perhaps you would pay your respects to the baron and baroness. Learn as much about them as possible.'

'Miss Norton, please talk to Miss Storm-Fleming. I find it curious that this young widow spends so much time travelling. Is there more to her holidays than she admits.'

'Holmes, do you not think it would be better if I questioned Miss Storm-Fleming?' I asked. 'After all, she and I have already become acquainted...'

'No, Watson, I think you are in a better position to question the Von Sterns. They came to you asking for help with the anonymous notes they claim to be receiving. Take advantage of that... Besides, old fellow, I would not want you to jeopardize your friendship with someone who may prove to be a fine woman.'

I nodded in agreement. 'Yes, Holmes, of course, very wise.'

'Time to begin, I believe,' said Holmes, just before he manoeuvred a large slice of mutton onto his fork. 'There are several matters I must look into, including the activities of our bearded stoker.'

We rose and began to make our way to the door. But before we could travel half way through the obstacle course of tables and chairs, we were spotted by a boy in uniform, who had just darted through the doorway.

'Commodore!' he called out, somewhat out of breath. He scurried past amused diners and stopped short when he reached us. 'The captain wants to see you in his cabin right away. He said the man you wanted to meet has arrived.'

'Excellent! That would be Mr Strickley,' said Holmes, clearly pleased that the investigation was once again moving forward. 'Let us not keep the captain waiting.'

When we arrived at the captain's sitting room, we found Strickley seated on a wooden chair, somewhat more subdued than when we last encountered him in the boiler room. Two muscular seaman stood like bookends on either side of him. Apart from these three men, there was no one else in the cabin. I was about to inquire as to the captain's whereabouts, when Captain E J Smith stepped through the doorway.

'Gentlemen, Miss Norton, thank you for coming so promptly.'

'Captain, would it be possible for these two gentlemen to wait outside?'

'I suppose the four of us can handle our guest. Bates, Johnson, wait outside the door, please.'

After the two crewmen left, the captain went to his desk and sat back in his big leather chair.

'Mr Strickley, the commodore tells me that you were impolite to him down in the boiler room. Do you have anything to say to that?'

The stoker was hunched forward in his chair. His posture suggested submission, but his eyes were filled with defiance.

'I wasn't rude to nobody. I just don't like a lot of accusations being thrown at me. I'm an honest working man, just trying to do his job.'

'Well then, how *did* you get those scratches on your face?' asked the captain, his voice firm, but calm.

'Like I told the officer here this morning, I fell into some scrap metal. That ain't no crime.'

'I doubt it,' I said, causing Strickley to sit up suddenly in his chair and look in my direction. 'I am a doctor and I have treated many injuries. Those scratches were not made by scrap metal. I would give ten-to-one odds that they were made by a hand.'

'All right. All right. It was a woman who scratched me. But it wasn't what you're thinking. I had a get-together last night with a young lady in steerage, that's all. I got a little too romantic for her, so she slapped me and ran off.'

'Did anyone see you with this young lady?' asked Holmes.

'No, we weren't exactly in a public place.'

'And do you recall her name?'

'No, I didn't even ask it. What for? We were just having a little fun together.'

'Captain, did you search the pockets of this fine example of English chivalry?'

'Yes, but we did not find anything – just a wallet, a comb and a few coins. There is nothing in his wallet except for a small amount of money and some personal papers. It is all over on the map table, if you would care to look.'

Holmes, who had been standing by the porthole, moved over to the table and examined the stoker's belongings. The contents of the wallet were arranged neatly on top of a nautical map.

'I see you play the horses, Mr Strickley. Here, on the back of this old betting slip, you have listed directions to two race tracks in the state of New York. Do you plan to place a few bets while you're in America?'

'Sure, I bet a few pounds. What of it?'

'Oh, nothing at all, except the money you have in your wallet will not make you a fortune. Unless, of course, you expect to have much more money when we reach America.'

'Just my regular pay, that's all.'

And I've noticed that you're not wearing your work clothes.'

'That's right. My back started acting up, so I reported in sick. I was resting in my cabin when the cap'n sent for me.'

'Allow me to compliment you on your shoes. They appear to be of high quality, and well kept. Not like the rest of your clothes, I'm afraid.'

'What are you saying?'

'Captain, you might want to ask whether any first-class passengers reported a pair of shoes missing recently.'

'I will do that, Commodore. Meanwhile, Mr Strickley, you are restricted to quarters until we reach New York. You will be informed of your next destination then. Any more questions, Commodore?'

'Thank you, not for the moment. Perhaps some time in his quarters will encourage him to tell us who hired him. It would be a shame for him to spend all that time in prison by himself. And I fear the judge will not feel generous towards an uncooperative robber who ties up elderly women.'

'You have no proof. I am innocent.'

'Good day, Mr Strickley,' Holmes replied.

As Holmes opened the door to invite the two seamen back into the captain's cabin, we saw Bishop outside, chatting with the two men. For just a moment, he and Strickley exchanged glances. Then Bishop, after tipping his hat to us, continued towards the wheelhouse.

Chapter Twelve

∽

THE AFTERNOON OF FRIDAY
12 APRIL 1912

A fter leaving the captain's cabin, Holmes, Miss Norton and I parted company to begin our separate investigations. My decision to take a walk around the boat deck proved to be a good one. I soon saw Von Stern and his wife approaching, walking arm in arm. The deck was filled with passengers enjoying the sunshine and fresh air. The starboard side of the ship, shielded somewhat from the brisk sea breezes, was by far the most popular.

'Good afternoon, Doctor,' said Von Stern. 'I see that you had the same idea we did. The sea air is quite invigorating, don't you agree?'

'Indeed, it makes me wonder why I continue to live in London. I suppose I have become used to the smell of fog and burning coal.'

'There are many advantages to city living... Elisabeth and I were hoping to use the gymnasium, but it is open to children only from one to three o'clock. So we decided to stretch our legs on deck instead. We have the squash-rackets court reserved for half past three.'

'Hans, why don't you invite Doctor Watson to play?' said the baroness. 'I will go to the gymnasium instead.'

'A pleasure, I am sure, Baroness,' I replied. 'But I do not have a racket or the proper clothing on board.'

'Everything you need is available in the changing room... So, it is settled. It is after three o'clock now. We will walk down together. On the way, we will stop at the inquiry desk and purchase tickets to the Turkish bath. I find it most refreshing.'

'Hans, isn't there another matter that you would like to mention to the doctor?' asked the baroness.

'Ah, yes,' said Von Stern. 'Doctor, we have received another anonymous note. This was slipped under our cabin door this morning.'

Von Stern handed me a folded piece of paper. Like the first note, the message was constructed from magazine type. Again, Baroness Von Stern's name was printed by hand, in pencil, along with a sum of money:

'Baroness Von Stern – The sum required to avoid scandal is 10,000 marks. You will be contacted.'

'What do you think about that, Doctor?' asked the baron.

'Well, like the first note, the words that are printed in pencil appear to have been written by a woman. And I will have to inspect the note more carefully, but the other words and letters may have been clipped from the *Strand Magazine*...'

A woman! Are you telling me that a woman has been threatening my wife?'

'It does appear to be the case, either alone or with an accomplice.'

'Very interesting. And have you come to any other conclusions?'

'None. As I said before, I am not a detective. All I can suggest is that you either report this to the captain, or wait until the blackmailer attempts to contact you. We might then be able to learn more.'

'Very well, we will wait,' said Von Stern, again illustrating a seeming unwillingness to consult the ship's authorities.

'I must say, Baron Von Stern, you appear to be taking this much more calmly than you did when we first met.'

'As I mentioned before, Doctor, my wife has nothing to hide. I can only assume that this is nothing more than a vicious prank. But I would very much like to know who is behind it.'

'I am very curious about that myself, and why someone would want to pursue Baroness Von Stern with an empty blackmail threat.'

'We will find that out, Herr Doctor. In the meantime, I suggest that we make our way down to the squash-rackets court. Elisabeth, will you manage?'

'Of course, *Liebchen*. I will be in the gymnasium. I will see you in our cabin before dinner.' Baroness Von Stern kissed her husband on the cheek and walked along the deck towards the gymnasium.

'And now, Herr Doctor, I hope you are a competitive man. As you will find out, one of my greatest joys in life is the thrill of victory.'

At half past three we were on the floor of the *Titanic*'s squash court. I must confess, my skills at that sport are somewhat limited. For many years, I had depended on morning or evening walks as my main means of exercise. But several years ago, when my growing waistline became a hindrance, young Wiggins invited me to try squash rackets – a game at which he had become quite accomplished. Wiggins and I began playing together once a week, and I soon found others at the club who were willing to share a court with a novice. Over time, by competing against keen players, my own skill at squash rackets increased. If Von Stern was as good on the court as he claimed, I had little hope of winning. Still, I was confident I could play a respectable game.

For the benefit of readers who are not familiar with the sport, squash rackets is played by batting a rubber ball against a wall in an enclosed court. *Titanic*'s squash-rackets court was located on the lower deck in the centre of the ship, just forward of the foremost boiler room. It extended two decks high, with a length of thirty feet and a width of twenty feet. There is a gallery for spectators at the aft end of the court at the middle deck level. That afternoon, a man and woman were looking down, I suspect more interested in the court itself, than the two players.

'Herr Doctor,' said Von Stern. 'I assume you play by the polite English rule that requires a player, upon hitting the ball, to back away, in order to give his opponent a free view of the ball?'

'Yes, of course, that is a basic rule of the game. Are the rules different in Germany?'

Von Stern's tone remained cordial, but I was offended by his inference that British sportsmanship made us weak competitors. I could not tell whether he was serious about the rule, or simply attempting to unnerve me.

'*Nein, nein.* We have the same rule. Only in my circles, we interpret it rather loosely. We find that that makes for a more exciting game. However, in our game, I will try to remember to play by standard conventions.'

'Thank you, Baron. I would appreciate that – especially since we have no referee here to call penalties.'

Von Stern's eyes showed a sudden flare of anger, but it disappeared quickly. The engaging smile returned to his face.

'Very good. Shall we begin, then?'

After a brief warm-up, a twirl of the racket gave the first serve to Von Stern. He began with a forehand service from a forward position in the service box, close to the wall. The ball bounced off the front wall at a wide angle, sending it to the back corner on my side of the court. I returned it with a drop stroke that hit the wall at the nick. Much to my surprise, the baron was able to meet the ball as it rebounded at a low angle off the floor. I was unable to reach his cross-court lob. The score was one–love.

Von Stern went on to win the first game, but I was very pleased by the close score of nine–seven. The baron appeared to be somewhat irritated as we began the second game of our best-of-five match.

I won the second game, ten–nine, after Von Stern called set two when the game was eight all. The baron made a fine recovery in the third game, winning by a score of nine–five. Still, my victory in the second game appeared to have shaken his confidence. In the third game, he began to play more aggressively, but lost some control. And from time to time, I found my returns blocked by Von Stern's movement about the court.

The score stood at three–two in the baron's favour when Von Stern lobbed a shot that rebounded off the front wall and flew over my head towards the back corner. As I ran backwards, I caught a glimpse of the baron moving sideways and to my rear. I shifted my balance to avoid a collision, but that simply sent me careening into the side wall and, finally, to the floor.

'Doctor, Doctor, are you hurt?' asked Von Stern, as he reached down to help me up. I did not accept his assistance. The fall had activated my old war injury, and my shoulder was throbbing with a dull persistency. And, I have to admit, I had little interest in receiving any support from the baron. I had little doubt that the 'accident' was intentional.

'Please, Herr Doctor, let me help you up!'

'Thank you. But I can manage.'

'You are rubbing your shoulder. Are you injured?'

'Not at all, it is just my old bullet wound causing a spot of bother. Just give me a minute and we can continue our game.'

'Are you sure, Doctor? You appear to be in pain. Would you not prefer to call the match a draw and move on to the Turkish baths? The steam would help your shoulder.'

'Indeed not, Baron. Let us continue.'

'Very well. But I must insist that I was at fault. The serve goes to you.'

'I will not disagree with you. Shall we take our positions?'

During the next rally, the baron and I again had a 'mishap'. As I ran forward to meet the ball, Von Stern's racket fell from his hand and clattered on to the floor in front of him. I managed to avoid tripping over the racket but the distraction caused me to miss the ball. Again, the baron conceded the rally to me, and he gained nothing. Perhaps his game was psychological – a move to jar me into losing control.

Much to my despair, the time had come to teach the baron that even British sportsmanship allowed for special measures in exceptional situations.

My opportunity came late in the fourth game, when the score was seven all. The ball was coming straight on at chest level and I was moving up into position. Von Stern was standing motionless in front of me, just out of the ball's path, but close enough to block my swing. But swing I did. My racket curved around like the swing of a pendulum. I missed the ball, but my efforts were not wasted. The racket came to a thudding halt on Baron Von Stern's breeches. The swing was not hard enough to cause the baron injury, or even serious pain. But much to my surprise, he chose that moment to make a belated effort to step aside. As he moved his right foot to the side, my racket collided with his back. Off balance, he began to fall forward. The ball, in turn, hit him just below the left eye. He shouted an oath, in German, as he dropped his racket and cupped his hand over the injured side of his face.

I grabbed his shoulders to steady him, then I carefully lifted his hand from his face.

'Baron Von Stern, please stand still, I am going to take a look at that.' I held open the lids of his eye, and asked him to look from side to side. 'Well, there is no apparent damage to the eye itself, but it looks like you are going to have a little discolouration for a while, I regret to say.'

As I continued to examine Von Stern's eye, I looked past him and saw the young officer, Bishop, watching us from the spectators' gallery. When he saw that I had spotted him, he moved along past the gallery opening and out of view.

'You and I both have had some bad luck with this game today, Herr Doctor. Now, it is I who must insist that we move on to the Turkish baths. We both have wounds to heal.'

'That sounds like a splendid idea, Baron. And perhaps a cold drink afterwards.'

I guided Von Stern to the door, as he continued to hold his hand over the injured eye. As we walked, I again looked up to the gallery to see if Bishop had returned. Instead, I saw Miss Storm-Fleming standing alone, her face expressionless. I waved to her but received only a half-hearted movement of the wrist in reply. Then, like Bishop, she moved away.

The *Titanic*'s Turkish baths included individual rooms for hot and temperate steam. The cooling room, where one goes to readjust to normal temperatures, was one of the most cleverly designed on the ship. It was decorated in seventeenth-century Arabian style. An elaborately carved Cairo curtain, placed in front of the portholes, gave the room a distinctly Eastern flavour. The walls were completely tiled in large green and blue panels, surrounded by a large band of tiles coloured in bolder hues. Bronze Arab lamps were suspended from gilt-coloured ceiling beams. There were low couches lining the walls, with inlaid Damascus tables between each. An elegant marble drinking fountain was at one side.

After taking steam at moderate heat, Von Stern and I, wrapped in thick, oversized towels, sat on couches in the cooling room. An attendant brought coffee and placed it on the table between us. The baron's eye appeared to be much better, but the bruising around the lower lid was much darker.

'Did I not tell you the baths were relaxing, Doctor? Or was the steam too hot for you?'

'No, the steam was fine. And the pain in my shoulder has diminished. Coming here was an excellent idea.'

We sat quietly for some time. It was the baron who finally broke the silence.

'Doctor Watson, I am curious about a rumour I heard earlier today. I understand that your friend, Miss Norton, had an intrusion in her cabin last night. Is this true?'

'I am surprised you have heard of it. Pray, who told you?'

'Word spreads quickly when so many inquiries are being made. Was anything valuable taken?'

'Not really; just a few personal items. I have no idea what the intruder hoped to find there. The more serious break-in was in the cabin next door, where an elderly woman was bound and gagged.'

'Very serious indeed. And are they making any progress in recovering Miss Norton's property?'

'Very little, I fear. But, as you know, the captain has instigated an inquiry.'

'You will let me know if you hear anything?' asked Von Stern.

'If you wish. But it is not a cause for concern. I am sure that it was just an isolated case, and that you and your wife are perfectly safe.'

'Yes, of course, I agree. But what with these blackmail notes, I cannot help but wonder whether there is any connection.'

'Oh, I doubt that very much. But certainly I will keep you informed, especially if I hear of anything that might link the two. Meanwhile, let us finish this excellent coffee.'

Half an hour later, I was walking through the corridors of C Deck, approaching my cabin door, when I heard the shout of a familiar voice and footsteps racing up behind me.

'Doctor Watson!' said the voice, as the footsteps slowed to a halt. It was Futrelle. 'Forgive me for chasing up behind you like this, Doctor, but I have some information that you might find interesting.'

'It must be very important,' I said, offering a calming smile and a handshake. I had forgotten how excitable Americans were.

'I do not know how important it is, but it is most curious.' Futrelle paused for a moment to catch his breath. 'I was here on C Deck a while ago when I saw Brandon stepping out of one of the corridors, and then walking down the forward staircase. He was carrying a bag under his arm.'

'Did you speak to him?'

'No, and I do not think he saw me... Anyway, I followed him, being careful to avoid being seen. When he got to the bottom of the stairs, he went over to the locked gate that leads to third class.'

'Did he attempt to pass through?'

'This is where it gets interesting, Doctor. When he got to the gate, he turned around to see if anyone was looking. I was near the top of the stairs, so I was able to conceal myself and thus avoid being seen. Anyway, a few moments later I heard the gate swinging open. I looked down just in time to see him removing a key from the lock... Now, where do you suppose he got it? I thought only the officers and crew had keys.'

'Where, indeed? Our gambler is a man of many talents.'

'That is not all. He closed the gate, but left it unlocked. I followed him down the corridor and saw him step into a storage room.'

'And...?'

'And a few minutes later I saw him come out, dressed in work clothes – the kind some of the crew wear. From there, he walked on and ended up unlocking another gate, this one marked "Crew Only".'

'Interesting, indeed.'

'I followed down the stairway, but was turned back by a member of the crew.'

'I greatly appreciate you telling me this, Futrelle. It could prove to be very useful.'

'It seemed like it was worth running down the hall to catch up with you,' he said, displaying a proud smile.

'My cabin is just down the hall. Let us go inside and discuss it further. I will order something cold to drink.'

Futrelle looked at his watch, then nodded.

I put the key in my cabin door and discovered that it had been left unlocked. When I opened the door, I was astonished to find the cabin in complete disarray.

'Good Lord, someone's broken in!' I shouted. The contents of the wardrobe and my suitcase had been emptied onto the floor and the mattress on the bed had been overturned. With the plans already stolen, I could not imagine what the intruder was attempting to find.

'Look at this place!' said Futrelle. 'They certainly were thorough. They have even torn the lining in your suitcase.'

'It does not appear that they have taken anything. Look, over here, they have left the spare cash I kept in the pocket of my overcoat.'

'Then what possible motive...'

'My notes! They've taken my notes on the code.'

'Code? What code is that?'

I continued to do an inventory of my belongings. 'It was an odd wireless transmission – something about a "Hot Russian Honey Bear". It may have something to do with the theft from Miss Norton's cabin.'

Futrelle was intrigued but I was too absorbed by the burglary to provide him with further details.

'I do not understand,' said Futrelle. 'If the culprits have already removed the item in question from Miss Norton's cabin, why have they searched your cabin as well?'

'That puzzles me too...unless, of course, we are dealing with a different intruder, who is still searching for the documents.'

'What next? Should I go to look for Mr Holmes?'

'Let me call the captain first. He should be informed and he may know of Holmes's current whereabouts.'

I picked up my cabin telephone and the switchboard operator put me through to the captain's cabin.

'Doctor Watson, this is most fortunate. I have people looking for you.'

'Is there something wrong?'

'Most definitely. Mr Bishop has been shot...dead. Mr Holmes is down where the body was discovered, and I am here questioning our suspect.'

'You have someone in custody?' My words came out in a stammer, as my mind raced to assimilate this rapid turn of events.

'Yes, we are holding someone...' The captain paused, his voice suddenly taking on a more consoling tone. 'Doctor, I am afraid it is your friend, Miss Storm-Fleming.'

Chapter Thirteen

THE LATE AFTERNOON OF FRIDAY 12 APRIL 1912

The cargo hold at the forward end of the orlop deck was a motor enthusiast's dream. A dozen or so fine automobiles were secured to the deck in neat rows, all pointed forward as if eagerly anticipating their arrival in New York.

Mr Murdoch, the first officer, who was sent by the captain to escort me to the hold, had prepared me for this impressive sight on our way down. Only one of the vehicles, a 25-hp Renault, actually appeared on the passenger manifest. It was owned by a Mr Carter. All the others were part of a private collection owned by a Mr Michael, a man who enjoyed his privacy. They were being transported quietly to his estate in New Jersey.

I have never been a fancier of automobiles. But I must say, this colourful assortment of machinery did capture my interest. During the course of the investigation, all of the canvas covers had been removed, revealing a proud display of everything the best European manufacturers had to offer. Mr Murdoch pointed out a few items – a bright red Bianchi, a 1903 Peugeot Phaeton and a yellow 1903 De Dion-Bouton Populaire.

And, in the middle of this amazing collection, I found Holmes, Miss Norton, Doctor O'Loughlin, the ship's surgeon, and Mr Boxhall, the fourth officer, all gathered around an open-topped motorcar.

'Watson, at last, I am glad they found you!' said Holmes, pausing only a moment to look up from his work. 'Tell me, what do you make of the wounds?'

Bishop's body was slumped back in the driver's seat of a Rolls-Royce Silver Ghost. There was one bullet hole to his forehead and another to his chest. I carefully examined each wound, and then moved the body forward to search for points of exit.

'There are no powder burns. I would say that the shots were fired at some distance – by a very good shot, may I add.'

'I agree,' said Holmes. 'And, as you have no doubt noticed, the bullet that made the head wound remains in the body. But the shot that was fired into the chest has passed through the body and has become lodged in the back cushion of the driver's seat... The good doctor here was about to lend me his medical instruments to remove it but I see you have your bag. Would you be so kind as to let me use a large scalpel and a pair of forceps?'

I reached into my bag and handed Holmes the instruments he had requested. He immediately cut a vertical gash through the leather across the bullet hole and probed with the forceps. Unsuccessful, he cut a horizontal line and probed again. After a few minutes, he removed the forceps and held the bullet under his glass. I was very much surprised to see a hint of a smile on Holmes's lips.

After holding the bullet out for all to see, he placed it in an envelope and wrote in pencil on the outside. He then entrusted it to Mr Murdoch.

'Mr Murdoch, may I have the weapon that was taken from Miss Storm-Fleming?'

Murdoch paused for a moment, then reached into his pocket and removed a small handgun.

'We have already verified that the gun has been fired twice, Commodore.'

'A Colt .25 automatic,' said Holmes. 'And with a pearl handle. Miss Storm-Fleming is, as always, a woman of style.'

Holmes paused, and then glanced at me with an apologetic expression.

'Mr Murdoch, would you examine the rear seat of the motorcar to confirm that there are no bullet holes?' said Holmes.

Murdoch appeared perplexed by the request, but nevertheless complied. He climbed into the back seat and examined the leather in detail.

'Nothing here that I can see, Commodore.'

'Very good. Now, please leave the vehicle, and I must ask all of you to back away some respectable distance.'

Holmes stepped away several paces and levelled Miss Storm-Fleming's automatic at the Rolls-Royce. Murdoch raised his hand in protest, but backed away quickly as he saw Holmes taking aim. The rest of us had already moved, we hoped, to safe locations.

One shot echoed across the deck...and then another. The sound was deafening. Most of us had covered our ears after the first round.

'You may all relax,' said Holmes. 'This first stage of our experiment is over.'

'Commodore!' exploded Murdoch, cautiously rising from behind a light blue Humber. 'I really must insist – you have no right to fire guns on board this ship.'

'My apologies,' said Holmes, returning the weapon to Murdoch. 'But it was necessary, as I am sure you will see in a moment. Watson, may I borrow those medical instruments again?'

Holmes probed through the leather deep into the rear cushions of the Rolls-Royce. Within ten minutes, he had recovered both chunks of lead. After observing them in some detail through his glass, he smiled, placed them in an envelope and pencilled a notation on the outside. He then handed the envelope to Mr Murdoch.

'Our work here is finished for now. Mr Murdoch, might I suggest that Doctor O'Loughlin and Mr Boxhall tend to the body, while you take Doctor Watson, Miss Norton and me to see the captain. And, if you would, please post a guard. We do not want any unwelcome visitors down here.'

I had been to the captain's sitting room several times before. And during the short time I knew the captain, I had come to respect him, and even look on him as a friend. But on this occasion, his official presence, and the power he held at sea, overshadowed any previous impressions I had.

Miss Storm-Fleming sat in a big leather chair, her full yellow dress covering its brown cushions. I must say, I admired her courage. Even under these difficult circumstances, she showed few signs of nervousness. Rather, she sat quietly, sipping her tea, as if she were paying a social visit. The captain appeared less congenial.

'Doctor Watson, Commodore, I am so very glad to see you!' said Miss Storm-Fleming, placing her teacup on a side table and rising from the chair. 'Perhaps you can convince the captain how silly this whole thing is.'

'I wouldn't use the word "silly", Miss Storm-Fleming,' said Holmes. 'After all, you were seen leaving the area of the shooting with a gun – a .25 calibre Colt, that had been fired twice. Nevertheless, I think I can convince the captain that the evidence is circumstantial, and there are no grounds to hold you for the shooting.'

'That is a most extraordinary statement, Commodore,' said the captain, leaning against the chart table, his voice calm. 'What new evidence do you have that would cause me to grant Miss Storm-Fleming her liberty?'

'Only that the shots that killed Mr Bishop did not come from Miss Storm-Fleming's handgun.'

'And how do you know this?' he asked.

Holmes took two white tea saucers and placed them on the captain's desk.

'Mr Murdoch, I earlier gave you two envelopes. One contains a spent bullet removed from the cushion behind the body. Would you place that in the saucer to the left.'

Murdoch turned to the captain. After receiving a nod, he complied with Holmes's request. Miss Norton and I exchanged smiles. She seemed elated by this opportunity to see Holmes at work.

'In addition, would you take the rounds I fired from Miss Storm-Fleming's gun and place them in the saucer to the right.'

Murdoch, after completing his assignment, left the empty envelopes on the desk and backed away.

'Now, Captain, if you will compare the rounds in the two saucers, you will see that there is a noticeable difference in size, and a slight difference in colour... The shapes are different, of course, but that is due to the surface into which each of them struck.'

Miss Storm-Fleming's eyes brightened.

'Yes, Commodore, I do see a difference,' said the captain, impressed, but still hesitant.

'And if you pick them up, you may notice a weight difference as well. It is small, but I am sure the scales in the ship's surgeon's office will support my statement. My guess is that it is about a 9 mm.'

'I do believe you may be right.' The captain, after comparing the rounds in two cupped hands, placed them back in the saucers. 'Mr Murdoch, when we have finished, please take these rounds to Doctor O'Loughlin and have them weighed. Remain there and observe the process.'

'Yes, sir.'

'Of course, Commodore, even if we prove that Miss Storm-Fleming's Colt was not the murder weapon, that is not absolute proof that she did not do the killing,' said the captain. 'There are no witnesses, and the second gun has not been located. Perhaps she fired both weapons.'

'And why would I do that?' asked Miss Storm-Fleming. She remained composed but was growing somewhat impatient with the captain's persistence.

'To create a confusion, perhaps...'

'A possibility, to be sure,' said Holmes. 'But it is a most complex and unlikely hypothesis... Miss Storm-Fleming, could you tell us what happened down on the orlop deck, and why you were there?'

Holmes gently motioned for Miss Storm-Fleming to be seated. He then pulled two wooden chairs from beneath the meeting table and offered them to Miss Norton and me. We sat and listened to Miss Storm-Fleming's remarkable tale.

'Well, as I told the captain, my late husband was a motorcar enthusiast. Over time, some of his enthusiasm rubbed off on me. When Mr Bishop offered to show me the collection in the cargo hold, I could not refuse.'

I thought back to my squash-rackets game against the baron, and how I had seen Bishop, and then Miss Storm-Fleming, in the viewing area. I had not yet told Holmes of this occurrence.

'He said the prize of the collection was a Rolls-Royce Silver Ghost, built in 1909. When we arrived in the cargo hold, he was quick to uncover it and climb into the driver's seat. We remained there for some time, discussing the features and performance of the Rolls, when I heard two shots fired in rapid succession. Mr Bishop first bent forward then, when the second shot hit him in the head, he was thrust back in the seat. I immediately took cover behind the Rolls, but it appeared to me that he died instantly.'

'Do you recall how long it was from the time you entered the hold until the shots were fired?' asked Holmes.

'I can only guess, but I'd say it was ten to fifteen minutes.'

'And did you see who fired the shots?'

'No, Mr Bishop had turned on the lights in the hold, but there were still areas of darkness. I only caught a glimpse of him.'

'You are certain that it was a man?'

'Yes, but I cannot provide any description beyond that... Tall, I believe... Doctoressed in a suit, not a crewman.'

'When did you fire your gun?' asked Holmes. 'And why, Miss Storm-Fleming, were you carrying it?'

'It is a habit I developed when I was living in New York. I seldom carry the Colt in England but, when I am travelling, I slip it into my bag. I suppose I am just apprehensive about travelling alone.'

'Please continue.'

'Well, when Mr Bishop was hit, I looked around and saw where the man was standing – about twenty-five or thirty feet away. He immediately ducked back into the shadows. After I had taken cover behind the Rolls, I remembered that I had the gun in my bag. I took it out and lifted my head just above the side of the door. I had to know whether he was still in hiding, or coming around after me. Just as I looked out, I saw him stepping forward, still in the shadows. But a ray of light did reflect off the gun. He was holding it directly in front of him. All I could think is that he was preparing to use it on me, and eliminate the possibility of a witness. I fired twice, and he leapt for cover. I was hiding behind the Rolls when I heard the sound of running. I looked up just in time to see him dashing through the door.'

'Did you pursue him?'

'Not immediately. I stopped to tend Mr Bishop but he was very clearly dead. As you know, Commodore, one shot hit him directly in the forehead... Anyway, I caught my breath and headed for the door. I am not sure whether I was looking to see that the killer was gone, or hoping to find help. As I stepped through the door, this big crewman ordered me to turn over my gun. I handed it to him, and then a moment later grabbed on to him and began to cry. When I regained my strength, I told him what had happened and took him inside to show him Mr Bishop's body.'

Miss Storm-Fleming's confident composure was weakening. It appeared that she was on the verge of tears. I wanted to step forward and comfort her but, wisely, resisted.

'I told him what had happened, but I do not think he believed me. He held my gun to his nose, smelled that it had been fired, and told me that he was taking me to see the captain.'

Miss Storm-Fleming's head was bowed, a single tear streaming down her cheek. She looked up at me asking, perhaps, what I thought of all this. In fact, I did not know what to think. Her story was generally plausible but why was she carrying a gun? And why, if she was accompanying Mr Bishop to the cargo hold, did she appear to be following him when I saw her from the squash-rackets court?

'Captain,' said Holmes, breaking a short spell of silence, 'I suggest that some effort be made to locate the entry points of the two rounds fired by Miss Fleming.'

'My thoughts, exactly, Commodore. Mr Murdoch, would you accompany Miss Storm-Fleming to the orlop deck and conduct a search. You can tend to weighing the bullets after that. Meanwhile, Miss Storm-Fleming, the evidence appears to be in your favour. You are at liberty to leave.'

'Thank you, Captain.'

'However, you are not completely beyond suspicion. Despite your claim of a man in the shadows, you were the only person found at the scene of the shooting. And while Bishop was not killed with your Colt, you still could have done the shooting with another handgun. If we find the second weapon hidden in the cargo hold, you could be back in custody again. And when we reach New York, I will turn the entire matter over to the authorities. They will, undoubtedly, want to question you further.'

'I understand, Captain.'

'And Miss Storm-Fleming, you will carry no more weapons on board this ship.'

'Yes, sir.'

Murdoch, who had been standing by the door, indicated to her to follow him. As she walked by, I said softly, 'I hope we will have an opportunity to talk later.'

She smiled and nodded, still holding back tears. A moment later, she and Murdoch were on their way to the cargo hold. Murdoch closed the door behind them.

'Well, Mr Holmes, what do you think?' asked the captain.

'Her story is most curious, but as you said, the evidence is in her favour. There were no powder marks on Bishop's body, which suggests that the gun was not fired at close range.'

'What about this mysterious man in the shadows that Miss Storm-Fleming mentioned?' asked Miss Norton. 'Who do you suppose he is?'

'When we find that out, we may be a step closer to finding our missing documents.'

The captain, who had been refilling his teacup, was taken aback by this remark.

'Mr Holmes, are you suggesting that these two incidents are related?'

'I think it is a strong possibility and our best lead yet in recovering the papers.'

'Murder! Espionage! Mr Holmes, I have kept your little intrigue quiet so far. But now, I am afraid it is getting out of hand. We must inform Mr Ismay, the owner of the line, about the situation. I will ring him now to see if he is in his suite. If he is, I must ask the three of you to accompany me there.'

'Very well,' said Holmes. 'My only request is that we do not go into any details about the nature of the stolen documents.'

'On that you have my agreement.'

The captain picked up the telephone. I walked to the teapot to see if enough remained to pour three more cups.

'Mr Ismay, please. Captain Smith here...'

Chapter Fourteen

~

THE EVENING OF FRIDAY 12 APRIL 1912

O ur journey thus far had been one of unparalleled comfort and elegance. At least, that is what we thought. Hidden away on B Deck, we found the best and most luxurious accommodation the *Titanic* – or any other ship in the sea – had to offer.

Mr J Bruce Ismay occupied a suite of cabins on the port side. Combined, cabins B52, B54 and B56 formed a spacious 'home away from home'. There was even a front porch – a private promenade overlooking the liner's imposing hull.

At the time Captain Smith called over the ship's telephone system, Mr Ismay was not in his cabin. His manservant, Mr Richard Fry, had answered, saying Mr Ismay was out having dinner but was expected back soon. He invited us to sit in Mr Ismay's suite while awaiting his return.

I had lost track of time. So much had happened in the past few hours. When we left the captain's cabin, we found that it was turning dark. Tired, I was invigorated by inhaling the fresh sea air. As we walked down to B Deck, I thought of Miss Storm-Fleming, walking with Murdoch in the ship's enormous hold, attempting to locate the shots she had fired earlier in the day.

The captain's knock on the door was answered by a slender, well-groomed man of medium height. He was dressed in a dark suit and tie.

'Captain Smith, gentlemen, madam, would you come in, please?'

We passed into a magnificent sitting room. Not, mind you, the luxury you would find in a fine country house. But still, by far the best stateroom I had seen during my six decades on this earth.

'Mr Fry, this is Commodore Giles Winter, Doctor John Watson and Miss Christine Norton. As I mentioned on the telephone, we have a matter of some delicacy to discuss with Mr Ismay.'

'Yes, of course. Mr Ismay is due back shortly. May I get you something to drink while you are waiting?' The captain nodded.

Mr Fry noticed Miss Norton's eyes, bright with wonder, as she looked about the room.

'Mr Ismay is quite proud of these suites. They are the best you will find on any liner.'

Indeed, our surroundings were most impressive. The sitting room was decorated in what Mr Fry described as Louis XVI style, with oak panelled walls. There was a large, round oak table at the centre of the room, surrounded by four thickly cushioned chairs, upholstered in a muted floral pattern. In addition, there was a corner writing table with a chair, and two other chairs. The light from a chandelier reflected off the large white moulded squares that covered the tall ceiling. It brought out the colour and intricate detail of the thick red and white carpet.

Mr Fry had removed a tray from a large cabinet and set it on an octagonal coffee table next to the sideboard. It held a flask of sherry and several fine crystal glasses. He filled four of them and handed one to each of us.

'Perhaps you would feel more comfortable seated next to the fireplace? Or, if you would prefer, I could show you the rest of the suite?'

Miss Norton accepted Mr Fry's offer of a tour, while Holmes, the captain and I adjourned to the private promenade running alongside the suite. The promenade was enclosed, with large screened windows that were open to the outside air. We looked out across the sea as the waves sparkled in the waning moments of twilight.

'What sort of man is Mr Ismay?' I asked, taking a sip of my sherry.

'Likeable, but a perfectionist,' said the captain. 'He wants every last detail to be perfect and he expects everyone who works for him to feel the same way. I respect that in him, although I find it a little trying from time to time. To his credit, he respects my position as captain and does not try to run the ship. He has hardly been to the bridge at all.'

'But can he be trusted with highly confidential information?' asked Holmes, turning from the window and looking the captain in the eyes.

Captain Smith had just lit a cigar, and was in the process of building a cloud of blue smoke about his head. Despite the light sea breeze passing through the promenade, the cloud remained in place.

'God knows Mr Ismay has kept enough business secrets in his time. Still, I will, as you asked, withhold particulars about the stolen documents. And, at least for the moment, I see no reason to reveal your true identity, Mr Holmes.'

'Thank you, Captain. That will reduce the possibility of complications occurring in the future.'

We were interrupted as Mr Fry walked through the door, carrying the sherry tray. Miss Norton followed. There was a cheerful look on her face as she glanced about the promenade.

After placing the tray on a small square table, Mr Fry approached the captain.

'Sir, if you do not require anything further, I will attend to my duties. I will, of course, tell Mr Ismay that you are here, as soon as he arrives.'

'Thank you, Mr Fry.' The efficient manservant made one last offer of hospitality to the rest of us, then departed.

'Well, Miss Norton, did we miss anything?' I asked.

'Indeed you did,' she said, with some satisfaction. 'It is a huge suite. There are two bedrooms, two dressing rooms and a bathroom. It is all so beautifully decorated. And he has it all to himself, for his family saw him off when he boarded but are not travelling with him.'

Miss Norton and I sat on the settee, while Holmes and the captain settled into round-backed chairs on either side. I refilled my sherry glass, as well as those of my companions. Captain Smith, his glass still half full, declined. We sat quietly, listening to the sound of the *Titanic* cutting through the waves. There was little to be said. It was a time for contemplating the day's events.

It was not long before a slender man of average height stepped through the doorway. As I had noticed from a distance in the dining hall, he was not a young man. Still, he was younger than one might expect, considering his high position. His dark moustache turned upwards as he greeted us with a smile. We rose to shake his hand.

'Mr Ismay,' said the captain, 'this is Commodore Giles Winter, Doctor John Watson and Miss Norton.'

'Yes, Commodore, it is a pleasure. I heard you were on board examining our ship for military potential in the event of war. Forgive me if I do not turn her into a troop transporter just yet. We'd like to enjoy her a little longer in her present condition.'

Holmes responded with a hearty chuckle. 'Oh, I doubt that we would ever use her for that. There is far too much luxury here for military purposes.'

Mr Ismay smiled politely, and then turned his attention to me. 'And Doctor Watson, I must say, I have always wanted to meet you and your associate, Mr Holmes. I sent him an invitation to a party once but I never received a reply.'

'I must apologize for my friend. He is a very private individual, and answering letters was never his forte.'

'In any case, I am very pleased to meet you. I have enjoyed your stories for years... And Miss Norton, I hear you liked the tour of my little cabin. This place will fetch a good price on future runs, but I felt I needed to try it out first before I recommended it to future passengers.'

'That is indeed the only way to make sure none of the doors squeak.'

'And, as a matter of fact, Miss Norton, none of them do.'

Mr Ismay reached down and filled a glass with sherry. Captain Smith, with introductions out of the way, got down to the matter in hand.

'Mr Ismay, I asked Commodore Winter...'

'I received your report about poor Bishop. What *is* going on on board my ship?'

The captain summarized what had happened thus far up to the questioning and release of Miss Storm-Fleming.

'And you are sure that this woman, Miss Storm-Fleming, had nothing to do with it?'

'We do not think she committed the murder, but she may know more than she has told us. That is why I invited the Commodore, Doctor Watson and Miss Norton here. They were assigned by the British government to transfer some highly confidential documents to the American authorities. Those papers were stolen from Miss Norton's cabin last night.'

Mr Ismay stood there in silence, his lips parted.

'The commodore believes that there may be some connection between Bishop's death and the theft of the documents,' said the captain. 'We have no direct evidence of this but the coincidence is worth investigating.'

'Captain, do you mean to say that there may be spies on board this ship who are running about shooting people? Do you suspect that Bishop may have been involved in all this?'

'Nothing is certain at this point, Mr Ismay, but we are looking into all possibilities,' said Holmes. 'Our immediate purpose, in addition to finding Mr Bishop's killer, is to recover the documents.'

'And what is the nature of these papers, Commodore?'

'I fear that I am not at liberty to go into details, Mr Ismay. But it is vital that they do not fall into the hands of a foreign power.'

Mr Ismay shook his head. 'In the forty-five years since my father founded this company, there has never been such a scandal aboard a White Star ship... We will, of course, provide every assistance to you in recovering the documents. But I must ask you to help us in return by doing your work as discreetly as possible. I will not have the passengers on this ship alarmed. Is that understood?'

'We will do our best, Mr Ismay,' said Holmes. 'The captain felt it was necessary for us to take you into our confidence at this point. And that was a reasonable request. Rest assured, we are just as concerned as you are to prevent rumours from spreading around the ship.'

'Yes, of course... Well, keep me informed, Captain. And give the commodore our complete support... By the way, how long have you known about this?'

'I was told by British authorities just before our departure.'

'Then proper protocol was followed. You have acted correctly, Captain. I appreciate your coming to me now.'

'Thank you, Mr Ismay.'

The meeting with Mr Ismay was less difficult than I had expected. We received his cooperation, without having to share too much confidential information. We could proceed with confidence, knowing that we could act with the authority of the captain and the White Star Line.

It was getting late. All of us were hungry, but also very tired. The captain invited Holmes, Miss Norton and me to join us in his cabin for a light dinner. Before we left Mr Ismay's cabin, he made a telephone call and placed an order for dinner for four.

Shortly after we arrived in the captain's sitting room, the food arrived. The steward uncovered a large tray filled with hot and cold meat, along with fruit, vegetables and cheese. It was accompanied by warm bread and a pot of tea.

We each helped ourselves substantially – that is, except for Holmes, who nibbled at a little beef, then poured a cup of tea and placed some cheese on the saucer. Few words were exchanged as we ate. The captain and I took second helpings. Holmes stood quietly, sipping his tea and staring out of a porthole.

I was concluding my meal when there was a knock at the door.

'Yes, Phillips. What is it?' said the captain.

'Excuse me, sir, but I have two important messages. One is for you, and the other is for the Commodore. I was about to look for him but I see that he is here.'

'Thank you, Phillips.' The captain took the envelopes and handed one to Holmes.

Phillips was about to leave, when he turned and fished a piece of paper from his jacket pocket.

'Oh, and one of the crewmen asked me to deliver this to you. Mr Murdoch sent it up from the hold.'

'Mr Phillips, you are a wealth of information today,' said the captain. 'Have you and Bride been getting any rest?'

'Some, sir. There are quite a lot of messages from the passengers. My finger is quite painful from tapping the key.'

'See to it that you and your finger get some rest. The same goes for Mr Bride.'

'Yes, sir. We will attempt to.'

Phillips left, after nodding to the rest of us, and adding an extra smile for Miss Norton.

The captain unfolded Murdoch's note first.

'It seems that Mr Murdoch and Miss Storm-Fleming have recovered one of her bullets. It was embedded in a wooden pallet that was propped up against a wall – just about where she said it would be. They are still looking for the other one.'

'That is good news for Miss Storm-Fleming,' I noted.

'Indeed,' said the captain, using a table knife to open the envelope of his wireless message.

'This is from our London office,' he said. 'I did some checking of my own in relation to Miss Storm-Fleming. I asked our people at White Star to make some inquiries.' Captain Smith studied the note. 'Let us see...thirty-four years old...middle name Janet...no police record... periodic mentions in the social pages of the newspapers...a frequent international traveller. I am afraid this is not very helpful... What about your message, Mr Holmes? Does it shed any light on this matter?'

Holmes, who had returned to staring out of the porthole, paused for a moment, and then turned to rejoin the conversation. 'No, I'm afraid not. Just a word of encouragement. He unfolded the note, which he had been holding in his hand, and began to read.

My dear Commodore,
I do not have to remind you how imperative it is that the documents in question be recovered immediately. We are all depending on the efforts of you and your companions. In my opinion, the matter could not be in better hands. Good luck!

Sincerely,
WC.

'Holmes, who is this WC?' I asked. 'Does he work for your brother, Mycroft?'

'More the other way around,' he said. 'Mycroft and I agreed on a few coded terms before I left, including the use of initials instead of names. This particular message is signed by Mr Winston Churchill, First Lord of the Admiralty.'

Chapter Fifteen

THE EARLY MORNING OF SATURDAY 13 APRIL 1912

Those of you who have read my work know that I am a man of few complaints. Indeed, I considered myself to be most fortunate to take part in the maiden voyage of this magnificent liner. But I must say that sea travel holds little appeal for me. I missed the comfort of my home in London and the company of my books. Perhaps even more, I missed long walks down London streets, watching people from all walks of life going about their daily routines. And, of course, there were the street urchins, those delightful little adventurers who were so full of energy and dreams, despite their poverty and limited prospects for the future.

I particularly remember the day I caught one of these enterprising tykes, all of eight years old, attempting to pick my pocket. I told him that I would not send him off to jail if he would accompany me to visit a friend. The friend in question was Inspector Wiggins of Scotland Yard, who was once himself a child of the streets. It just so happened that when the attempted theft occurred, I was on my way to have tea with the inspector.

We met at a small café along the Victoria Embankment. Wiggins was not in uniform, but the boy was quite skilled at identifying police officers. I thought for a moment that the young man was about to bolt. But a smile from Wiggins and the offer of a custard pastry encouraged him to give us a little more time from his busy day.

After tea, and second helpings of pastry, Wiggins took the boy for a walk along the Embankment. I do not know what was said during that conversation but I do know that the boy has stayed out of trouble. I know this because Wiggins looks in on him from time to time.

These things occurred to me as I stood in my cabin, preparing to meet Futrelle for breakfast. At Holmes's suggestion, I had knocked on the writer's door before retiring for the evening. He gladly accepted my invitation to assist in the investigation. His wife, after three full days of activity, had expressed a desire to sit quietly, reading. She willingly gave him permission to play the detective, provided he returned in time to dress for dinner.

Futrelle and I were to spend the day in the second- and third-class sections of the ship, making discreet inquiries. Our orders from Holmes were simply to 'go everywhere, see everything, and overhear everyone'. Admittedly, our prospects for gleaning useful information were limited. But then, where better to hide the documents than a place far removed from the area where they were stolen? There was also Futrelle's earlier sighting of Brandon unlocking a gate and entering the third-class section. The captain had said this was completely unauthorized and threatened to place Brandon under arrest. But at Holmes's request, he agreed simply to assign a crew member to keep Brandon under observation.

Miss Norton's assignment was to work with the captain and crew in conducting the investigation into Bishop's death. That included the continued interrogation of the stoker, Strickley, who had thus far refused to divulge any information. He continued to insist that he had nothing to do with the break-in.

Holmes declined to discuss the details of how he planned to spend his day. But he did say that he had several lines of inquiry to follow involving our suspects. His most telling comment was that Miss Norton and I should not expect to see Commodore Winter until evening. From this I deduced that Holmes was about to abandon temporarily his disguise as the crusty commodore, and assume some new and less conspicuous identity.

At half past eight, I had just adjusted my tie and was brushing the jacket of my oldest brown suit, when I heard a knock at the door. I was surprised to find Miss Storm-Fleming outside, looking warm and comfortable in her golden brown dress and yellow woollen shawl.

'Good morning, Doctor Watson. I would like to talk to you for a few minutes, if I may.'

'Miss Storm-Fleming, please forgive me but I was just leaving for a meeting. Perhaps you would care to join me on deck for a moment, before my appointment?'

She answered my invitation with a mischievous smile. 'I brought a visitor,' she said.

'A visitor? I don't...'

She looked down the corridor to her right and beckoned to her guest. A moment later, a small boy came forward and stood by her side. He was dressed in a dark blue suit with a matching blue cap.

'This is my friend, Tommy,' Miss Storm-Fleming said. 'Tommy, meet Doctor Watson.'

Attempting to conceal my puzzlement, I extended my hand to the short, young gentleman. 'How do you do, young man?'

He looked at me, wide-eyed, and then back at Miss Storm-Fleming. Then, after placing the book he was carrying under his arm, he reached out and shook my hand.

'I hope we do not disturb you, but I told Tommy earlier that I would introduce him to you, and this seemed as good a time as any.'

With a burst of energy, Tommy suddenly chose that moment to overcome his shyness.

'Doctor Watson, I have read everything you have written about Mr Holmes! I brought this book, hoping you would sign it for me. My mother said I should not bother you, but...'

'No bother at all, Tommy. How old are you?'

'I'm ten now, eleven next month.' He hesitated for a moment, looking down at his book, and then up at me. 'Do you suppose Mr Holmes would let me join his Baker Street Irregulars? I'm really observant and he wouldn't even have to pay me...'

'I am afraid all those adventures happened a long time ago, Tommy. All of the Irregulars are grown up now. One even works for Scotland Yard.'

Tommy's excitement crumbled as he listened to the bad news.

'But I am sure that if Mr Holmes ever decides to recruit a new team of Irregulars, he would be proud to include a fine young man like you. I will mention your name to him.'

'My surname is Roberts. I live in London with my parents when I am not at school.' He reached into the pocket of his trousers and pulled out a wrinkled business card. 'This is my father's card, from where he works. If you contact him, he will give me the message. He reads your books too.'

'Cox & Co., a very fine bank. I go there myself... Let us see, what have you here?' I took the book he was holding and walked over to the dressing table. *The Hound of the Baskervilles*, I remember that case very well. Have you read it?'

'Twice, I'm on my third time now.'

I opened the book to the title page and began to write. 'Three times!

I am flattered. How do you find time to play with your friends, with all this reading?'

'On this trip, he has been standing by the rail most of the time, watching the children play down on the third-class deck,' said Miss Storm-Fleming.

'A little bored, Tommy?'

'Yes, sir.'

'Well, me too sometimes.' After completing the inscription, I returned the book to him. 'There you are, young man, and I will let you know if Mr Holmes needs any help.'

'Why don't you run along now, Tommy,' said Miss Storm-Fleming. 'I need to speak to Doctor Watson. And don't forget to say, "Thank you".'

'Thank you, very much, Doctor Watson.'

'My pleasure, Tommy.'

The boy turned and walked towards the door.

'Oh, Tommy, before you leave, what is the number on the outside of my cabin door...without looking, now?'

'Why, C28, sir.'

'Excellent! You are a very observant young man. You will make a fine detective.'

The boy grinned from ear to ear, grasped his book tightly and skipped out of the door.

'Thank you, Miss Storm-Fleming, for that introduction. I approve of your taste in friends. Shall we walk towards the hall?'

'I made friends with you, did I not?' She smiled, but her face lacked the energy and spirit that I had seen so often over the past few days. I could tell that at this particular moment, she was very much in need of a friend.

'I understand that you and Murdoch found one of the rounds fired from your gun. Did you have any luck in finding the other?'

'No, but they are still looking.'

'Do not be concerned — I think the captain believes you. He is suspicious, though, that you may not be telling him everything.'

'And what is your opinion, Doctor Watson?'

'I must confess, I sense there is something more.'

Miss Storm-Fleming lowered her eyes and then folded her arms, as if feeling a chill in the air. After a moment's contemplation she began walking faster along the hall. 'If there is something more, do you trust me enough to remain my friend?'

'Indeed, Miss Storm-Fleming. I would also like to think that you trust me enough to confide in me.'

'And is there anything *you* would like to tell *me*, Doctor Watson?'

We turned to each other and smiled.

'Whatever your deep, dark secret, take care,' I said. 'You have had more than enough adventure for one voyage. Try to be a typical passenger, for a change.'

'Why, Doctor Watson, I would never dream of being typical,' she replied, as she hastened her step away from me.

Then she was gone, leaving only the scent of perfume and the warmth of her smile.

Chapter Sixteen

THE MORNING OF SATURDAY
13 APRIL 1912

Oatmeal porridge, vegetable stew, fried tripe and onions, Swedish bread and marmalade and, of course, tea. The third-class dining room offered a hearty breakfast and delightful conversation. Futrelle and I had seated ourselves at a long table, next to a Scandinavian family. Jan and Lise Svensson, their son and two daughters were on their way to Massachusetts, where Jan had a position assured on his brother Sven's fishing boat. Both Jan and Lise were fluent in English and their children were rapidly developing a basic knowledge of the language. In their early thirties, the couple had mixed feelings about leaving their home and loved ones. But Sven's letters had gone into detail about how living in America had offered opportunities for his own children, and how happy his family was. And, above all else, Jan and Lise wanted a better life for their children.

The Svenssons said they were finding their first trans-Atlantic crossing to be the thrill of a lifetime. They occupied a four-berth cabin at the ship's stern on F Deck. This afforded them easy access to the dining room, where they also ate lunch and dinner. The dining room was bright and cheerful, with white enamelled walls. The long tables were tastefully decorated and the wooden chairs, though uncushioned, were quite comfortable.

Futrelle told the Svenssons that he was preparing a newspaper article on the *Titanic* and, consequently, he was gathering information on each class of service. They were more than happy to offer their own evaluation of steerage and its facilities – information that proved useful to Futrelle and me as we planned our day's activities.

Mrs Svensson said the General Room was comfortable, though not well equipped with recreational opportunities for the children. Fortunately, the Svensson children had found playmates and, for the most part, they had improvised games and activities to occupy their time. She noted, however, that the General Room did have a fine piano, and some of the passengers whiled away the hours playing some enjoyable tunes.

Mr Svensson said he had spent little time in the two bars but he did enjoy an occasional trip to the smoking room, where he could light up his pipe and play a recreational game of cards with the other men. When he grew tired of cards, he tried chess, draughts and dominoes. Most of all, he enjoyed meeting other passengers, and discovering where they had been and where they were going.

Mrs Svensson said she had been concerned about the hundreds of men who, travelling alone, were berthed in the forward end of the ship. Some were in six- or eight-berth cabins, while others, mostly immigrants, shared dormitory-like areas on G Deck. While families and single women were berthed far away, in the aft end of the ship, all steerage passengers shared decks and public rooms during the day. She admitted that she had no reason to believe that any of these men were dangerous. Still, she kept a careful eye on her children.

Though not sharing his wife's concerns, Mr Svensson did say that there were a few troublemakers on board. The steerage bar on the forward end of E Deck seemed to be a gathering point. Word had already spread about a shouting match that had erupted the night before, when the crew attempted to close the bar for the night. A group of gamblers, who had been drinking whisky much of the evening, had objected to the game being interrupted. They then apparently moved the late-night session into one of the cabins.

After finishing our tea and wishing the Svenssons good luck in America, Futrelle and I continued on to the bar at the forward end of the ship. We had little to go on, so seeking out trouble seemed to be as good an idea as any.

We made our way up to E Deck, and travelled along a corridor that connected the forward and aft steerage accommodation. It was called 'Park Lane' by the officers and 'Scotland Road' by the crew. The sound of our footsteps echoed down the steel-walled hallway as we walked along the linoleum-tiled floors. This was a far cry from the regal pathways of first class.

As we walked along the corridor, Futrelle and I poked our heads into some of the open doorways. This area was largely taken up by quarters for cooks, stewards and waiters. There was a good deal of running about, as these industrious crew members travelled to and from their duties. A few, who were having a rest or were off duty, relaxed in their bunks or sat in chairs reading. After passing through the crew area, we found ourselves in a short section of corridor with third-class cabins on either side. Not much activity here. The passengers were away enjoying the various entertainments provided.

At the forward end of the corridor, we rounded the corner and found ourselves at the entrance to the saloon. The room was open, although alcoholic refreshments were not yet being served.

The saloon was small, compared to those in first class. The oak-panelled walls and teak tables and chairs created an atmosphere that was simple, but cheerful. Cheerful, that is, except for the dreary-looking souls who were seated around two tables joined together at the rear of the room. Their faces were unshaven and their clothing was unkempt. They appeared to be very tired, but still they went through the motions of a poker game.

One man was clearly winning. A mound of red, white and blue chips lay on the table before him. Unlike his companions, he was fresh and neatly dressed. His grey tweed suit was crisply pressed, and he wore a newly cut carnation in his lapel. This dapper card player, much to my surprise, was Hugo Brandon.

'Why Doctor Watson, Mr Futrelle, whatever are you doing down here?' Brandon rose and beckoned us over. His companions remained seated and eyed us suspiciously. 'Are things getting a little dull in first class?'

Futrelle replied. 'No, no, not at all. I am writing an article on the maiden voyage of the *Titanic*, and the captain has given me permission to roam about. Doctor Watson very kindly offered to accompany me. But what about you? Surely you are not preparing a travel review.'

Brandon laughed. 'Writing is not my forte. But I do enjoy a good game of cards. And while the games in first class are for far higher stakes, I find them a little tame. Playing with my friends here helps to sharpen my skills for bigger games.'

The men at the table continued to stare at Futrelle and me. Aside from Brandon, this was not a congenial group.

'Oh, I do beg your pardon, allow me to introduce you to my companions.' Brandon grabbed his walking stick from the table and used it as a pointer. 'The gentleman to my left is Charlie, and there is Kurt, Willy and Swede. Swede, incidentally, does some wonderful card tricks. Perhaps we can persuade him to show you some, after he has finished his coffee.'

Swede said nothing. Instead, he picked up the coffee pot at the centre of the table and poured a half cup. He then reached inside his coat and pulled out a dull, metal flask. However, the motion of his arm was interrupted when the tip of Brandon's walking stick tapped the side of the flask.

'Now, Swede, as a friend, I cannot allow you to overdo it on the spirits. Remember, you have a busy day planned today, and it is still only mid-morning.'

Swede begrudgingly put the flask back inside his pocket.

'I only wanted a touch to get my blood moving.'

'Then try a little more of this excellent coffee,' replied Brandon, filling Swede's cup to the top. 'That'll bring you to life.'

My attention was fixed, not on Swede's problem, but on a small bottle containing a clear liquid. It was on the table next to Kurt, resting on a folded handkerchief. Brandon looked at me, and then at the bottle.

'Oh dear, what have we here?' said Brandon. 'More spirits? Gentlemen, if you are going to insist on drinking, I may have to step away from the game. And I know you would all like the chance to win your money back.'

'I understood that there was some trouble last night,' I said. 'Do you happen to know what it was all about?'

Brandon, his temperance speech interrupted, stroked his chin, as if trying to recall anything out of the ordinary. Suddenly, he smiled and pointed his finger in my general direction.

'I think I know what you are referring to. These gentlemen and I were in this room just before ten last night, when the barman announced that he would be closing down soon. Naturally, it was thought that this was a little early and some raised objections. There was a minor confrontation that eventually involved some of the crew. After a time, I was able to convince them all that we could continue the game just as comfortably in their cabin. And that is all there was to it... My word, has that story spread all over the ship?'

'Oh, no, indeed not. A man in the dining room happened to mention it.'

'Good, you know that these stories can get out of hand.'

'Well, Mr Brandon, gentlemen, we must be getting on,' I said. 'Perhaps we will meet you again later.'

'Nice to see you, Doctor, Mr Futrelle. I would invite you to join in the game but, as you can see, everyone is eager to win their money back. You are most welcome to stay and watch.'

'Thank you, but, as I said, we must be on our way. Mr Futrelle has a good deal of research to do for his article.'

We shook hands with Brandon, and exchanged nods with his companions.

When we were back in the corridor, I placed my hand on Futrelle's shoulder and looked back towards the door to the bar.

'What did you think of the bottle, the one on the table?' I asked.

'Very unusual. It seemed as though the handkerchief was being used to pad the bottle from the surface of the wood.'

'That is exactly what I thought. Let us proceed on deck to tell the captain.' I reached into my pocket and pulled out a deck map that the captain had given us before we began our tour. It was at that moment that Brandon and Swede chose to step through the door from the bar. Brandon was carrying the coffee pot.

'Lost?' said Brandon. 'Swede and I were just about to get more coffee. Perhaps we can help you.'

'We can manage. But thank you for the offer.'

'No trouble at all. In fact, I know a short cut. It is around the corner, to the right. Just follow me.'

Futrelle and I exchanged glances, then followed Brandon's lead.

Swede, instead of accompanying his companion, followed behind us. The journey was only a short one. Soon after we rounded the corner, we approached a stairwell.

Brandon hurried on ahead, stepping down the stairway instead of up. 'We will have to go down a couple of decks first,' he said. 'This stairway only goes up one more deck. But if we go down to G Deck, we will reach a corridor that will take us back to the lifts.'

I smiled, looking back briefly to determine Swede's location. 'On second thoughts, I think we will go back the way we came. Futrelle and I want to speak to some of the crew on our way out.'

Brandon appeared disappointed that his offer of help was rejected. 'Are you sure? There are some interesting crew areas here as well.'

'Quite sure.' I changed my direction. 'Thank you, very much.' After a few steps, Futrelle and I stopped short. Swede was holding a shiny revolver. It was pointed directly at me.

'I got 'em, Mr Brandon.'

Futrelle turned his head back towards Brandon, who was climbing back up the stairs. 'I say, Brandon, does your friend always carry a gun when he gets coffee?'

Brandon laughed. 'Sometimes the kitchen is reluctant to fill the pot.'

Brandon too was carrying a revolver, somewhat smaller than Swede's military issue. He motioned for me to walk down the stairs.

'We will be putting our weapons away, gentlemen. We do not want to disturb the passengers and crew. But just remember, we are still holding them in our pockets. And we have nothing to lose if you force us to use them. But we cannot allow you to report us to the captain.'

We continued down the stairs, with Swede close behind us and Brandon leading the way. As we made our way down one deck, and then another, we crossed paths with a young steward who was scurrying up the stairs with a tray full of dirty dishes. It occurred to me that bumping the tray out of his hands might create a sufficient distraction to allow us to overcome our captors. But I decided that such a move would place this innocent passerby at too great a risk.

The stairway ended at G Deck, where Brandon motioned for us to continue down a dark corridor. At the end of that hallway we found a hatch in the floor, with the doorway open.

'Down the ladder, gentlemen,' said Brandon. 'And please mind your step.'

Swede was the first to descend, and I followed. The chamber was dark but there was enough light for me to see that I was in a familiar area. It was the cargo hold where the motorcars were stored, where Miss Storm-Fleming had her unfortunate meeting with Bishop. My mind raced through the possibilities. If I could somehow break free, this cavern provided ample opportunities to hide. I would, of course, be apprehended in time – unless I was able to make my way into the adjoining luggage or post rooms. My prospects for finding help in those areas were not great but the next section was the forward boiler room, where I was likely to find some very strong and hearty members of the crew. Then there was Futrelle to consider. What if he was not able to break free? I decided that he would be no worse off, and perhaps even safer if Brandon knew I was on my way to find help.

Swede was well below me, and about to step off the ladder onto the floor. I was not a young man, but I had always made time to exercise and keep healthy. After glancing upwards and seeing Futrelle in the hatchway, I let go of the ladder and jumped directly on top of Swede. He let out a startled cry and fell to the floor. I could hear the sound of his gun clanking on to the deck.

I too had fallen flat on my back and a sharp pain was penetrating my shoulder and arm. Fortunately, my legs felt fine and I was able to get to my feet. I was surprised to see that Futrelle had not moved. He was still in the hatchway, apparently under Brandon's watchful eye. Brandon was not even calling to his companion. He apparently felt that Swede could handle any difficulties.

Brandon's judgement proved to be correct. Swede, still on the floor, grabbed my leg just as I got to my feet. I heard the sound of metal sliding briefly along the deck and a moment later Swede was on top of me. I felt a stinging blow to the back of my head, and then drifted off into unconsciousness.

Chapter Seventeen

THE AFTERNOON OF SATURDAY 13 APRIL 1912

I followed the roar of the rushing water. The pathway was wet and my feet slipped as I ran. Sweat poured from my brow, yet the cold, damp air penetrated my clothing. I paused to button my coat to the collar but this was only for a moment. I continued even faster, mindful of the danger that awaited my friend.

After a time, the trail turned sharply towards the sound of the water. The path was level here and it was easier to keep my footing. I trudged along the wet ground until I reached a wooden bridge. It was there, in the mist, that I saw my friend, Sherlock Holmes, fighting hand to hand with a man dressed in a black cloak.

I stepped forward to join Holmes in the struggle but my foot broke through the planks as if they were paper. I saved myself from plunging into the falls below by grabbing the rail.

Ahead, Holmes and the cloaked figure continued their battle. For them, despite their chaotic movements, the planks held firm.

The cloaked figure raised his hand, which held a sturdy walking stick. As his arm moved back to strike a blow, his cloak fell away, uncovering the military uniform he wore underneath.

The stick swept downwards, but Holmes moved to the side and avoided what would have been a crushing blow to his head. His opponent, attempting to regain his balance, twisted around. Through the mist, I saw the face of Colonel James Moriarty. He was laughing at me, as his arms surrounded Holmes in a tight grasp.

Just then, the deck of the bridge fell through. I looked in horror as I saw my friend and the colonel, still in combat, plummet towards the raging water.

I stood there, looking down and listening to the steady roar of the falls. But then I heard another sound directly behind me – an animal. It was a deep, penetrating growl that developed a gurgling resonance as saliva filled the beast's mouth.

I continued to look towards the falls, terrified that the slightest movement would invite an attack. Slowly, I turned my head, while grasping the end of the bridge railing. There, crouched on top of a boulder, was a beast of enormous proportions. Its black, moist coat shimmered in the faint rays of light that penetrated the mist. The hound's eyes blazed with a yellow glow. Its huge white teeth were fully exposed behind its dripping jowls.

I tried to move, but I found that my arms and legs were frozen in place. I sensed that the creature knew this, and was waiting there, taking its time to strike. The wait was not long. With a sudden wail, it sprang forward, propelling its huge mass on to me. We crashed into the bridge rail, and then down, down towards the dark, rushing water.

I continued to fall, powerless to save myself. Suddenly, I heard someone calling my name. It was a calm voice, but not a friendly one. It repeated my name over and over again.

'Doctor Watson, Doctor Watson... Good, I see you are coming round. I would never have forgiven myself if Swede had damaged you permanently.'

Brandon stood in front of me, holding a lamp beside his face. Swede was seated on a crate, fingering his open flask. Futrelle, sitting up and alert, was bound hand and foot. I tried to raise my arm to rub my throbbing head but discovered that I was bound as well.

We were in the ship's hold, in an area used for storage of various odds and ends. Judging by the V shape of the room, we were in the forward-most area of the deck. I could hear a roaring sound through the heavy steel hull, as the ship cut its way through the water. Futrelle and I had been thrown on a pile of empty sacks, which were slightly moist. There was a chill in the air, and I longed for the warmth and comfort of my cabin.

'How are you, Doctor? Is there anything I can do for you?'

I blinked, attempting to clear my vision. 'You can call a steward. Ask him to send two aspirin and someone to untie these ropes.'

'We will attend to the aspirin, but I am afraid I cannot help you with the other. By the way, Swede apologizes for hitting you with his gun but you should not have tried to escape.'

I turned to face my fellow prisoner. 'How are you, Futrelle?'

'As well as can be expected in the circumstances. I was just trying to get Brandon here to explain what this is all about. So far, no luck.'

Brandon smiled. 'Oh, I'll be happy to explain, although I am a bit surprised that the two of you have not been able to deduce it for yourselves.'

'What do you mean by that?'

Brandon put down the lamp and sat on a nearby crate. 'Just that here, I have two of the most famous mystery writers of our time. Doctor Watson, you record the cases of Sherlock Holmes. And Mr Futrelle, you have your fictional detective, Professor Van Dusen, whom you call The Thinking Machine. Yet, neither of you have the slightest notion of what I have planned... But then, you have been investigating and asking a lot of questions. Perhaps you know more than you will admit to.'

'Perhaps,' I said, doing my best to outbluff this old poker player. 'But, for the sake of the details, pray start from the beginning.'

'I would be glad to, Doctor. Well then, I suppose if you want me to give you the complete story, I should tell you about a boy growing up in London.

'I had a comfortable upbringing, good parents, a fine education. I also had a great love of games – anything competitive. At the university, I excelled at football and cricket, but most of all I loved evening card games with the members of my teams. If someone outstripped me on the playing field, I knew it would not be long before I would be collecting their weekly allowance at the poker table.'

Truly, Brandon had a captive audience but I still had the freedom of protest. 'This is all very fascinating, Brandon, but I do not see...'

'Background, Doctor. I want you to understand today's events in the light of what I have discovered in life. It is only then that you can understand, and perhaps accept, what is about to happen.'

'Then please continue.'

'Thank you, Doctor. Well, life was good and I felt quite content with my studies and sport. Still, my existence appeared to lack meaning. I had no direction that would allow me to make my mark on the world. Ironically, it was a game of poker that helped me to find that direction.

'I was playing with some of the older students and losing rather badly to a fellow named McKee. The rest of us looked on McKee as an odd sort, because he belonged to some peculiar political groups, and his bookshelves were filled with Marx, Engels and other socialist thinkers. But in his favour, he was a good card player and a congenial fellow, so we invited him into our games.

'We were about to conclude for the night, with McKee holding most of the chips, when he offered a most interesting wager. He said he would bet all his winnings on one hand of poker. If he lost, we would recover our losses. But if he won, we would agree to accompany him to a meeting of the Marching Together League, a student socialist society. At first I refused, thinking that my evening's losses were hardly worth diminishing my reputation, especially if my parents ever found out. But McKee assured me that my attendance would remain secret, and if anyone did find out, he would support my story that I was there to repay a poker debt. I did end up accepting his wager, as did the two other players at the table, who had lost even more than me.

'Well, McKee's luck held out, and on the following Thursday night we found ourselves at a smoky Oxford bar, listening to fiery rhetoric from some highly intelligent speakers. Except for one well-known history teacher, I did not recognize any of them. Yet, within their own circle, they were well regarded and respected. I began to consider my own values and soon concluded that money – while a worthy goal in games of chance – should not be used by the powerful to oppress the weak. Within a fortnight I had decided to join the Marching Together League.

'After coming down from Oxford I told my father I wanted to take some time to see a bit of the world before entering the bottom rungs of his brokerage business. He seemed disappointed, but agreed to fund my trip as a graduation present. I said I would return in no more than six months, after touring Europe and visiting friends of my father along the way. He wanted this to be a business education, as well as a cultural experience. I felt guilty but deep in my heart I did not consider my acceptance to be an out-and-out lie. After all, I did plan to visit his friends and might, ultimately, decide to return to my father's business. But, in the meantime, my travels would complete another type of education that began with the Marching Together League. I would make contact with socialist organizations throughout Europe, and look for opportunities to build a stronger alliance.

'I looked up one of my father's friends in Paris, but abandoned my business pursuits after this one stop. Instead, I devoted my time to the mission given to me by the league. The money given to me by my father was a more than ample stake to begin a successful career as a card player... Sadly, I never saw or contacted my parents again. I understand that my father died last year. You must understand, gentlemen, I loved my parents. I bear a great burden of guilt. Yet, I could not return to them and explain why I did what I did. They would never have understood.'

'That's a fine biographical account,' said Futrelle, 'but it does not explain why we are here, bound from hand to foot.'

Brandon, who had come to look somewhat melancholy, quickly regained his earlier enthusiasm. 'Yes, gentlemen, to the point. As you know, the launching of this ship was greeted with a good deal of trumpeting. In fact, the *Titanic* is seen as a symbol of the infallibility of the British Empire and the capitalist system. If this ship sinks on its maiden voyage, the loss of confidence by capitalist countries will be immeasurable.'

'You mean to sink the *Titanic*!' I shouted. 'Hundreds of innocent people would die! You cannot be serious!'

'Oh, I am very serious. And as for those who will die, well, my burden of guilt will grow immensely. But remember, thousands, even millions die in wars. This one incident will bring us a giant step closer to world socialism.'

'Brandon, stop this insanity!' said Futrelle. 'This ship does not have enough lifeboats. Only a fraction, if any, will be saved. And do not forget, you and your men will die too.'

'No, no, not if we follow our plan.' Brandon was pacing back and forth, like a professor before a blackboard. 'A ship will be waiting for us a mile off the starboard side at around midnight. It has instructions to signal to us, to guide our approach. At 1 am two nitroglycerine charges will be set off by timers. One, in fact, is right here in this hold. Another is elsewhere in the ship.'

I looked around the hold but did not see any signs of a bomb. 'Give it up, Brandon. Sinking a ship will not further your cause. If anything, the authorities of the world will band together to destroy you and your organization.'

'And who will tell them that we did it? The two of you will be the first to die. And as to the cause, we have every hope that it will be seen as an accident – an exploding boiler or a collision with an iceberg. We will have to wait and see.'

'Brandon, I beg of you, give this up now,' I pleaded. 'Kill us if you like. There will not be any witnesses. But do not continue with your terrible plan.'

'Well, Doctor, I am a sporting man. I could kill you both right now. But if the two of you are clever enough, there is a small chance that you could concoct some means of escaping and of warning the captain. As I recall, Mr Futrelle's Professor Van Dusen was somewhat of an escape artist.' He pulled a watch from his pocket. 'It is now just past 4 pm. The charges have been planted and my friends and I must make preparations for our departure. Remember, both charges go off at 1 am... But no more clues. Goodbye, and good luck.'

Chapter Eighteen

THE EVENING OF SATURDAY
13 APRIL 1912

Escape is an art that is distinct from the science of deductive reasoning.

Deductive reasoning involves examining factual evidence and, through analysis, reconstructing past events. It is rather like locating the pieces of a puzzle, and then putting them together.

Escape, on the other hand, requires one other thing – an overpowering will to survive. You must truly believe there is a way out, if only you can find it.

Futrelle and I clearly understood the importance of our challenge. The survival of everyone on board the ship depended on our ability to free ourselves and warn the captain. But despite this awesome responsibility, we found ourselves completely perplexed.

Brandon and Swede had taken the lantern with them, leaving us in total darkness. While other holds on the ship had electric lights, I had seen no evidence of a switch or light fixtures in this small chamber. I sat there, attempting to remember everything I had observed during our conversation with Brandon.

We were encased on all sides, above and below, by solid steel. Futrelle, who had been conscious throughout our ordeal, identified our prison as the forward-most cargo hold on the orlop deck, just in front of the hold where the automobiles were stored.

After Brandon and Swede left, we had heard the sound of chains being looped through the handle of the steel door to the adjoining hold. They had not gagged us, since shouting would do us no good. After the shooting, the captain had forbidden entry to the scene of the crime. Only senior officers were allowed in. Brandon cleverly saw this as an opportunity to conceal his activities.

The forward wall also had a covered opening. It was labelled 'chain locker'. That offered some hope, since the ship's huge anchor chain was far too large to occupy only one deck. If we could enter the locker, we might be able to climb to a higher level and escape through an unlocked door. Even if we were unable to leave through the opening, we might be able to attract the attention of people on the other side.

The crates lining the walls around us were not labelled. We had no clue as to their contents, though the lack of refrigeration indicated that they were not perishable.

The floor and ceiling both had large hatchways, through which crates and other cargo could be lowered. Unfortunately, both were covered by huge metal plates. The bottom hatch cover was piled high with crates. I suspected that the cover on the upper hatch might be weighted in a similar manner.

I sat shivering on the stack of burlap sacks, struggling to loosen the ropes that bound my hands and feet. Though I could not see Futrelle in the darkness, I could hear rustling and grunting sounds, as he strained his muscles in a tireless effort to regain his freedom.

'Futrelle, do you think you might be able to free your arms or legs?'

'Not a chance. If anything, the ropes seem to be getting tighter.

Perhaps it is the dampness. How about you?'

'No, I have the same problem.'

'Watson, do you think he is really serious about sinking the ship? I did not see any bomb in here.'

'It could be in one of the crates, or behind one. For the sake of the people on this ship, I think we must assume that he is telling the truth. We must find a way to alert the captain.'

We sat in silence, considering the alternatives. In addition to being bound, we could not move along the floor. Our captors had looped a rope through a hole at the base of a metal stanchion that ran from the floor to the ceiling. The ends of the rope were tied to our wrists. We had only a few feet of slack.

'Futrelle?'

'Yes.'

'As I recall, did not your story, *The Problem of Cell 13*, involve Professor Van Dusen escaping from a prison cell? I cannot remember the details. How did he get out?'

'Well, he bet some men that he could escape from a prison cell within a week.'

'I fear that we do not have that long, but please continue.'

'Let us see... He went into a cell with only the clothes on his back, some toothpaste and twenty-five dollars in cash. He was not allowed any contact with the outside world, and only his captors knew that he was there.'

'Then what?'

'To cut a long story short, he unravelled a long thread from his socks and tied one end to a rat he had captured in his cell. He sent the rat through an old drainpipe to a playground just outside the prison wall. The rat carried a ten-dollar bill, and a note asking whatever child found it to give the note to a particular newspaper reporter. When the reporter returned with the boy, he found the drainpipe and attached some stronger string to the thread. Van Dusen then pulled the end of the string into his cell, creating a means for sending small objects through the pipe.'

'Amazing! What happened then?'

'He used nitric acid, which he had received through the drainpipe, to cut through the bars of his window. Then he cut through a cable outside the window, placing that side of the prison in perfect darkness. That allowed him to leave through the window.'

'What about the prison gate?'

'He walked through, disguised as an electrician.'

I sat for a moment, considering Futrelle's extraordinary narrative.

'I regret, Futrelle, that I do not think there is anything in that story that can help us in this particular situation.'

There was silence, then my fellow prisoner spoke in a subdued voice. 'No, I suppose not... Did you and Mr Holmes ever plan an escape?'

'We were seldom in such a situation, although a few of our clients had narrow escapes.'

'Such as...'

'Well, I recall one case where a young engineer was locked inside a hydraulic press and the ceiling began to come down slowly upon him.'

'What did he do?'

'Very little, I fear. Just as he was about to be crushed by the machine, a woman confederate of his captor opened a side door and allowed him to pass through.'

'He escaped unharmed, then?'

'Unfortunately, his captor cut off his thumb with a butcher's cleaver as he made his escape through a window. But other than that, he was fine. But I suppose that does not help us much either. That is, unless one of Brandon's henchmen decides to take pity on us.'

'I do not consider that to be a possibility.'

'Neither do I...'

We stopped speaking for what could have been fifteen minutes, as each of us continued to struggle with our ropes. We tried fraying the rope that bound us together by rubbing it against the supporting post but with no success.

'Watson, do you suppose there's a trap door or anything beneath this pile of sacks? I mean, it is a possibility.'

'I suppose we could move the sacks and examine the floor. Of course, bound to the post as we are, we would not be able to climb down there, even if there is a hatch.'

'It could be that there's someone below us.'

By sliding back to the metal post, Futrelle and I were able to get to our feet. We found that the slack in the rope allowed us both to stand in a crouched position. With our feet bound, it took considerable time and effort to kick the sacks away and expose the floor beneath them. At this point, we both sat down again and felt the floor with our fingertips.

Futrelle uttered an oath under his breath.

'My dear Futrelle, what is the matter?'

'I tore my trousers on a jagged piece of metal, bent up from the floor. I may have cut myself too.'

'Futrelle, can you manoeuvre your hands over to the metal and cut the ropes?'

I heard him sliding along the floor, and then stop suddenly.

'Watson, could you slide towards the post? I need a little more slack.'

I slid backwards, and soon heard a sawing sound as the edge of the metal rubbed against the rope.

Futrelle stopped for a moment. 'I think I have almost done it.'

'Splendid! Keep going.'

Soon, Futrelle was free from his bonds. He then caught his breath, and set to work untying me. When my hands were free, I reached into my jacket pocket and pulled out a box of matches. Despite the dampness, I was able to light one on the first try.

'Is there anything in here we can burn?' I asked.

'Perhaps one of these sacks is dry enough to make a torch.'

'I do not understand why there are no electric lights. The other holds have them.'

Futrelle looked around in the dim glow of the match. The opportunity was short, since the flame soon reached my fingers. 'Perhaps there are lights and we just have not seen them. Even with Brandon's lamp, it was still pretty dark in here.'

'I am certain that there is no switch by the door,' I said. 'Where else would one be?'

Futrelle scrambled about the floor for a while, then returned with a long, square piece of wood. 'I found this by the crates. We could try wrapping some cloth around it.'

I managed to remove my tweed waistcoat and, after wrapping it tightly around the end of the stick, I used the rope to secure it in place. It served well as a torch and burned brightly.

'But it will not last for long,' I said. 'I suggest we make haste.'

It did not take long to solve the mystery of the missing switch. I found a light fixture on one wall, with a string dangling below. One quick tug at the switch produced an even glow.

'I will try to push these crates over so they do not block the light,' said Futrelle.

'No! Wait! Remember the bomb. You might set it off. We will just have to make do with the light we have now.'

Futrelle nodded, somewhat embarrassed by his rash suggestion.

'Where do you suppose the bomb is?' Futrelle asked.

'Well, I've been thinking about that. On the night we left Cherbourg, Holmes and I were in the smoking room, listening to a conversation between a passenger and the ship's designer, a Mr Andrews. Andrews said that the ship has sixteen watertight compartments, and that it can remain afloat with any two of them flooded – or any three of the first five flooded. I would say that the bomb is likely to be next to a bulkhead somewhere further down.'

We faced each other for a moment, then walked to opposite corners of the hold. Futrelle was the winner.

'Just our luck!' said Futrelle. 'Here it is, in a shadow. All I can see is a bunch of wires, some metal thing and a glass bottle all jammed together in a wooden box.'

'Perhaps we should try moving it into the light?'

'We could set it off,' Futrelle cautioned. 'First let us see if there is a way out. If Brandon was telling the truth about it going off at one o'clock, we still have lots of time left. What time is it, by the way?'

'Half past seven.'

We decided to leave the bomb alone for the moment, and spend some time examining possible escape routes. Our findings were far from promising.

As we expected, the door to the next hold was held firmly in place by the chain. On the opposite wall, the cover to the chain locker was fastened by some very large bolts. We could reach the cargo hatch above by climbing on top of the crates but the metal cover would not move an inch. We tried moving crates to reach the hatch cover on the floor but they were too heavy for the two of us to handle. If we had a crowbar or some other means of prying them open, we could perhaps unpack them until they were light enough to move. But that might take hours, and the prospects of escaping by that route were not that good, even if the crates were removed. My previous study of the ship showed that that there was another hold below us, and there was no indication of whether we could move freely to the next compartment.

'Perhaps we could short the electric lights,' Futrelle offered. 'If that blacked out other parts of the ship, they might send an electrician down to find the trouble.'

'And if it does not, or if they decide to leave the problem until morning, we will be left in the dark. We would have virtually no chance of defusing the bomb. Not that either of us knows anything about defusing a bomb.'

'I suppose... I wish we could ring for room service. I am extremely hungry.'

I smiled and nodded in agreement.

'Futrelle,' I said. 'There may be another way.' I was surprised to hear my voice cracking. 'It would not save us, but it may save the other passengers.'

'What is it?'

'We could try to defuse the bomb. If we succeed, then well and good. If we fail, and the bomb goes off, it will only flood two of the holds.'

'And kill us.'

'And, as you say, kill us. But the ship will not sink, at least until the second bomb goes off at 1 am. And the threat of two flooded holds might cause the captain to abandon ship.'

'But there are not enough lifeboats.'

'Some would be saved. And if the captain calls for help early enough, another ship might come before the *Titanic* goes down.'

'I consider our duty is clear.'

We carefully moved the box containing the bomb to the opposite wall, under the electric light. For some time, we kneeled next to it, examining the complex network of wires and components.

'The bottle of nitroglycerine is down underneath all this other apparatus,' I said. 'If only we could just remove it, that would make the whole process simple.'

I tugged gently at the spool-like piece of metal above the bottle, but it held firmly in place.

'We could try pulling some of the wires,' Futrelle said.

'That might trigger it, but then again, perhaps not.'

I tried tugging at another component, which caused a brief whirring sound that made me think twice about continuing that particular approach.

'If we had a straw and could remove the stopper on the bottle, we could siphon the nitroglycerine out of the bottle and into another container. Then the bomb would be harmless.'

I wiped the sweat off my brow. 'Not the most helpful suggestion, Futrelle.'

'Do you have a better idea?'

'Confound it, Futrelle, I am a doctor, not an explosives expert!'

'Apologies, old fellow. An unusual situation for both of us.'

'There is a wire here that is lightly soldered into place,' I said, pointing to a thin strand covered in red insulation. 'I am going to give it a tug.'

'I am with you, Watson. Proceed...but gently, if you please.'

I took a deep breath, then gently placed my fingertips on either side of the wire, down near the connection. I placed the forefinger of my other hand on the component just below the connection, and began to work the wire back and forth.

'What the devil is that!' I gasped, backing my hands away from the device.

Someone was rattling the chain outside the door. I looked up at Futrelle and he looked back at me with an expression of utter delight.

'We're saved!' he said. 'The ship is saved!'

'Unless it is Brandon coming back to check up on our ropes,' I said, keeping my voice down. 'Quickly, to the door! We will need to grab whoever it is when he comes in.'

Futrelle and I stood on either side of the door, our backs to the wall. Suddenly, I remembered something and ran back to switch off the light.

The door opened before I could return to my position. I saw the silhouette of a stooped man. He had a full, fluffy beard and mumbled to himself as he peered through the doorway. It was clearly not Brandon, but I wondered whether it might be one of his henchmen.

He slowly lifted a lamp from the floor, and pointed it directly at me. He suddenly backed away in surprise but then braced himself on the door frame and moved forward cautiously.

''Ere now, who is that lurkin' about in the dark? Come out in the light now, yer 'ear?'

Futrelle took no chances. He lunged at the stooped figure as he stepped into the room. Both fell to the floor with a thud. I turned the light back on and studied the features of our visitor, who was now lying flat on his back, with Futrelle on top of him. He was an elderly man with a weathered face and a bushy beard and eyebrows. The white hair behind his receding brow was long and uncombed. The man's grey, battered coat did not appear to be that of one of the crew. But then, he did not appear to be a passenger either, since his clothing contained a layer of soot.

'Futrelle, I suggest that you help our visitor up to his feet to allow him to explain who he is and what his business is down in the cargo hold.'

Futrelle helped the man to his feet. Our visitor showed little gratitude. Instead, he brushed himself down and scrutinized each of us from head to toe.

'What I am doin' 'ere is no concern of yours,' he said, continuing to brush dust from his sleeves. 'And what do you mean by jumpin' on me like that? Seems to me I did you gents a favour by lettin' you out of 'ere.'

I was beginning to feel a little guilty. While we were justified in being cautious, he had indeed done us and everyone on board a great favour.

'My apologies but we had to make sure that you were not in league with the man who locked us in here. But what *are* you doing down here yourself?'

The man grinned wryly, stood up straight, and used both hands to pull the beard from his face.

'My dear Watson, I was simply looking for you.'

'Holmes!'

'Indeed it is. And I am most relieved to find that I have not lost my touch with disguises. You must admit, this one had you completely fooled.'

Chapter Nineteen

'Holmes, you amaze me! After all these years, you still surprise me. How on earth did you find us down here?'

'When you failed to return, I went down to third class to find you. I could not locate you in any of the public areas, so I decided that my best course of action was to follow our mysterious gambler friend, Mr Brandon. I found him in the bar.'

'But why the disguise?' asked Futrelle, nervously dividing his attention between Holmes and the bomb.

Holmes looked curiously at Futrelle, and then back at me.

'My dear fellow, what do you have back there?'

'It is a bomb...but it is not set to go off until one o'clock.'

Holmes folded his arms, nodded and stared at me with calm resignation. He made me feel like a schoolboy causing mischief in the teacher's absence. After scratching his chin, he walked to the corner of the room and glanced down at the bomb.

'One o'clock, you say?'

'Yes, Brandon plans to sink the ship,' I replied. 'He thinks, somehow, that this will further the cause of Marxism. He does not seem to know anything about the stolen documents.'

'I see... Well, this adds a new dimension to our mystery. I suggest that we go on deck and report to the captain.'

We debated, for a moment, whether one of us should stay behind to stand guard over the bomb. We decided that it was well enough hidden to avoid notice during the short time we were gone.

On the way up to the captain's cabin, Holmes continued his account of how he had located us in the cargo hold. I was surprised to hear that he had resorted to a talent he had picked up years ago from London's criminal element.

'When I entered the bar, Brandon was seated at a table with his companions. He was pointing out something on a large sheet of paper, which was unfolded and spread across the table. I moved in more closely and discovered that it was a set of deck plans for the ship – the same kind that the captain gave to us. From time to time, he would take the pencil he was using as a pointer, and mark something on the map.

'At the conclusion of this discussion, Brandon folded the map and put it into his coat pocket. He then stood up, picked up his empty beer glass and walked to the bar. I followed him and, in fact, was able to begin a casual conversation with him. He did not recognize me, of course, since I was no longer in the guise of Commodore Winter.'

'But again, I must ask you, Mr Holmes, why the new disguise?' asked Futrelle, as we hastily made our way past the post office and up the stairway that bordered the squash-rackets court.

'I started the day by making enquiries in areas of the ship where passengers and crew might have been intimidated by the sight of an officer in uniform. I decided, for a time, to take on a less assuming civilian identity.'

'How did you find us?' I asked. 'Were you able to deduce something from your encounter with Brandon?'

'Not exactly... I picked Brandon's pocket,' said Holmes, taking some satisfaction in this feat. 'And I must say, his set of deck plans was most helpful. The hold where he had imprisoned you, and hidden the bomb, was circled.'

'Outstanding, Holmes! You may not only have saved our lives but also the ship.'

'I fear, Watson, that I may also have given the game away. Brandon will undoubtedly become suspicious when he notices that his deck plans are missing. All the more reason to make haste in reaching the captain.'

We found the captain on the bridge, going over nautical charts with the officer of the watch. When he saw us at the doorway, he seemed somewhat irritated. I suspect our appearance may have had something to do with it. After our ordeal in the hold, Futrelle and I were badly in need of a bath and fresh clothing. And then there was Holmes...

'I will be with you in a moment, gentlemen. Please step into my sitting room.'

'I think, Captain, that we should talk to you at once,' said Holmes.

The captain peered at Holmes over his reading glasses and then, without saying a word, he followed us into the adjoining room and closed the door.

'Still masquerading in that outfit, Mr Holmes? You look like a character out of Dickens.'

'Captain, listen carefully,' said Holmes. 'There is a bomb in the forward cargo hold of the orlop deck. It is set to go off at one o'clock.'

'A bomb! What the devil are you talking about? Who put it there?'

'Brandon. He and a small group of anarchists plan to sink this ship. They also plan to steal a lifeboat and row for a waiting ship around midnight.'

'Anarchists! From what country? What do they want?' The captain was clearly rattled by the news, but I sensed no panic or hesitation in his voice.

'There is no time to discuss that now. Do you have anyone on board who can defuse a bomb? It is attached to a bottle of nitroglycerine.'

The captain thought for a moment. 'So far as I know, there are no experts on board... I seem to recall Hanson, one of our electricians, saying that he used to set munitions charges when he was in the navy.'

'Then I suggest, Captain, that we find him and ask him to inspect the device.'

The captain reached for the telephone. 'Mr Boxhall, please come into my sitting room immediately.'

'There is no great danger, Mr Holmes. A bomb can damage the ship, but it cannot sink her. Several holds would have to be flooded and...'

'There are two bombs.'

'What! Where is the second?'

'As yet, we do not know.'

'Good God, man! What has been going on here? Does this have something to do with those stolen documents of yours?'

'Nothing, sir,' said Holmes, folding his arms and looking the captain squarely in the eye. 'In fact, if it hadn't been for our investigation, you would never have known about the bombs until one o'clock, when they explode.'

'Both at one o'clock.'

'Yes,' said Holmes, reaching into his coat pocket. 'I have Brandon's copy of the deck plans here.' Holmes laid them out flat on the table. 'This may help us to locate the second device.' Holmes looked at the plans for a moment, then pointed. 'Here is the location of the first bomb. If it goes off, it will flood these two holds.'

The captain studied the plans, stroking his beard with one hand, and using the other to point to various positions on the paper. 'If those two holds are flooded, all he has to do is flood two more in the forward section of the ship. That will sink us. Or he could hit one or two holds in the rear – I would have to consult Mr Andrews about that.'

The captain again picked up the telephone, this time to find the young ship designer.

'Holmes,' I said. 'Should we not be doing something to take Brandon and his cohorts into custody? They might be persuaded to tell us where the second bomb is hidden.'

'Agreed, Watson, but first things first. Defusing the first bomb should ensure the safety of the ship. And with Mr Andrews's help, finding the second bomb should not be too difficult. There are only so many places where an explosion would be effective. As for Mr Brandon and his friends, they are fanatics. There is no guarantee they would co-operate, even at the cost of their own lives.'

The captain put down the telephone just as Boxhall entered the room.

'Good, Mr Boxhall, I have a little task for you to perform... Gentlemen, Mr Andrews will arrive shortly to assist us.'

The captain explained the situation to Boxhall, who took the news with as much professional demeanour as could be expected. Smith then ordered the officer to find Hanson, confirm that he did indeed know about explosives and take him to where the first bomb was hidden.

'It is now nine o'clock – so please lose no time. If Hanson is unable to defuse the device, we will have to find someone else who can. Mr Futrelle here will go with you and show you the exact position of the bomb. The rest of us will be attempting to locate the second charge. Understood?'

Boxhall accepted the assignment with calm resolve. 'Yes, sir. Right away.'

'Oh, Mr Boxhall,' said the captain, reaching into a desk drawer. 'You might need this.'

The captain pulled out a silver-coloured revolver. After checking the chamber, he handed it to Boxhall.

'These are dangerous men, Mr Boxhall. They may come back.'

The young officer seemed somewhat less assured than he had a moment earlier, but he put the weapon in his coat pocket without hesitation. Then he and Futrelle left, making their way to the bridge.

'And speaking of our Mr Brandon...' said the captain, 'it is time that he and his friends learned that this ship and this crew are not to be trifled with.'

Once again, the captain picked up the telephone.

Chapter Twenty

ি

Junior Electrician William Hanson was sitting on a crate, wiping his hands nervously on a large red handkerchief when we arrived. He was describing the bomb's triggering device to Boxhall and Futrelle, who were stooped next to it, examining its contents. The bomb had been moved to directly under the electric light, which provided a clearer view of its inner workings.

Hanson stood as the captain walked through the doorway, followed by Andrews, Miss Norton and myself. Before leaving his cabin, the captain had ordered a search of the ship to find Brandon and his friends.

'Thank you for coming, Mr Hanson,' said the captain. 'Needless to say, this goes far beyond your normal duties.'

'Anything I can do to help, sir.'

'Was I correct about your service experience? Are you acquainted with such a device as this?'

'Well, sir...' Hanson cleared his throat. 'I was never what you would call an explosives expert, but I am trained to follow standard procedures for handling ordnance.'

'But can you defuse this bomb, and another one like it?' The captain's voice was calm, but firm. 'If you are unable to, we will attempt to find someone else. But I do hope that you can, for it is nearly 9.30.'

'Yes, sir, I think I can...' Hanson was visibly nervous, but he had courage. 'No guarantees, mind you. But given the time we have left, I am probably your best chance.'

A thought occurred to me. 'Captain, could we not simply throw the bomb over the side? It might be safer.'

'I would not advise it,' said Hanson, taking command of the situation. 'Once that thing is wired, it is a hair trigger. It might explode, maybe near some people, while it is being carried to the deck. And besides, it would definitely explode when it hit the water, and probably blow a hole in the side of the ship.'

'Your point is well made, Hanson,' said the captain. 'Proceed.'

Hanson's eyes widened as he looked at the captain, and then the bomb. It reminded me of the first time I performed surgery. Of course, in that instance, there was only one life at stake.

Hanson rose from the crate, wiped his hands one more time, and approached the bomb. Futrelle and Boxhall backed away to give him room. At that moment, a man in uniform stepped through the door. It was Commodore Giles Winter.

'Captain,' he said. 'I came as soon as I got your message. What *is* all this about?'

The captain played along with the charade. 'A bomb, Commodore... planted by anarchists. I am expecting them to be brought before me any moment. But our immediate concern is this bomb...this one, and another planted somewhere on board the ship.'

'Any progress in finding the second device?' Holmes said, showing mild concern.

'Your friend, Miss Norton, is assisting Mr Andrews in a search.'

'How much time do we have?'

'One o'clock. I thought it wisest to restrict knowledge of the danger to as few people as possible. We have some sound theories on where the second bomb might be hidden.'

Attention shifted back to Hanson and the explosive device.

'Do you require any assistance, Mr Hanson?' asked Boxhall. 'I have spent a little time with explosives, so if I could be of... '

'No, no thank you, sir. Another set of hands would not do any good. In fact, sir, I think you all would be well advised to leave the room.'

The captain remained silent for a moment. He was not the type of man to seek safety, while a member of his crew was in danger.

'We all have work to do. Our most important task is to assist Mr Andrews in finding the other bomb... Carry on, Mr Hanson.'

Smith began to herd us towards the door. As the last of us stepped over the threshold, the captain turned towards the electrician.'

'Mr Hanson,' he said.

'Yes, sir.'

'You have our thanks and our prayers.'

'Thank you, sir. I will report back once I have finished.'

We passed through the next cargo hold and into the post room. There, we saw Andrews and Miss Norton peering over the deck plans, which were laid flat on a sorting table. The post-room crew had gone off duty, and they were alone in the room.

'Do you have anything to report, Mr Andrews?' asked the captain.

'We checked all the positions marked in pencil, and we found nothing.'

'Do you need any help – search parties...that sort of thing?'

Still studying the plans, Andrews replied, 'I am hoping that we can reason with them. Assuming Brandon knew what he was doing, it must be strategically placed.'

Holmes slid himself between Andrews and Miss Norton, to gaze at the plans.

'Let me see,' said Holmes. 'Mr Andrews, if I recall correctly, the ship can remain afloat with any two of its sixteen holds flooded. Is that not the case?'

'Or any three of the first five.'

'What other factors are important?' Holmes used the stem of his pipe as a pointer. 'This first bomb was wedged in a corner between the bulkhead and the hull. Might we expect the second bomb to be placed in a similar position?'

Andrews squeezed in closer to the plans and ran his finger along the length of the ship. 'It would be the best way of ensuring success, from the anarchists' point of view, but look here. The coal bunkers are up against the bulkheads throughout the mid-section of the ship. Access would be very difficult in most areas.' Andrews paused, and looked up at Holmes. 'Although, igniting the coal dust would tend to amplify the explosion... But no, that is a little far-fetched.'

Holmes walked towards the aft wall, which had a box of parcels in front of it. A canvas was draped over it and tied down at each corner.

'What about here?' asked Holmes. 'According to the plans, there is a coal bunker on the other side of this bulkhead.'

'You are quite right, Commodore,' said the captain, walking to Holmes. 'But as you can see, that box goes all the way up to the hull. There is no room for a bomb.'

'What about the hold on the port side?'

'A baggage locker, locked and filled to capacity,' said the captain.

'Commodore Winter may be on to something.' Andrews abandoned his deck plans and strode rapidly over to the pile of parcels. 'An explosion here would flood two more compartments. The hull plating is thicker on the other side of the bulkhead, but the exploding coal...'

'Possible, Mr Andrews, but not very likely,' the captain replied. 'This room is secured after the post-room crew goes off duty. After that, there are regular safety checks. There would be no time to come in here, unstack the parcels, plant a bomb and restore everything to its original position.'

'If they used a bomb like the other one, it would have a twelve-hour timer,' Boxhall said. 'They could not set it up for any longer than that.'

'And the best location would be at deck level,' Andrews added. 'An interesting thought, anyway, Commodore.'

'This canvas has been cut,' Holmes said. 'Mind you, I did not say torn. It has been sliced with a knife.'

The captain kneeled down next to Holmes and examined the opening in the thick cloth. He then looked at Holmes, but did not say a word.

Holmes lifted the bottom of the canvas, revealing the end of a parcel. It was wrapped neatly in paper, with the string tied in a bow. The end of the package was stamped in red with the letters 'WWU'.

'WWU?' said the captain, feeling the end of the package. 'What do you suppose that means? Some university, perhaps?'

'Workers of the World, Unite!' shouted Miss Norton. All eyes turned immediately to the young woman, who seemed a little embarrassed by the sudden attention. 'I mean, I saw that before, somewhere...read it in some magazine, I think.'

'Very good, Miss Norton!' said Holmes, smiling. 'I think we may be on to something. Did you notice that the string is bowed at the end of the parcel? That is a little unusual... I think I will attempt to pull it open to see what happens.'

I was not entirely sure that pulling on the string was a good idea. After all, it could have been attached to the triggering device. But there was no time to protest. Holmes reached over and untied the string with a firm yank. Moments later, he was pulling away the paper, and removing a square of cardboard. This uncovered a round opening in the package.

'Does anyone have a match?'

Boxhall pulled a match from his pocket and gave it to Holmes, who struck it against a crate and used it to illuminate the interior of the box.

'Well, well, well... I see a bottle, and some electrical items. I believe we have found our second bomb.'

'Incredible!' exclaimed the captain. 'How did it get down at the bottom of the pile? One of the post-room crew must have...'

'Or, someone posing as a member of the crew,' Holmes interjected. 'In any case, the bomb was placed here, in this position, at the beginning of the voyage. After that, setting the timing device became a matter of opening the end of the package and turning a switch. Any skilled thief could accomplish that without anyone noticing.'

'Ingenious,' said Futrelle. 'In fact, if you do not mind, Commodore, this kind of thing might be a nice touch for one of Professor Van Dusen's adventures.'

'Indeed, Futrelle,' said Holmes. 'I am sure the anarchists will raise no objection if you include it in one of your stories.'

Hanson chose that moment to walk into the room. His big red handkerchief was soaking wet as he mopped the sweat off his hands and face. As he walked into the room, he looked like a man who had just run a mile in the hot sun.

'Well, sir, the bomb is all taken care of. I have removed the triggering device. So if you don't mind, I will run up to my quarters and...'

'No time for that now, Hanson. You will find bomb number two inside that box.'

Boxhall ran back to steady the man, whose legs seemed to be giving out beneath him.

The captain spoke. 'And now, gentlemen...Miss Norton, now that the danger to the ship has passed, let us pay our respects to Mr Brandon and his friends. If the search party has not yet discovered them, we know where they will be at midnight.'

Chapter Twenty-One

Midnight on Sunday 14 April 1912

I must confess to being a creature of comfort. Nothing pleases me more than sitting in front of the fireplace, catching up on my reading. But to his credit, Holmes has sent frequent ripples through what might have been a life of tranquillity. How many times have I been pulled away from my easy chair, or left my dinner on the table, to go running into the night on some adventure? And my life has been the richer for it.

But there is one form of discomfort that I simply cannot abide. Old soldier that I am, I have never become used to the penetrating chill of a cold wind. And there is no wind worse than the kind that occurs on the open sea.

I was contemplating the warmth of my cabin that Saturday night as I crouched behind the lifeboat, with my service revolver in my coat pocket. The wind was whipping across the deck and the temperature was below freezing. All in all, this was not my idea of a pleasure cruise.

Fortunately, none of the passengers was partial to bitter cold weather either. They were all below enjoying the comforts of the ship. The captain had posted men inside to be on the lookout for Brandon's men, and at the same time to redirect any passenger who might want to wander out on deck.

Holmes and Miss Norton were at my side. It was our job to stand watch on the port side of the boat deck, along the second-class promenade. The captain, Futrelle and Boxhall were guarding the starboard side. Other members of the crew were posted by the boats at the forward end of the ship.

I remembered Brandon's words well. A ship would be waiting for him and his four companions at midnight, a mile off the starboard side of the ship. It was now approaching 11.30. If they were to make their rendezvous, they would have to arrive soon to take one of the lifeboats.

Miss Norton's teeth were chattering. In the dim glow of the ship's lights, I saw Holmes give her a disapproving look.

'Miss Norton, silence is essential.'

'I do not think they are coming,' she whispered. 'Not if they know that Doctor Watson and Mr Futrelle have escaped.'

'We cannot be sure of that.'

Boxhall had issued each of us with a heavy coat. He said he had worked on deck many a time without getting cold. After a while, however, I noted that they were not designed to keep a man warm while sitting still.

Miss Norton moved close to me. Why had such a young girl chosen such a dangerous career? Being a courier was difficult enough, but this...? If Brandon and his friends did come on deck, I resolved that my chief responsibility would be to protect her. Why had she insisted on joining in this vigil?

There was a glow on the deck of the ship. Ice was forming! An odd chase this would be if we all ended up sliding into each other...

'I say, Holmes,' I said, quietly. 'Do you remember the Roylott case, when we stood watch outside the house at night, and the cheetah and baboon were roaming the grounds?'

'Yes, Watson, I remember. That was a long time ago. As I recall, it was much warmer...'

'Quiet,' urged Miss Norton.

I was about to make a brief reply, when she put her fingers over my lips and whispered, 'No, please, listen!'

There was a clattering sound coming from the raised area, just forward of the aft funnel. In the dim light, I saw several figures moving about. Quietly, they moved towards the ladder and then disappeared. Moments later, one man, dressed in dark clothing, made his way across the deck. I did not need to see his face. The height and breadth of the man immediately told me that it was Swede.

The huge figure disappeared behind a lifeboat, while the others remained hidden around the corner. From time to time, we heard rustling and clanking sounds. While the temptation to leave our hiding place was overwhelming, we remained in the shadows, listening and watching.

Several minutes passed, during which we heard nothing but the sound of the wind whistling across the deck. Then there was a faint clanking of metal, followed by a cranking sound. The lifeboat forward of Swede began to rise, up, up and over the rail, until it was positioned above the water. Then Swede emerged, cautiously walking to the centre of the deck. He looked all around, fore, aft and up to the raised roof. Deciding that all was clear, he motioned to his friends to come out of hiding.

Swede returned to the lifeboat and lifted the edge of the canvas cover, as his companions hurried across the deck and stood anxiously by the rail.

At that moment I felt a tap on my shoulder. Holmes moved casually out on to the deck. His revolver was pointed directly at the men.

'Stay where you are, Hugo Brandon.' His voice cut through the wind, and the five men searched quickly through the darkness to trace its source. Within moments, all eyes were fixed on Holmes. 'You will not be going anywhere tonight,' Holmes said.

Brandon stepped forwards, peering into the darkness. 'Commodore, is that you? Why yes, I believe it is.'

A man in the shadows reached slowly into his coat. Charlie, Kurt, Willy? I could not tell.

My revolver in hand, I quickly took aim. I did not have time to fire. There was an explosion and flash from Holmes's gun. The man twisted and fell to the deck, holding his right shoulder.

Unfortunately, the revolver's recoil caused Holmes to lose his footing momentarily on the icy deck. Brandon and his men used the opportunity to jump for cover behind a lifeboat. It was directly in front of the boat that had been positioned over the water.

Holmes, regaining his balance, ran back to Miss Norton and me, pushing us to the deck as he skidded to a stop.

'That should bring the captain and his men,' Holmes shouted. 'Would you prefer to put down your weapons now, or wait for them? It makes no difference to me.'

'We will wait for a while, if you do not mind,' Brandon replied. 'If I were you, I would forget about us and conduct a search of this ship. As Doctor Watson may have told you, we planted two bombs. And you do not have very much time.'

'Oh, the one in the post room. It is already defused, but thank you.'

A gun fired, chipping a splinter of wood from our lifeboat. A flurry of shots followed. But they were not aimed at us. The attention of Brandon and his gang was now drawn to the captain and his men, who emerged from both forward and aft positions. As the ship's crew began to shoot, our adversaries were caught in a crossfire. Clearly, they could not hold their position behind the lifeboat.

Suddenly, there was a chugging, mechanical sound. The lifeboat over the water was being lowered. Swede and the wounded man jumped over the rail, but both were hit by gunfire and fell limply over the side. Moments later, the three remaining men came out of hiding, their guns blazing. Two of the men held their ground until they fell to the deck. But Brandon, after firing two shots, jumped over the rail. By this time, the lifeboat must have been half-way to the water. The gambler was taking the biggest gamble of his life.

The captain and his men came out from their positions of cover and rushed across the deck.

'Raise that lifeboat!' the captain shouted.

Boxhall ran to the motor and reversed its direction.

We all gathered by the rail as the lifeboat rose from the darkness. It was empty.

Ten minutes later, Holmes, the captain and I approached Miss Norton and Futrelle, who were standing on the starboard deck.

'Do you see anything?' I asked.

'We think we see a ship's lights about a mile out, but we are not sure,' said Miss Norton.

Then the five of us went to stand by the side of the rail, waiting quietly, looking out across the water. It was not long before we saw a blinker signal sending a short message.

The captain chuckled. 'They are signalling "WWU" – Workers of the World, Unite.'

'Captain, may I use that signal lamp over there?' Holmes asked.

The captain nodded and, smiling curiously, switched on the device.

'Holmes, I didn't realize that you knew Morse code,' I said.

'I have learnt a few new skills over the years, Watson.'

Holmes took the device in his hand and switched the light on and off. There was no reply from the mysterious ship.

The captain was laughing heartily but the rest of us remained in the dark.

'Holmes, whatever did you say?'

'What any good Englishman would say, of course. "Rule, Britannia."'

Chapter Twenty-Two

THE MORNING OF SUNDAY 14 APRIL 1912

S herlock Holmes shook his head as he closed the cover of his watch.
'Time, Watson. Time is running short.'

Our deadline for recovering the plans was fast approaching. The *Titanic* would be docking in three days. Over the past twenty-four hours we had saved the ship from disaster and eliminated one red herring, Brandon, from our list of suspects. Still, it seemed we were no closer to succeeding in our investigation.

Saturday night's *mêlée* on the boat deck had not gone completely unnoticed. The bitter cold had discouraged most passengers from going outside. Those who tried to brave the weather were prevented by the captain's men, who gave the explanation that emergency repairs were being made to some of the ship's equipment. Still, a few passengers had asked about gunshots that appeared to be coming from somewhere outside. This was explained away as electrical explosions, confirming that the deck was no place to be while repairs were under way.

Saturday night's freak storm had left as suddenly as it had appeared. Fair weather had returned.

The captain had invited Holmes, Miss Norton, Futrelle and me to breakfast in his sitting room. Except for Holmes, all of us had begun filling our plates with eggs and bacon, and also fruit, which had been laid out on a small table. I had not eaten dinner the previous evening, and the smell of hot food suddenly brought my appetite back.

Our meal was interrupted by a knock at the door. 'Come in!' called the captain. A young officer entered. He was a man of disciplined demeanour and a hint of determination in his eyes. The captain put his breakfast aside, rose and motioned for the young man to step forward.

'Gentlemen, Miss Norton, I don't believe I have introduced you to Mr Charles Lightoller, my second officer,' said the captain. 'He is one of my most trusted and valued men. No doubt you have seen him attending to his duties over the past few days.'

I expected a round of introductions. Instead, the captain folded his arms and got right to the point. 'I have taken the liberty of divulging your mission and Mr Holmes's identity to Mr Lightoller. He will be available to assist you when I am otherwise occupied.'

Holmes responded calmly to this surprise announcement.

'We must surely be taking up too much of your valuable time, Captain. Mr Lightoller, we are very pleased to have your assistance in solving our little puzzle.'

'I must say, Mr Holmes, I was quite amazed when the captain told me who you really are. I am at your service.'

The captain introduced the rest of us and invited Lightoller to join us for breakfast. He then returned to his easy chair and picked up his plate of bacon and eggs, which he had barely had a chance to touch.

'I fear that I have another puzzle for you to work on, Mr Holmes,' said the captain, beginning his breakfast at last.

There was a knock at the door, which Holmes answered. It was Bride.

'A message for the captain, sir.' Bride tipped his hat to the rest of us and left.

The captain again set his plate aside, rose and unfolded the wireless form. 'Well, well, more good news,' he said, a tone of sarcasm in his voice. Listen to this: "Captain *Titanic* – Westbound steamers report bergs, growlers and field ice in forty-two degrees north, from forty-nine degrees to fifty-one degrees west, 12 April. Compliments, Barr.'

'Who is Barr?' asked Miss Norton.

'He is the captain of the *Caronia.*' The captain folded the message and appeared lost in thought.

Encouraging some eggs on to my fork, I inquired, 'Are we going to be passing through that area?'

'We are heading in that general direction. But nothing to worry about. I will inform the officers and we will keep watch for any signs of ice.' The captain put the message in his coat pocket.

'Captain, you were saying something about a puzzle,' said Holmes.

'Oh, yes. It seems that our stoker friend, Mr Strickley, has disappeared.'

'What!' I said. 'I thought he was confined to quarters.'

'He was, but apparently he did not take my orders too seriously. When we find him, he will go straight to the brig. But so far, no luck.'

'Have you begun a search?' asked Holmes.

'Every available man. With all the intrigue lately aboard this ship, my men are becoming quite experienced at conducting searches.'

The captain looked each of us in the eye, then returned to his easy chair and his breakfast.

'Do you have evidence that he escaped on his own?' Holmes inquired.

The captain dropped his knife and fork on his plate, showing signs of a man whose patience was wearing thin.

'You suspect foul play, Mr Holmes? At last, I thought, I could get back to the serious business of running a pleasure cruise... I swear, sir, if I did not know better, I would say this ship was under the curse of Jonah.'

Miss Norton poured the captain another cup of tea. 'Now, Captain, your breakfast is getting cold.'

Taking a deep breath, the captain forced a smile and picked up his knife and fork, slowly lifting a slice of melon to his mouth.

'Rest assured, Miss Norton. This captain is always in control. But Mr Holmes, why the concern?'

'I believe Mr Holmes might be referring to Bishop,' said Futrelle, who had already devoured his breakfast. 'We still do not know who killed him. If, in fact, someone shot Bishop to keep him silent...'

'Exactly, Futrelle,' said Holmes. 'Captain, I would like to inspect Strickley's quarters immediately. I may be able to determine whether we have another murder on our hands, or if Mr Strickley is simply absent without leave.'

'Very well. Mr Lightoller, would you assist Mr Holmes?'

'Yes, sir, a pleasure... Mr Holmes, do you suspect that Strickley's disappearance could be related to the theft of the documents?'

'It is possible. We also have few clues as to their whereabouts. Strickley's disappearance may serve to enlighten us.'

'It is Sunday, and I am expected in the dining room at 10.30 to conduct Divine Service. Would any of the rest of you care to join me? A prayer would be helpful to all of us,' said the captain.

'My wife and I were already planning to attend,' said Futrelle. The writer looked at his watch. 'Doctor Watson, Miss Norton, shall we meet there in an hour?'

'I must accompany Holmes. Perhaps Miss Norton...' I responded.

With a firmness of tone that reminded me of my late wife, Miss Norton said, 'You have had quite enough adventures yesterday. You will take a turn on the deck with me, then we will go to the service.'

Holmes chuckled and walked over to the table of food.

'I must agree, my dear Watson. You are officially off duty until after church.'

Miss Norton grabbed my arm and began to lead me to the door.

'She Who Must be Obeyed,' I said, resignedly, waving goodbye to the others.

☙

Chapter Twenty-Three

THE LATE MORNING OF SUNDAY 14 APRIL 1912

T he morning was bright and clear, and a number of passengers were enjoying the opportunity to take a pleasant stroll on deck.

As Miss Norton and I ambled along the boat deck, I took particular pleasure in watching the children play.

'Thirty-one, thirty-two, thirty-three...' said one young girl as she faced the deckhouse, her hands covering her eyes. Her companions were scurrying to find a place to hide. One ambitious young man was nervously inspecting a lifeboat, trying to find a way inside.

As we continued, I spotted a familiar face. The boy was sitting next to a deckchair, playing with some toys.

'Well, well,' I said. 'If it isn't our young detective, Tommy Roberts. And how are you this fine day?'

'Doctor Watson! Would you like to play? I am pretending that...' Tommy stopped and stared at my companion.

'Oh, Tommy. I would like to introduce you to my friend, Miss Norton.'

'Pleased to meet you, Tommy. What is that you are playing with?'

Tommy smiled, thrilled by this interest in his new game. 'Found these in the wastepaper basket...little tables and chairs, cabinets, even some little people.'

'What fun,' said Miss Norton. 'I once had a doll's house with pieces like that...'

'I am using them to make Mr Holmes's sitting room, just like you described it in your books, Doctor Watson.'

'I am most impressed, Tommy. That is a very good representation.'

'I just wish I had some more pieces. There's a lot missing.'

'Just use your imagination. Remember, Mr Holmes uses his imagination, along with deductive reasoning, to solve crimes.'

Tommy paused for a moment to consider this.

'Tommy, have you seen Miss Storm-Fleming lately?' I asked.

'Not since yesterday. She was talking to that man, the German.'

Miss Norton and I exchanged glances. 'When was this?'

'Just before dinner, I think. They were in the library. I went there with Mother, so she could get a book.'

'Thank you, Tommy. I have been looking for her. Perhaps we will see her at the church service.'

'Church! Oh my gosh! I told Mother and Father that I would be back to get dressed... Excuse me.' The young man abruptly got to his feet and ran down the deck, leaving his toys behind.

Miss Norton laughed. 'I hope he is not in too much trouble.'

I stooped down and scooped up Tommy's toys. 'I am sure he will want these. I will return them to him at church... I wonder if Holmes knows that our sitting room has become the latest vogue among children.'

My companion smiled. 'Fame can affect judgement, Doctor.'

'A point well taken, Miss Norton.' I grinned. 'But rest assured, the fresh sea air and a rousing sermon from the captain will soon restore my humility.'

Miss Norton took my arm. 'Lead the way, Doctor Watson.'

We arrived well before the service was due to begin. I was surprised to see that a large congregation had already assembled. Many viewed this as a fine opportunity for conversation and meeting new people. It was a family occasion, and the only one that brought together passengers from first, second and third class.

It was a special treat for steerage passengers. They were staring wide-eyed at their luxurious surroundings, while chatting quietly and pointing about the room.

The Futrelles had already arrived and were engaged in a conversation with Baron Von Stern. Moriarty was standing in a cluster of well-dressed people, some of whom I recognized as being among the first-class passengers.

Miss Storm-Fleming had just paid her respects to the captain and was circulating through the crowd. I waved and she returned my gesture with a broad smile, walking briskly in our direction.

'Doctor Watson, I have been looking everywhere for you!' She spoke warmly.

Somewhat overcome by this greeting, I muttered a less than satisfactory reply.

'I was rather involved in a matter that took some time...'

'And what kind of business would keep you so busy in the middle of the Atlantic Ocean?' she asked.

'Nothing of any consequence... Just helping Futrelle with research for an article he is writing on the *Titanic*'s maiden voyage.'

Miss Storm-Fleming's eyes remained warm and bright but there was a momentary change in her expression that indicated she was not fully pleased with my explanation.

'And how are you, Miss Norton? Are you enjoying the trip? Quite exciting, is it not?'

'Yes, very much so,' Miss Norton replied. 'I am happy to see that you are enjoying it too...after everything that happened.'

'I have always had a talent for springing back from adversity. Hardships along the way are part of life's great adventure.'

'Have they made any progress in finding Bishop's killer?' Miss Norton asked.

'I do not believe so. I was just talking to the captain and he did not volunteer any information. Have either of you heard anything?'

'Not a word,' I replied. 'If only Holmes were on board. This is the kind of mystery he thrives on.'

'Yes, if only he were.' Miss Storm-Fleming's eyes were fixed on mine. 'Doctor Watson, people are taking their seats.'

'Please do join us.'

'Thank you, but please do not say anything about my singing, Doctor. I am very sensitive on that point.'

The captain led the service from the White Star Line's own prayer book, and the music was provided by the ship's orchestra. The opening hymn was familiar, but one I had not heard in some time. Miss Storm-Fleming's voice was clearly distinguishable from my neighbouring worshippers.

> Eternal Father strong to save,
> Whose arm hath bound the restless wave,
> Who bids the mighty ocean deep
> Its own appointed limits keep:
> O hear us when we cry to Thee
> For those in peril on the sea.

I adhered to Miss Storm-Fleming's request not to comment on her singing.

The service was strangely moving. As I glanced about the room, I sensed a unity among the ship's passengers. There was a common bond, perhaps brought on by this reminder that we all came from the same Maker.

Captain Smith led the formal service. He gave a respectable reading of various prayers and Bible passages. It ended promptly on time with the hymn, 'O God, Our Help in Ages Past'. Miss Storm-Fleming, again, sang with enthusiasm:

> O God, our help in ages past,
> Our hope for years to come,
> Our shelter from the stormy blast,
> And our eternal home.

Following the benediction, the band played a festive recessional. Conversation grew louder as friends gradually made their way to the reception room, outside the dining room. As we continued towards the big open doors, Miss Storm-Fleming took my arm and pulled me to one side, away from the path of the moving crowd. Miss Norton, who had moved slightly ahead, soon noticed that we had paused and she waited for us.

'Doctor Watson, I know how much you enjoy the company of your fellow musketeers, but would you join me for dinner tonight?' Miss Storm-Fleming asked, hesitantly. There was an uneasy timbre to her voice. 'As you know...this has been a difficult journey for me...and what must you think of me...? An opportunity for quiet conversation would greatly restore me.'

'Miss Storm-Fleming, it would be a great pleasure. Shall we say 7.30 in the restaurant?'

She nodded her acceptance and, seconds later, was on her way.

I watched as she left the room. Miss Norton joined me.

'What did she want?' Acting as both a friend and a professional, she had easily overcome the urge not to pry.

'Dinner,' I replied. My voice sounded weak. I cleared my throat.

'Doctor Watson,' said the captain, coming up behind us. 'How did you like the service?'

'It was very pleasant. I had no idea that you were such a good preacher.'

'A captain has to be a jack of all trades.' He pulled an envelope from his pocket. 'I have just been handed a note. It is addressed to you.'

I ripped it open. I had noticed immediately from the handwriting on the envelope that it was from Holmes. The note contained a most curious request.

'What is it?' asked Miss Norton.

'The commodore wishes us, together with Futrelle, to meet him next to the fourth funnel.'

Chapter Twenty-Four

༄

THE AFTERNOON OF SUNDAY
14 APRIL 1912

After eating a light lunch, Miss Norton, Futrelle and I went to the boat deck for our rendezvous with Holmes. He had asked us to meet him there at precisely two o'clock, and we arrived with minutes to spare. Instead of finding Holmes, we were greeted by Mr Lightoller.

'Gentlemen, Miss Norton, the commodore has asked me to escort you to the base of the fourth funnel. He is already there.'

'I wish Holmes had told us what this was all about,' Futrelle said. 'I mean no offence, Doctor, but I must say, I do get annoyed by his sense of drama from time to time.'

'Patience, Futrelle,' I said. 'Over the years I have become used to Holmes's little surprises. And besides, they are good fodder for my stories in the *Strand*.'

Lightoller motioned us towards the aft end of the ship. 'This way, please.'

We arrived at a gate and the second officer reached for his keys to open it. We walked across a short span of deck reserved for the crew and passed through another gate to the second-class promenade. The view caused me to shiver because this was the area where we had stood for so long in the cold. There was no evidence of our recent confrontation with the late Mr Brandon and his men.

'We must climb the ladder to the raised roof,' Lightoller said. 'That is the way to the base of the funnel.'

As I mentioned earlier, the fourth funnel was a dummy. Unlike the other three, it was not designed to vent smoke from the boiler rooms. Instead, it was situated above a shaft from the turbine room and used for ventilation. As we stood on the raised roof, a thought occurred to me. We were standing directly above the first-class smoking room. Could tobacco consumption on board be so high as to require an entire funnel?

Lightoller opened a door and we found ourselves in a large open room. Below was the shaft leading down to the turbines. I glanced over the rail and suddenly felt a touch of dizziness. The lights and roar of the turbine room were far, far below.

Miss Norton glanced about the room. After looking in my direction and shrugging her shoulders she turned to Lightoller. 'Where is Mr Holmes?'

Lightoller smiled and, without saying a word, pointed a finger skywards.

'Oh, my word!' gasped Miss Norton.

We all gathered around the rail and looked up through the long funnel. There was an obstruction that was partially blocking the bright, blue light of the sky. The obstruction was moving.

Miss Norton immediately climbed the ladder that brought her to the base of the funnel.

'Mr... Commodore! Commodore Winter!' she cried, her voice echoing back. 'Please return at once – it is too dangerous!'

In fact, Holmes was on his way down. Minutes later, he stepped off the ladder on to the floor of the chamber.

'Miss Norton,' he said quietly, sounding somewhat annoyed, 'Good Lord, you remind me of our dear departed Mrs Hudson.'

Miss Norton stood her ground. 'What were you doing up there? You could have been killed.'

'My dear young woman, I am in excellent condition and not quite as old and frail as you might think.'

'I did not mean to imply... What *were* you doing up there anyway?'

'Merely following up a clue...or at least an idea I had. It appears that my hypothesis was incorrect.'

'What hypothesis?' I asked.

'It concerns our little cypher about the "Hot Russian Honey Bear". As you recall, our mysterious passenger sent a confederate a message, upon the ship's arrival in New York, to meet him by the "pipe organ in the smoking room". It occurred to me while standing on deck that the four funnels might look a bit like a pipe organ. I decided that it would be worthwhile to check the one funnel that might possibly be accessible to a passenger. A trifle foolish, I now believe.'

'You found nothing?' asked Futrelle.

'Nothing.'

'What about your search of Strickley's cabin? You had hoped to...'

'Nothing of consequence, Mr Futrelle. I am afraid, thus far, this has been a very unproductive day.'

'But Holmes, why did you ask us to meet you here?' I inquired.

'Time is growing short. I thought it best that we got our little team back together and off in pursuit of more facts.'

'I agree wholeheartedly,' said Miss Norton, still somewhat annoyed by Holmes's gymnastics display. 'But could we talk outside, in the sunshine?'

'Of course, Miss Norton.' He picked up his jacket and hat. 'And I apologize if I disturbed you just now. I promise to keep my feet firmly planted on deck until we reach New York.' He smiled at her.

After a moment's pause, her face, too, brightened into a warm grin. 'I dread to think what mother would have said if she had seen you up there!'

We continued down to the deck and on through the gates to the promenade deck. It was not long before we were approached head-on by Mr Boxhall. He was walking at a crisp pace.

'Excuse me, Mr Lightoller,' he said, paying his respects to a superior officer. 'The captain wants to see the commodore at once.'

'Why, what's happened?'

'It's the missing stoker, Strickley... They have found his body.'

Lightoller showed us the way to the crew's hospital, which was situated on the forward end of C Deck between the crew's galley and the firemen's mess. Strickley's body was stretched out on the examining table. Captain Smith stood by as William O'Loughlin, the ship's surgeon, and J Edward Simpson, the assistant surgeon, examined the deceased.

The two surgeons made quite a team, indeed. Doctor O'Loughlin was a fine old gentleman who enjoyed walking about the ship conversing with passengers. We had met briefly when Holmes and I accompanied the captain and his officers on their inspection of the ship and then later near the motorcars. Simpson was a much younger man. He had a reputation for being more gregarious and, according to fellow shipmates, had a somewhat mischievous sense of humour.

'Doctor Watson, it is good to see you again. I am glad you could come as this may interest you.' Doctor O'Loughlin beckoned me to move closer to the examining table. I greeted him, 'You remember Commodore Winter?'

The captain then introduced Futrelle and Miss Norton. O'Loughlin seemed perplexed by the presence of these two newcomers – especially the young woman – but said nothing.

'Well then, back to work,' said O'Loughlin. 'Doctor Watson, I think you will agree that there is no doubt about how Mr Strickley died.'

Even from a distance, I could see the line of blood around the stoker's throat. On closer examination, I saw that the wound was not deep. But there was a thin, red indentation that ran all the way around the neck. The colour of the face confirmed my conclusion.

'This man was garrotted to death,' I said.

'Precisely,' said O'Loughlin.

Holmes stepped forward to conduct his own examination. 'Where was the body found?'

'The kitchen staff found him in a sack in the potato store,' Simpson interjected. 'The poor chap's foot was sticking out of the end of the sack. He...' The young doctor was silenced by a disapproving look from the captain. 'We believe he walked down the corridor with his killer, who somehow got him into the food storage area and did the deed.'

'Did anyone see them walking together?' Holmes asked.

'No one we could find,' the captain replied. 'We are questioning the crew. Meanwhile, we are completely in the dark.'

'Captain, I would like to examine the food storage area and the corridor from Strickley's cabin.'

'Certainly, Commodore. Mr Lightoller will assist you. And gentlemen, Miss Norton, I must remind you again, discretion is of the utmost importance. We are trying to keep the knowledge of this incident to ourselves.'

'Of course,' said Holmes. 'We fully appreciate your many responsibilities as captain of this ship.'

I was relieved to see that the captain remained calm and in command of the situation, his mild outburst at breakfast being only a temporary indulgence. I had no doubt that this was a man who could remain strong and decisive through any ordeal.

But I found myself frustrated by our lack of progress in finding Miss Norton's lost plans. And, beyond that, we were contending with two unsolved murders and the aftermath of a political conspiracy. Yet, despite all this nefarious activity, I found my thoughts constantly returning to Miss Storm-Fleming's dinner invitation. Why did she want to see me privately? Clearly, she knew more than she was telling. Did she have some information to convey about the plans, or one of the murders? I would soon find out.

Chapter Twenty-Five

The Evening of Sunday 14 April 1912

By seven o'clock the temperature on deck had dropped dramatically. It was nearly freezing, and most of the passengers had retired to the comfort of the ship below decks. Holmes, after assuring me that there was no more I could do this evening, had rushed off to continue the investigation on his own. After years of following Holmes's methods, I knew that he could disappear for several hours – or days – and come back with amazing results. But I must confess, it always made me feel somewhat useless. In any case, we had arranged to meet at 11.30 in the smoking room. I would find out then whether or not he had made any progress.

I had time to spare before meeting Miss Storm-Fleming, so I wandered into the smoking room, which was on A Deck. There, I witnessed a most curious exchange between Captain Smith and Mr J Bruce Ismay. The two were engaged in what appeared to be a casual conversation. Having met Mr Ismay earlier, I decided that it would not be out of place to stroll up and pay my respects. The captain greeted me when I arrived.

'Doctor Watson, good evening,' he said cordially. 'We were just chatting about the weather. Have you been on deck lately?'

'Yes, just now. It certainly has taken a turn for the worse. Is this typical for this part of the Atlantic?'

'It is fairly common. We are a fair distance to the north.'

'But not to worry,' said Ismay. 'We are making very good time.'

I found this news far from pleasing, since time was our greatest impediment in recovering the plans.

Ismay then took a step towards me and looked about in all directions. After a moment's hesitation, he spoke in hushed tones.

'Doctor Watson, I am glad we happened to meet this evening. I have not yet had the opportunity to thank you for your heroic efforts yesterday. Imagine, anarchists on board this ship! If it had not been for you and your companions...well, the outcome might have been disastrous.'

'I must say, this voyage has been far more exciting than I had expected.' Once again, my sense of humour got the better of me. 'I realize that the White Star Line promises its passengers adventure, but I do not believe that this is what you had in mind.'

Ismay laughed politely. 'No, certainly not. But I am also very glad to see that you are keeping your sense of humour after the ordeal you have been through. Have you recovered?'

I gave the question serious consideration. 'Much to my surprise, I am feeling better than I have felt in months – perhaps even a trifle younger.'

Ismay seemed perplexed by my answer. But not the captain. There was a knowing look in the eyes of the old seaman.

'In any event I would appreciate it if you would pass along my heartfelt thanks to your friends,' said Ismay.

'I will do that, sir.'

The captain echoed Ismay's words of appreciation. He then turned to his employer and abruptly changed the subject.

'By the way, have you got that radio message which I gave you this afternoon?'

Ismay thought for a moment, then reached into his coat pocket. 'Yes, here it is.'

Smith opened the folded piece of paper and read the message. 'Thank you. I want to put it up in the officers' chart room.'

'Anything wrong, Captain?' I asked.

'No, no. Nothing really. There is just some ice ahead of us that we have to keep an eye on.'

He handed me the telegraph. It was from a ship called the *Baltic*. 'Have had moderate variable winds and clear fine weather since leaving. Greek steamer *Athinai* reports passing icebergs and a large quantity of field ice today in latitude forty-one, fifty-one North, longitude forty-nine, fifty-two West.'

I folded the message and returned it to the captain. 'Is this anywhere near us?'

'Nothing to worry about, Doctor. We will take all the standard precautions.'

I looked at my watch and discovered that there were only five minutes remaining before I was to meet Miss Storm-Fleming.

'Please excuse me, gentlemen. I have an engagement in the restaurant.'

'I will be there soon myself,' said the captain. 'The Wideners are honouring me with an invitation.'

'It was a pleasure to see you again, Doctor Watson,' said Ismay. 'I hope the rest of the voyage will be a little more relaxing for you.'

I arrived to meet Miss Storm-Fleming five minutes late, taking pride in the fact that I was only slightly short of breath. Fortunately, she had not yet arrived and I had time to compose myself.

'There you are! My apologies for my lateness.'

Miss Storm-Fleming was wearing the same red evening gown she had worn at our dinner party on Wednesday evening.

'I must say that you are looking most delightful tonight.'

'Thank you, Doctor Watson. But you have seen this old thing before.' She smiled, then held out her arm. 'Shall we find our table?'

Some distance away, I saw Moriarty standing next to the model of the *Titanic*. I was surprised to see that he was not dressed for dinner. The colonel was talking to one of the ship's junior officers. He appeared to be excited about something, and from time to time looked away from the unfortunate young man and glanced about the room. Upon seeing Miss Storm-Fleming and me, he abruptly abandoned his conversation and stepped hurriedly in our direction.

'Doctor Watson, Miss Fleming, have you seen the captain? I need to speak to him urgently.'

'I saw him in the smoking room not ten minutes ago. Why, Colonel, what is the matter?'

'A most annoying thing has just happened. Someone has broken into my cabin.'

'What! Do you have any idea who may have done it?'

'No, none at all. I had been out for a stroll on the deck and returned to my cabin to prepare for dinner. The door was unlocked, which surprised me since I was sure I had secured it before leaving. I assumed, at first, that a careless stewardess was responsible. But when I opened the door I discovered that the room was in complete disarray. The mattress was overturned and my clothing was scattered about.'

'Was anything missing?' asked Miss Storm-Fleming.

'I do not think so. Apart from a little cash and some inexpensive jewelry, I keep all of my valuables in the ship's safe. Everything seems to be there.'

'I am very sorry, Colonel,' said Miss Storm-Fleming. 'You do not expect that kind of thing to happen on a ship like this.'

Moriarty nodded, and it appeared for a moment that he was about to walk away. But instead he turned to me and spoke softly.

'Pardon me for asking, Doctor, but I heard a rumour that Miss Norton's cabin was broken into earlier in the voyage. Do you know anything about that?'

'There was a burglary in Miss Norton's cabin on Thursday night. The worst part of it is, the villains also broke into the adjoining cabin, where an old woman was sleeping. They tied her up, but she was not harmed.'

Moriarty raised his eyebrows, but Miss Storm-Fleming did not look surprised.

'Villains? There was more than one intruder?' Moriarty asked.

'The captain investigated. It appears that two men were involved.'

'And was anything taken?'

'I do not believe so...nothing of importance, anyway.'

I had played poker long enough to know that I had some talent for bluffing. Moriarty appeared to believe me. He had said nothing about the break-in that took place in my cabin. Did he know? Had he, in fact, been the intruder? And was he being truthful about the burglary, or was his story intended as a red herring to divert suspicion from himself?

'This is most peculiar, Doctor. I wonder whether there is any connection between the two incidents?'

'I do not know... Tell me, Colonel, did anyone know that you would be away from your cabin?'

Moriarty thought for a moment. 'No one that I know of... Although, I did run into our German friend, Baron Von Stern, on deck. He began talking about my late brother. He seemed to think that I should write a biography. While I have no interest in such a thing, I did not see any harm in discussing it. It passed the time as we strolled along the deck.'

'How long were you together?' asked Miss Storm-Fleming.

'Perhaps half an hour. Why? Do you suspect the baron?'

'Not at all,' said Miss Storm-Fleming. 'I just wondered whether someone might have seen the two of you and taken advantage of the opportunity.'

'Well...if you will excuse me, Doctor, Miss Storm-Fleming, I must make my way to the smoking room to see the captain.'

'He is expected here shortly,' I said. 'He has a dinner engagement.'

'Then perhaps I will meet him on his way – thank you.' He nodded to each of us as he left.

The dining room was already full of people, but the head steward had reserved a quiet table for us at one side of the room.

'Doctor Watson, is it not shocking about the colonel? And your friend, Miss Norton! What *is* going on?'

'I am sure I do not know... And you left out the small matter of a murder.'

'Two murders, if my information is correct.' She studied my reaction.

'You have heard about Strickley, then?'

'Is that his name? I just heard about a body being found down below. How did *you* find out about it?'

'The captain asked me to help the ship's surgeons perform the post-mortem.'

'And I know something else – there was some kind of disturbance on deck last night after your mysterious disappearance. Passengers who tried to walk there were turned back by the crew – something about an electrical problem.'

Stunned by this admission, I decided to confront her.

'Miss Storm-Fleming, just who are you? You are not an innocent widow, that is for certain.'

'That may be true. But I am your friend, and I am in trouble. I have no idea whether they will believe my story about Bishop once we reach New York.'

'I am not sure that I believe your story either...not that I think you killed Bishop. But I saw you from the squash-rackets court – you were not walking with Bishop, you were following him.'

Miss Storm-Fleming's eyes were open wide and beginning to fill with tears. She put her hand on my arm.

'I had personal reasons for following him... I cannot tell you about that now. But I need to know what is going on. You are in the middle of something, I can tell... I need to know that you are on my side, and that you will help to clear my name.'

'You seem to know a great deal already. In fact, you are exceptionally well informed.'

'Perhaps I have friends in high places.'

I was losing my patience with her, and it showed.

'I can see that I was wrong to bring this up,' she said. 'Let us just forget it and see if we can have a quiet dinner.'

'We will let it pass for the moment but sometime you must give me some answers,' I replied.

We ordered a bottle of wine and, much to my surprise, soon found ourselves in a relaxed and warm conversation. We spoke of departed loved ones and how difficult it was to fill the emptiness. The time passed quickly and soon we were finishing our coffee.

'Thank you for a wonderful evening, Doctor Watson. I hope I have not been too trying.'

I smiled and reassured her that that was not the case.

Across the room I saw Captain Smith and his dining companions. It appeared that he too was about to retire.

'Miss Storm-Fleming, if you will excuse me, I need to speak to the captain.'

'Please do, I shall retire to my cabin.'

'Shall I accompany you?'

'No, no, please go ahead. I will be fine.'

I called out to her over the roar of conversation, 'Miss Storm-Fleming, please be careful.'

She turned to glance at me, smiled and left the room.

On my way to the captain's table I passed the Von Sterns, who were finishing their main course of roast duckling with apple sauce.

'Doctor,' said the baron, rising to shake my hand. 'We saw you when we came in but we did not want to disturb you. Would you care to sit down?'

'No, no, thank you. I just wondered whether you heard about Colonel Moriarty.'

'What about the colonel?'

'Someone broke into his cabin this evening.'

'No!' he said. 'I do not believe it. I was just talking to Herr Moriarty. Was anything taken?'

'It does not appear so, but he is very disturbed.'

'I am disturbed as well,' said the baroness. 'First these terrible blackmail notes, then the burglary at Miss Norton's cabin and now this. Have you made any progress in investigating the blackmail?'

'I am afraid not, Baroness. But I do not think these burglaries are related to the blackmail notes. Try not to worry.'

Von Stern walked behind his wife and put his hands on her shoulders. 'My wife is a very sensitive woman, Doctor, but she will be fine... Meanwhile, my dear, our dinner is getting cold. Are you sure you will not join us, Doctor?'

'Thank you again, but I must be on my way.'

I arrived at the captain's table, just as he was bidding his dining companions good night.

'Ah, Doctor Watson. Have you met my friends – Mr and Mrs Widener and their son, Harry; Mr and Mrs Thayer; Mr and Mrs

Carter, and Major Butt.'

We exchanged greetings.

'Perhaps, Doctor, you would accompany me to the bridge? It is almost nine o'clock and I have a busy day tomorrow.'

I told the captain that I would be most pleased to. We said goodnight to the others, who were clearly not ready to leave.

As we left the dining room, I asked the captain if he had seen Moriarty.

'Yes, another entry in our log of murders and burglaries – not to mention shooting. I will look into it in the morning. How is your investigation?'

'I am still in the dark. But Holmes asked Miss Norton and me to meet him in the smoking room at 11.30. Maybe he will have something to report then.'

In the short time it took to get to the bridge, we made no progress in solving the mysteries on board the *Titanic*. But the walk did give me an opportunity to breathe some fresh air and compose myself again before meeting Holmes and Miss Norton. There were only a few men on the bridge when we arrived.

'All in order, Mr Lightoller?' the captain asked.

The second officer was standing by the wheel when we arrived.

'Indeed, sir. We are keeping a lookout for icebergs. Mr Murdoch will be relieving me at ten. How are you, Doctor Watson?'

'Very well, thank you.'

'There is not much wind,' said Smith.

'No, it is very calm. A few waves would make any icebergs easier to spot... Of course, there would be a certain amount of reflected light from the icebergs.'

The captain nodded and stroked his beard.

'Forgive me, Captain, but all this talk is making me a little concerned,' I said.

'I have been through iceberg warnings all my career and I have never hit one. Besides, we have some very reliable lookouts up in the nest who would warn us in plenty of time. And, as you know, they say this ship is iceberg-proof. Do you not trust our engineers?'

We all laughed and this helped to put my mind at ease.

'Well, Doctor, I am going to retire. Please stay on the bridge for a while and keep Mr Lightoller company, if you wish. He likes a good mystery story as well as the next man.'

'Thank you, Captain. I may take advantage of your offer.'

'And Mr Lightoller...'

'Yes, sir.'

'If it becomes at all doubtful, let me know at once. I shall be just inside.'

Chapter Twenty-Six

ॐ

THE NIGHT OF SUNDAY 14 APRIL 1912

By 11.15 pm, social activities on board the *Titanic* had nearly ended for the night. This city of 2,200 people was going to sleep. The public rooms were quiet, and most of the passengers and off-duty crew had retired to their cabins. The smoking room was still open but only a handful of passengers remained. At a side table, a marathon poker game continued. Other passengers were enjoying brandy and cigars at their tables, or standing by the fireplace. As I entered, I waved to Major Butt, Harry Widener and Mr Carter, who were seated near the bar and having a spirited conversation.

In this relaxed atmosphere, I found myself marvelling at the beauty and elegance of this ship. Even out here, on the cold Atlantic, I could come to this fine room and feel a sense of warmth. I studied the rich mahogany panelling, inlaid with mother-of-pearl. The painted windows, which lighted the room during the day, contained images of landscapes and ancient ships. I reflected on how man had come so far, and could create comfort amid such forbidding surroundings.

Holmes and Miss Norton had not yet arrived, so I removed my

overcoat and walked over to the large, open fireplace. The painting above was a powerful image of a ship entering Plymouth Harbour. On the hearth below, the flames were beginning to die. I had hoped for a roaring fire to remove the chill from my bones. Instead, I stopped an elderly steward and asked him to bring me a brandy.

As I held my hands to the weak flames, I listened to two men as they discussed our likely arrival time in New York. One estimated that we would arrive on time, and the other thought we might get in a few hours early. The steward, to whom I had just spoken, was still taking orders and overheard the conversation.

'I think we will do better than that,' said the steward.

'Why do you say that?' asked one of the men, who spoke in a French accent.

'Because we are making faster speed than we were yesterday.'

'And what do you know about it?' the other man asked.

'I heard it from the engine room.'

The man with the accent smiled and looked at his companion. 'That does not mean anything.'

The steward, not to be dismissed so lightly, offered to prove his point.

'Gentlemen, come and see for yourself. It is hard to tell here but you might notice that tonight the ship's vibration is much greater than it has ever been. And if you will accompany me to the passageway just outside, you will see that the change is quite evident.'

The two men chuckled, shrugged and told the steward to lead the way.

After warming myself by the fire, I found a secluded table where Holmes, Miss Norton and I could discuss the day's events without being disturbed. It was not long before they walked in side by side. Neither appeared to be in the best of spirits.

'Watson,' said Holmes, draping his overcoat on an empty table and flopping down in a chair, 'I hope that one day when this story can be told, you do not mention these long stretches of failure. My enquiries today were less than successful.'

'And I would prefer that you kept my name out of it entirely,' said Miss Norton. 'This is not one of my better moments.'

Unlike me, Holmes and Miss Norton had changed and were wearing more comfortable attire – that is, assuming they had taken the time to dine.

'I just ordered a brandy,' I said. 'But it appears that I should have ordered three. Please remember, we might have been more successful if we had not been interrupted by a political incident.'

I saw the steward and waved him over to our table.

'Yes, sir, I will bring your brandy right away. And may I bring anything for the rest of you?'

The commodore and Miss Norton also asked for brandy.

'With or without ice, sir?'

'Without ice, by all means,' said Holmes. 'I am still shivering from being out on deck.'

Miss Norton nodded.

'Very good,' said the steward, before heading off in the direction of the bar.

'Where have you two been all evening?' I asked. 'I have not seen hide nor hair of either of you.'

'Miss Norton has been kind enough to keep an eye on our chief suspects, and came back with a very satisfactory report, I might add,' said Holmes.

'Did you not see me in the restaurant? I was there,' Miss Norton smiled. 'I assumed you must have been distracted.'

I ignored her remark and asked a question that had been gnawing at me since dinner.

'Did you see the baron approach Moriarty on deck?'

'I did.'

'And where was the baroness at the time?'

'I am uncertain. She was with the baron just before he ran off to catch up with Moriarty. Then she bustled off in the direction of the stairway. I decided it would be better to keep an eye on the two men.'

'Following the baroness might have been more interesting,' I replied. 'Did you hear that Moriarty's cabin was broken into this afternoon – at least that is what he said.'

'I did,' said Holmes. Miss Norton looked surprised. 'I did not have an opportunity to tell you as we walked in, but I would say that Frau Von Stern is at least our chief suspect in this burglary, and perhaps your break-in as well, Watson.'

'If she was looking for the plans, that means the Von Sterns do not have them,' I said.

'That would appear to be the most likely hypothesis, but still...'

Holmes was interrupted by the arrival of the steward carrying three glasses of brandy on a tray.

'There you are, gentlemen, Miss. That should take the chill out of you.'

'Let me give you something for your trouble... ' I reached into my jacket pocket for some change. Instead, I removed a few items of miniature furniture.

Holmes handed a few coins to the steward, who smiled and walked away.

'What have you there, Watson? Are you planning new furniture for your flat?'

I laughed, and emptied the full contents of my pocket on to the table.

'Tommy's toys. I had forgotten all about them. I put them in my dinner jacket pocket in hope of returning them this evening.'

'Tommy?' said Holmes.

'A small boy I befriended. Miss Norton has met him. He left these toys when he ran off to church. Incidentally, he is a great fan of yours. And listen to this – he asked to become a Baker Street Irregular. Can you imagine that? He could not believe that all the Irregulars were grown up now.'

'Well, if I were not in the guise of Commodore Winter, I would introduce myself... But on to the matters at hand.' Holmes examined the toy sofas, tables, cabinets and fireplace casually as he spoke. 'As I mentioned earlier, my efforts were less than successful today. There is a sad lack of evidence on the disappearance of Mr Strickley. I tried questioning the crew and others who might have been witnesses, but that too produced dismal results. Tomorrow we must reassemble and...'

Holmes was staring intently at the toys on the table. He had arranged them in a pattern. It appeared to be a formal setting of some kind.

'What is it, Holmes?'

'Do you recognize it, Watson? Do you see it?'

'See what, Holmes?' Miss Norton appeared puzzled as well.

'My God, Watson, look around you!'

I looked more closely and ventured a guess. 'The smoking room? The furniture does look familiar, but...'

'I tell you, Watson, if I am right about this, I will personally decorate your friend Tommy as the greatest Baker Street Irregular of them all.'

'Finish your drinks quickly. We are going to take a trip down to the reception room.'

Miss Norton and I stared at each other in wonder. 'The model of the *Titanic*?' I said. 'But that is locked in a glass case.'

'Locks can be opened,' he said. 'In fact, I would consider it to be highly likely that the late Mr Bishop had a key.'

'Is not that a little far-fetched, Holmes? You think someone might have cleared out a section of the model and hidden the plans inside?' asked Miss Norton.

'If I am wrong, I will be duly embarrassed. But at the moment it is the best hypothesis we have.'

'We will need a key, Holmes, and the captain is asleep.'

'We will go down and take a look first. If it appears the thing has been tampered with, we may have to wake him up.'

'I would hate to be the one to do it,' I said. 'Hell hath no fury like...'

At that moment, we felt a jarring motion and the toys began to move across the table. So did our brandy glasses. At the same time, there was a low, continuous noise, which could best be described as something between a whine and a roar. It went on for a nerve-wracking period of time. In fact, it was less than a minute.

'What the devil was that!' I shouted. Other passengers were looking excitedly about the room. Even the marathon card game was temporarily interrupted.

'If we were not out in the middle of the Atlantic, I would say we had run aground,' Miss Norton suggested. 'You do not suppose something is wrong with the engines, do you?'

Holmes had risen from the table. 'Let us go on deck.' He appeared calm, but there was a distant, somewhat concerned look in his eyes.

We left the table and made our way quickly to the promenade deck on the starboard side of the ship. That is when we saw it. In the starlit night, a mighty tower of ice was visible directly behind the ship. Rising just above the boat deck, the iceberg did not appear to be particularly menacing. Yet we had clearly made contact, perhaps below the water. The three of us stood at the rail and watched the iceberg disappear from sight.

The few of us who had been on deck and had actually seen the iceberg became instant celebrities. Latecomers were eager to find out what had happened. We explained what we had seen. As I was pointing out the direction of the iceberg to an excited passenger I felt a hand tugging at my forearm.

'There is no time for this now, Watson, we have work to do.'

Holmes, Miss Norton and I walked quickly along the deck to the forward end of the ship. As I glanced back to take another look at the gathering crowd, I found myself slipping on a solid object and falling backwards. Fortunately, Miss Norton caught my arm and I regained my balance.

Holmes, who was well ahead, stopped and looked around. He saw the white chunk of ice gliding forwards on the deck. Stopping it with his foot, he picked it up and walked back towards us.

'Are you all right, Watson?'

'Yes, I am not hurt. Is that what I slipped on?'

He handed it to me. 'Indeed, here is a souvenir for you. A genuine piece of an iceberg. It must have fallen off when we made contact... Are you able to carry on?'

'Of course.'

'Then let us proceed. We must get down to that model.'

We returned to the interior warmth of the ship and walked down the main staircase until we reached the reception room on Saloon Deck D. The lights had been dimmed, but the room's furnishings were still clearly visible. We could not see the model of the ship from the grand staircase. It was to the right, by a wall that surrounded the boiler casing below the first smokestack. I looked at the dining-room doors on either side of this partition, wondering whether anyone would enter unexpectedly.

Upon reaching the case, Holmes peered through the glass and examined the upper portions of the model in great detail.

'I cannot tell anything from here. We will have to get inside.'

'Shall I get the captain?' I asked.

'No,' said Holmes, reaching inside his coat. 'Let me try something else first.'

Holmes held a leather case in his hands. It was a case I had seen before while assisting Holmes on missions of questionable legality.

'Your old burglary tools!' I exclaimed. 'I must say, you did come well prepared.'

Holmes selected one of several lock-picks from the case and poked it into the opening. 'This one should do the trick. It is a relatively easy lock.'

Moments later, Holmes was lifting the glass lid from the case. He then reached inside and tugged at various portions of the model to determine where it might separate.

'Do make haste, Mr Holmes,' said Miss Norton. 'Someone might come.' We could hear, through the stairwell, voices and movement from the decks above. Passengers, who had been awakened by the encounter with the iceberg, were beginning to stir.

'I am well aware of that. This should only take a...' A long section of the boat deck came away in Holmes's hand.

It was like opening a treasure chest. We all looked over the top of the case and peered inside.

'My God, look!' Miss Norton, who was not much taller than the case, was struggling to reach inside. 'You were right, the plans! Thank God!'

'Well, Watson, it looks like I will not be eating humble pie after all.'

'I would not speak too soon, Commodore...or should I say, Mr Holmes?' Baron and Baroness Von Stern were approaching us from the grand staircase. The baron was holding a gun.

'Good evening, Baron,' said Holmes. 'Up a little late, are you not? I am afraid the dining room is closed.'

'We are not looking for a midnight snack. My wife and I were following you. We had camped on deck, outside the smoking room and were about to retire for the night when the big iceberg passed...a magnificent sight, by the way. We saw you run outside, and then down along the deck.'

'What have I always told you, Watson, persistence pays off.' Holmes, while doing his best to appear calm, had raised his hands and was staring at the baron's gun.

'By the way, Miss Norton, I owe you my thanks,' said Von Stern. 'If you had not now mentioned Mr Holmes's name, I never would have realized that I had defeated the great detective.'

'Are you going to kill us?' Miss Norton asked.

The baron appeared puzzled by the question, then glanced at his wife.

'I am not sure. I suppose I had not really thought about that. Now, we cannot be having you go to the captain before we reach New York. Hmm, what do you say, my dear?'

'I hear voices, Hans. Let us move into the dining room.'

'I suppose that is a good idea. But first, Elisabeth, Miss Norton has something for us. Would you take the plans from her? And, my dear, please be careful not to walk into my line of fire.'

Miss Norton hesitated, then held out the plans. Frau Von Stern snatched them and walked back quickly behind her husband.

'Scoundrel!' said Miss Norton.

'Scoundrel, you say? Need I remind you that the engineering principles that make your submarine possible were stolen from us by British spies. You did, however, seem to make some modifications that appear very interesting. We must take them back to Germany for more detailed examination.'

'Hans!'

'Yes, my dear, I know. Gentlemen, Miss Norton, would you please step inside the dining room. We will decide in there what to do with you.'

The baron waved his gun and I decided that we had no choice but to comply. As I opened the door, I looked at Holmes. I could see that his keen mind was looking for some method of overcoming our adversaries. But the baron was a trained agent. I did not think it likely that he would make a mistake.

The interior of the restaurant, like the lounge, was dimly lit. We stepped inside and moved back as the Von Sterns entered the room. The baroness closed the door behind her.

Von Stern looked around the room and pointed to a chair that was standing along the wall.

'My dear, would you remove the small cushion from that chair and bring it to me? I think it is best that we deal with this problem in a prompt manner. But I do not want to make too much noise.'

I looked around and saw that a champagne bucket was resting on a nearby trolley. I began to reach for it, planning to make a desperate move to knock the gun from the baron's hand. Much to my surprise, Holmes signalled me to stop.

'What goes on here?' said the baron. 'Doctor Watson, I must insist that you keep your hands up. There is no point to your foolish bravado. I would have shot you before you had even reached that bucket.'

'No, no, Baron,' said a woman's voice. 'I am quite sure I would have shot you first. But let us not argue over trifles. Please drop your gun.'

Miss Storm-Fleming emerged from behind a post, to the baron's right. She was holding a silver revolver.

'Miss Storm-Fleming, you realize, of course, that I am pointing my gun at your friends. Surely you do not want to see them die.'

'You won't shoot, Von Stern. The moment your gun fires I will kill both you and your wife. And in case you did not know, I too am a trained marksman.'

The baroness, who had the cushion in her hand, suddenly threw it across the room in Miss Storm-Fleming's direction. As it went sailing by, the baron began to turn. Miss Storm-Fleming's eyes remained fixed on the baron. She fired her gun and the baron's body was jolted back by the impact. He reached for his chest, looked back to his wife and fell to the floor.

'Miss Storm-Fleming!' I exclaimed. 'I am very glad you arrived, although I am uncertain as to what is happening.'

'Did I not tell you to trust me, Doctor Watson?'

Holmes smiled at Miss Storm-Fleming and delivered a cordial salute. He walked over to the baron's body, pushed it with his foot, bending over to retrieve the gun.

Miss Norton lowered her hands. 'This is astounding,' she said, mopping her brow on her sleeve.

The baroness stood in shocked silence. Suddenly, she broke down in tears and ran to the body of her husband.

'Hans, Hans, please, you cannot die!'

The baroness was on her knees, pulling at her husband's shoulder, trying to turn the body face upwards. She stopped abruptly to take a handkerchief from her sleeve. The movement seemed awkward and the handkerchief appeared to shine. Miss Storm-Fleming fired again. The baroness crumpled forward, falling on her husband's body.

Miss Storm-Fleming walked over to the lifeless couple. Kneeling down on one knee, she examined the two bodies. After reassuring herself that the Von Sterns were no longer a threat, she removed a derringer from the baroness's hand and the submarine plans from her coat. She then got back to her feet and walked towards Miss Norton.

When the two women were face to face, she lifted her arm and held the plans in front of her.

'Here you are, Miss Norton. And in future, you might want to take better care of government property.'

Chapter Twenty-Seven

MIDNIGHT ON SUNDAY 14 APRIL 1912

The *Titanic* was utterly motionless in the water. But it was far from silent. High above the boat deck the ship's huge funnels were blowing off steam with a mighty roar.

Holmes, Miss Norton, Miss Storm-Fleming and I were making our way forward to the bridge, where we planned to tell Captain Smith the sad news that he had two more deaths to deal with. We were all reluctant to burden the captain with more problems, since we knew he would be fully occupied with the ship's structural damage. At that point, we had no idea how serious the damage really was.

The other passengers and most of the crew were also in the dark. A number of people, awakened by the commotion, were braving the cold to see what all the fuss was about. Some were bundled up in their warmest clothing, while others were wearing coats over their pyjamas. They stood along the rail, shivering and staring out into the dark – but there were no answers to be found. When asked, the crew would speculate that the ship had lost a propeller blade, or that they had stopped to avoid nearby icebergs. No one really knew for sure.

But for me, at least, one big mystery had been solved. Miss Storm-Fleming was an agent of the American government. She had been assigned to protect the plans, and all the while keep her identity secret from her British counterparts. (Did Mycroft know?) I had many questions to ask her, but they would have to wait until after we had seen the captain. I restrained my curiosity, knowing there would be plenty of time to talk later on.

As for the Von Sterns, there were questions about them that would never be answered. Clearly, they were agents of the German government. And quite obviously, they did not steal the plans from Miss Norton's cabin. But I had little doubt that they had broken into my cabin, and that of Colonel James Moriarty. And what of Moriarty? Was he our thief? If so, who was he working for? One thing was certain: Moriarty could not escape in the middle of the Atlantic Ocean. We would soon be dealing with him.

We arrived at the bridge at an opportune time. Captain Smith was returning with Thomas Andrews, Chief Officer Wilde and Fourth Officer Boxhall. They had been inspecting the ship's damage.

'My apologies, Commodore, I do not have time for you at the moment!' the captain said curtly as he opened the door to the bridge.

'Captain, if you please, it is quite urgent.'

'Sir, I am afraid you do not know the meaning of the word!' He paused and his voice suddenly lowered to a calmer tone. 'Very well, I suppose you all want to come...and Miss Storm-Fleming, too. Come with me, then.'

Andrews appeared to be both perplexed and impatient with the encounter. He had a look of urgency on his face.

Once inside, the captain spoke at once. 'Mr Andrews, please get started on your calculations. Commodore, would you – and only you – step into my cabin. You have one minute.'

Holmes and the captain disappeared behind closed doors. Meanwhile, Andrews unrolled plans of the ship's structure and studied them intently. From time to time, he would jot something down with a pencil or consult his slide rule. He worked furiously, but the resigned expression on his face told me he was merely confirming facts that he already knew.

Several other men were on the bridge, including Chief Officer Wilde, First Officer Murdoch, Fourth Officer Boxhall and Sixth Officer Moody. Murdoch was nervously looking over Andrews's shoulder, until impatience caused him to walk over to the ship's wheel. Gripping the wheel, he looked forward, out of the window, and appeared lost in thought. Wilde was to the rear of the bridge, consulting a White Star manual, while the other two officers spoke quietly to each other in the background.

In just over a minute, the captain and Holmes returned to the bridge. Much to my surprise, the captain appeared unaffected by their conversation. Equally to my surprise, there was a look of alarm in Holmes's eyes.

'Any progress, Mr Andrews?'

'I will be finished in a moment, Captain.'

The captain, forced to wait for answers, looked at each of our faces. We were all eager to know what was going on, but none of us dared to ask.

'I was just telling the commodore that the ship is very seriously damaged. At this moment, we are awaiting word from Mr Andrews on whether she will last the night. But I must tell you, we are in a very grave situation.'

'Was it the iceberg, sir?' I asked. 'We got just a brief glimpse of it...'

'Yes, Doctor. Mr Murdoch here was on duty when he got a call from Mr Fleet in the crow's nest that there was an iceberg right ahead. Mr Murdoch responded quickly by hard-a-starboarding and by reversing the engines. He had intended to steer to port around the iceberg, but it was too close. The huge mass of ice below the water scraped us along the starboard bow. While Mr Murdoch had immediately closed the watertight doors, it did not solve the problem. There is a good deal of water down below and it is coming in fast.'

We all took a moment to consider the captain's horrifying account of our situation. I thought back to the debate that had taken place between Mr Andrews and Mr Stead, and their discussion of the lack of lifeboats.

'Sir, the lifeboats...?' I could not complete my sentence.

'Well, Doctor, if the worst happens, let us just hope there are other ships nearby.'

We all stood quietly as Andrews completed his work. Before he did, Mr J Bruce Ismay stepped inside, wearing a suit over his pyjamas and a pair of carpet slippers.

'Any word yet, Captain?' He stopped short when he saw four visitors. 'What are these passengers doing here?'

'They have my permission, Mr Ismay,' the captain replied.

Ismay nodded, suddenly realizing there were more important questions at hand.

Andrews rose from the table. 'I have something for you now, Captain, and I fear that it is not good news.'

Captain Smith put his hand on Andrews's shoulder. 'Go ahead, Mr Andrews.'

He looked the captain in the eye, then turned back to the other officers. 'This ship has an hour and a half left. Possibly two. Not much longer.' Again, silence. It was broken by the captain.

'Are you certain?'

'The evidence is here,' Andrews replied, directing Smith to look at the plans on the table. 'This ship can float with any two of her sixteen watertight holds flooded. She can even float with all of her first four holds gone. But she definitely cannot float with all of her first five holds full.'

'But this ship cannot sink,' Ismay protested.

'I am afraid it can, sir,' Andrews said. 'We have water in the forepeak, holds Number 1 and 2, the post room, boiler rooms Number 5 and 6...' Andrews picked up his pencil and drew a long line from the bow of the ship going back. 'That iceberg cut a narrow gash in the starboard side of the ship nearly 300 feet long. We never expected that would happen.'

'But the watertight holds...' Ismay said.

Andrews again pointed to the diagram. 'Once the first five compartments are flooded, the bow will sink so low that the water in the fifth compartment will overflow into the sixth. Then the water in the sixth will overflow into the seventh, and so on... The ship will sink. There is no doubt.'

The captain decided that it was time to end the conversation.

'Mr Wilde, uncover the lifeboats. Mr Murdoch, alert the passengers. Mr Moody, get out the lifeboat assignments. And Mr Boxhall, wake up Mr Lightoller and Mr Pitman. Tell them to report to me immediately. I will go to the wireless to send out a distress call.'

Holmes, Miss Norton, Miss Storm-Fleming and I left the bridge and moved down to the forward end of A Deck. We were drawn there by the cries and cheers of a strangely festive group of first-class passengers. As we pushed our way through the small crowd, I was nearly knocked over by a middle-aged man carrying a football-size block of ice.

'Sorry, old man,' he said, grabbing my forearm. 'Are you hurt?'

He was breathing rapidly and a frosty cloud formed between us each time he exhaled.

'Not at all.'

'I was in a hurry. I wanted to get below to show this prize off to some friends.'

He proudly displayed his clear, shining trophy, which glimmered in the electric lights like a giant diamond.

'Tell me,' I said, pointing forward. 'What is all the excitement about?'

'Why, the sporting match of the year! When we passed the iceberg, big chunks fell down on to the well deck. Some steerage passengers are down there throwing them around, having a fine old time. Looks like great fun. I got one of them to toss this up to me. I suppose those of us in first class will have to be satisfied with being spectators, what?'

As he disappeared around the corner, Miss Storm-Fleming spoke softly, 'Do you suppose we ought to tell them? They do not know, and there are only a couple of hours... So many could die tonight...'

'Perhaps we should leave that to the experts,' I said. 'I am sure the captain has a plan that will prevent panic and save as many as possible. And there is a lot of shipping in this area. In this age of wireless communication, we will be surrounded with help in no time.'

She nodded, but did not seem to be entirely convinced. We walked forward to join Holmes and Miss Norton at the rail.

Below, the scene was just as our new acquaintance had described it. Men, children and even a few young women were kicking chunks of ice between imaginary goals. There was no precise means of keeping score but that did not dampen their enthusiasm.

The cheers of both athletes and spectators blended with the roar of the funnels, which were still belching up steam from the boilers below. In the distance we could hear the sound of the ship's band, as it played lively ragtime tunes.

Then, from above, I heard a 'pop'. Within moments, a bright burst of light spread across the sky. Rockets were being fired from the bridge deck. There was a cheer from the excited crowd. But I noticed that a few passengers standing nearby were suddenly subdued by this display. Frequent travellers, especially, knew the meaning of distress rockets.

Some of the crew were now trying to break up the crowd on A Deck and get the passengers to assemble inside.

'Will everyone please move back to the first-class lounge,' shouted a steward. 'We will begin lowering the lifeboats shortly. The captain has ordered women and children first. I repeat, women and children first.'

There were no outward signs of alarm from the passengers. In fact, a few ignored the warning completely and stayed by the rail.

My companions and I, setting an example, immediately responded to the steward's orders.

As we moved back through the long corridors, one young woman said to her husband, 'Well, I am not going out in one of those little boats. I would freeze out there. This ship is as steady as can be.'

Her husband agreed, but was less certain. 'Yes, it does not make much sense,' he said. 'It must be some regulations they have to follow. You know White Star, everything by the book.'

As we neared the lounge, Holmes moved to the right and opened a door. He motioned for the three of us to enter. We found ourselves in the reading and writing room, which was unoccupied. After we were all inside, Holmes closed the door, shutting out much of the noise and commotion. The curtains had been drawn across the large bay window, giving us privacy from the passengers who were walking outside along the promenade deck.

The room must have been recently used, because yellow flames were blazing in the fireplace. We gathered closely in comfortable chairs and leaned forward towards the heat.

'As you know, our situation is precarious,' said Holmes. He paused, but no one said a word. 'In addition to the question of our personal safety, we have the responsibility of completing our mission and delivering the plans to the American authorities.'

Holmes's hands were pointing forwards, with fingertips touching, as he stared into the flames. I had often seen him in this pose at our Baker Street flat, mostly when he was deep in thought.

'Miss Norton,' he said, 'you must board a lifeboat as quickly as possible. It is your responsibility to ensure that the plans arrive safely.'

For a moment, it appeared that our young friend was going to raise her voice in objection. But she stopped short when Holmes turned his head to look at her.

'Yes, Mr Holmes, I will.'

'And Miss Storm-Fleming, I consider it your duty to accompany Miss Norton. In view of all the efforts that have been made to steal the plans thus far, she might need your help.'

Miss Storm-Fleming left her chair and sat on the floor in front of me, next to the fire. She smiled at him, then turned to the fire and began to warm her hands. 'My superiors gave me *two* assignments. One was to look after the submarine plans. The other was to make contact with you at the end of the voyage and take you to your American contact. If I let you drown, I will have failed in one of my missions. That would taint my record.'

'Miss Storm-Fleming, you must get to a lifeboat,' I said. 'Holmes and I will proceed shortly, after a rescue ship arrives. This is not certain, but the odds are with us.'

'Well, Watson,' said Holmes. 'If I thought it would do any good, I would tell you to try to get into a lifeboat too. They might allow men to board later on. But I know what the answer would be. So perhaps you would like to accompany me in a search for Moriarty. There are one or two matters of interest that I would like to discuss with him.'

'Are you not forgetting that we have friends on board? Mr Futrelle and his wife, especially,' said Miss Norton. 'Should we not we find them and try to warn them?'

'And young Tommy and his parents...' added Miss Storm-Fleming.

'Yes, of course, you are quite right. We must make an effort to find them while there is still time.'

'It is a large ship,' I said.

'Yes, indeed it is,' Holmes replied. 'Perhaps we should split up. Miss Norton, please come with me. We'll search A Deck.'

I looked at Miss Storm-Fleming and she nodded.

'We will go up to the boat deck.'

'Very well,' said Holmes. 'We will meet again at 1.15. Go to the boat deck below the forward funnel, on the starboard side, but if matters begin to look difficult, please go to a lifeboat.'

Holmes was the first to rise from his chair. Soon, the rest of us headed slowly towards the door.

We paused before leaving. Inside this room there was warmth, elegance and, dare I say it, friendship. But we all knew full well that the clock was ticking. Before the night was out, this luxury room on the world's largest ocean liner would be filled with icy water and lying on the ocean floor.

Holmes extended his hand to me, and I grasped it firmly.

Then he opened the door.

Chapter Twenty-Eight

THE EARLY HOURS OF MONDAY
15 APRIL 1912

The *Titanic* had developed a perceptible tilt. Both Miss Storm-Fleming and I noticed it immediately as we stepped out on to the boat deck. Much to our surprise, there was no panic. People seemed to realize that the ship was in trouble but they had no idea of their immediate peril. In fact, one member of the crew, who was assisting with the loading of a lifeboat, told me that the *Titanic* could not possibly sink in less than eight hours – plenty of time for rescue ships to arrive. Speaking as a veteran, it was his opinion that the ship would not sink at all.

'I may stay on board while the ship is towed back to Belfast,' he boasted. 'I will book myself a first-class cabin and have a grand old time.'

The *Titanic* had sixteen lifeboats under davits, as well as four Englehardt collapsible boats, which were stored elsewhere on the boat deck. Thus far, six of the craft had been launched, none of which had been filled to capacity. The crew was having a difficult time getting people to board the boats. So rather than waiting for greater cooperation from the passengers, they launched them. Officers reasoned that once the boats were safely in the water, they could come back and rescue swimming survivors.

Miss Storm-Fleming and I had a decision to make. With precious moments remaining, was there anything we could do to rally the passengers? Could we save lives by going from group to group, urging people to board the lifeboats? And what if some action on our part had just the opposite effect? A panic might slow the loading of the lifeboats and result in a greater loss of life. And who were we to question the wisdom of an experienced crew? We decided to proceed with our mission and, if possible, offer our assistance to the captain.

We began our search for Tommy and the Futrelles on the starboard side of the ship. There was no sign of them. We were impressed, however, by the sight of the ship's band standing outside the gymnasium playing lively tunes. I could not help but admire these fine men, whose music did so much to raise the spirits of those on board.

On the port side we found Mr Lightoller preparing to lower a boat. The second officer, while guiding reluctant women and children into the craft, was simultaneously carrying on a conversation with a steward.

'I am sorry, Hart, I am needed here and I have no one spare. You will have to manage by yourself.'

'It is the language more than anything, sir,' said Hart. 'So many of them cannot understand English. I just cannot persuade them to move. Finns, Swedes, they do not understand.'

'Perhaps I can help,' said Miss Storm-Fleming. 'Linguistics was always one of my stronger subjects.'

Lightoller interrupted his work. 'Miss Storm-Fleming,' he said with some surprise. And Doctor Watson. Would you accompany Mr Hart down to steerage?'

'Yes, of course, just show me where to go,' said Miss Storm-Fleming.

'And me too,' I added.

'Very good. But make haste,' said Lightoller. 'There are still plenty of boats, but they are going fast.'

Hart guided us to the foot of the main steerage staircase, aft on E Deck. The area, surrounded by plain white walls and low ceilings, was mobbed with families. Some appeared frightened, while others just looked confused. I felt especially sorry for a young mother, who was trying to keep her children together amid the moving crowd.

Hart took charge of the situation. 'I'm going to find the interpreter and see how he is doing. By now, he should have a group assembled to go on deck. Please gather together some families, as many as you can, and follow the same route back to the boat deck. Do you think you can do that?'

'Indeed,' I replied.

'Good luck then, and God bless you.'

Hart disappeared into the crowd.

The steward had not exaggerated the difficulty of the task. It required conveying the urgency of the situation, without creating panic. Miss Storm-Fleming did a magnificent job carrying out her assignment, using several different languages. I helped with the English-speaking families. Soon, we had a group of about thirty people ready to go.

I led the group up the stairs and into the third-class lounge on C Deck. Miss Storm-Fleming took up the rear, ensuring that there were no stragglers. We continued across the open well deck, past the library and into first class. Before long we were making our way up the grand stairway to the boat deck.

It was a joy to see the first of these passengers heading towards the lifeboats. But I shuddered to think of the steerage passengers still below who would, quite probably, lose their lives in the next few hours. And what of the crew down below who were valiantly operating the pumps and keeping the electric power flowing?

I looked at my watch. It was 1.25. We were late for our rendezvous with Holmes and Miss Norton, so we moved quickly, running forwards along the starboard deck.

En route, we saw Futrelle. He was walking aft and appeared to be lost in thought.

'Futrelle, I am so glad that we found you,' I said. 'Where is your wife?'

'I put May in a boat not five minutes ago. She is safe now.'

'Futrelle, I...'

'Doctor, I have spoken to Holmes and Miss Norton. They told me everything.'

'Please, join us, Mr Futrelle. We are on our way to meet them now.'

'No, no thank you. I prefer to be alone with my own thoughts.'

'Futrelle...' I searched for the right words.

'But I must thank you, Doctor. My thanks to both you and Mr Holmes. It was truly a case to remember.'

He shook both our hands. Futrelle began to turn, but then paused. 'I do believe I have discovered a plan by which Professor Van Dusen could escape safely from this situation. I fear, however, that it is not for me.'

He smiled, waved slowly, and began to walk away.

Miss Storm-Fleming and I moved quickly to the forward funnel, where we hoped to meet Holmes and Miss Norton. Instead, we found only Miss Norton. She was pacing up and down nervously.

'Where have you two been? I thought of going to look for you, but...'

'Where is Holmes?' I asked.

'He has gone to meet Moriarty.'

'What! But why?'

'While we were returning to meet you, a page ran up and delivered a note. It was from the colonel. He said he knew the commodore's true identity, and demanded that Mr Holmes meet him immediately.'

'Meet him where?' I asked.

'Mr Holmes did not show me the note.' She reached into her pocket. 'But he did write a note of his own and asked me to give it to you.'

I hesitated before unfolding the paper, which I recognized as a sheet from Holmes's notebook.

My dear Watson,

I write these few lines as I prepare to meet Colonel Moriarty, who has sent me an invitation that I simply cannot resist. The colonel has written a note stating that if I do not meet him immediately, 'innocent lives will suffer'. It is hard to imagine more suffering than will take place on board this ship tonight, but nevertheless, my curiosity compels me to see what this vengeful creature has in mind.

Reading between the lines, I have deduced from his note that the colonel is a freelance agent who meant to profit from the theft of the submarine plans. I have no doubt that it was he who hired Bishop and Strickley to steal the plans, and then murdered them to prevent them from giving him away. He has, no doubt, friends in high places, since he knew that both I and the plans would be on board this ship. I would place his intellect at a level equal to that of the late Professor Moriarty. But I am afraid that he was not being honest earlier when he said that he had forgiven me for the death of his brother. That appears to be foremost on his mind at this fateful hour.

In a way, I must thank the colonel for providing an opportunity to face death in a way that is most satisfactory to me. As you know, I abhor inactivity, and this gives me the chance to use these final moments to pay my respects to those values I have held for so long. My only regret is that it prevents me from saying my proper goodbyes to you, old friend. I would have been lost on this mission without my

Boswell. Please make sure that Miss Norton and Miss Storm-Fleming board a lifeboat, and save yourself if you can. I regard you as the best and wisest man it has ever been my privilege to know.

Very sincerely yours,
Sherlock Holmes.

I passed the note to Miss Storm-Fleming and Miss Norton, who each read the letter in silence.

'We did find Tommy and his family,' said Miss Norton eventually. 'We told them about the ship and, with the help of Mr Lightoller, got Tommy and his mother on board one of the lifeboats.'

'That is indeed good news,' I said, finding that I had to clear my throat to speak. 'Thank you, Miss Norton. I just hope that Tommy does not lose his father tonight.'

'There's more. Before we went to the lifeboat, Mr Holmes took Tommy aside and spoke to him. I do not know what they said, but after a while, Tommy was grinning ear to ear. Then Mr Holmes handed something to Tommy, patted him on the back and took him back to his parents. He would not tell me what he said to Tommy. He just said he and the boy were having a little professional discussion.'

'You do not suppose Mr Holmes told him his true identity, do you?' said Miss Storm-Fleming, ever mindful of the absolute need for security.

'Oh, I doubt it,' I said with a smile. 'But then again...'

'Do you suppose we should look for him and try to help him?' Miss Norton asked.

'No, Miss Norton, you have your job to do and I have mine. After I put you and Miss Storm-Fleming into a lifeboat, I will try to track him down. He tricked me into missing the last fight he had with a Moriarty. This time, I plan to be there at his side.'

I expected to hear a protest from Miss Storm-Fleming, but she was silent. Instead, she took my arm and smiled at me in a way that seemed to reflect a knowledge beyond my mortal comprehension. Miss Norton took my other arm and the three of us walked over to the forward end of the boat deck.

I had been so preoccupied that I had not noticed how much the situation on board had deteriorated. By now the bow of the mighty ship was low in the water and the first signs of panic had begun to show. A group of men had gathered around a boarding lifeboat and were trying to push their way into the small craft. For a moment, it appeared that the boat, and all passengers on board, might be in some jeopardy. Could it hold up if the mob broke past the crew and tried to jump on board at once?

Suddenly, two shots rang out, sending bright flashes across the night sky. The mob immediately backed away, and gradually moved on to find better opportunities. Some of the crew and two bystanders then jumped on board the boat and forcibly removed two men who, without the support of the mob, offered little resistance.

'Women and children only!' shouted Chief Officer Wilde, who was in charge of loading the boat. 'Last call. We will be lowering away in a few moments! Would all women and children please step forward!'

I looked at the small craft. It was Englehardt Collapsible C, which had been loaded into the davits of long-departed Lifeboat No. 1. The canvas sides looked frail, but I had no doubt that it would hold up on the calm sea. Inside, passengers were frightened and restless. I saw one young girl with a serious gash on her head, possibly the result of the recent altercation.

'Last call!' Wilde shouted again. 'We are about to lower away! There are still a few seats available!'

But there were no women or children nearby. I did, however, see Mr J Bruce Ismay, who was doing his best to assist Wilde with his duties.

'Lower away!' Wilde said.

'Wait a minute!' I shouted. 'I have two more for you.'

'Very good, Doctor. Get them on quickly.' Wilde held up his hand to the crewman who was handling the davits.

'Doctor Watson,' someone shouted. It was a familiar voice. I turned to see the stern face of Captain Smith. 'Why do you not join them? We have an injury on board and your medical knowledge is needed. No doubt it will be needed much more as the night progresses.'

'I am sorry, Captain. I cannot board ahead of the other men. Someone on board can bandage the girl's wound.'

'Doctor, there are already many men in those lifeboats – and many empty seats too. I am afraid we were not quite prepared to handle all this.'

'Nevertheless, as a man of honour. I cannot...'

I felt a stinging blow to the back of my head. And, for the second time on this voyage, I lost consciousness.

Chapter Twenty-Nine

҈

MONDAY 15 APRIL 1912

I felt a splash of icy cold water on my face, followed by a stinging sensation in my eyes and the taste of salt on my lips. And then, of course, there was that throbbing pain at the back of my head. Quickly I summoned the energy to sit up and rub the water from my eyes.

As my eyes cleared, I saw that Miss Storm-Fleming and Miss Norton were sitting on either side of me in a lifeboat. I strained to peer out into the darkness.

'The *Titanic*?' I said.

'Still afloat, but sinking fast,' said Miss Norton. She pointed back over her shoulder and I turned around, all the while dreading what I would see.

The *Titanic* was at a steep tilt, her bow well down in the water. But much to my surprise, the mighty ship's electric lights were still blazing away and the sound of the band penetrated the bitterly cold night air. But they were no longer playing lively ragtime tunes. I recognized the hymn. I had sung it at church services many times:

Nearer, my God, to Thee,
Nearer to Thee!
E'en though it be a cross
That riseth me;
Still all my song shall be,
Nearer, my God, to Thee.

The music blended with the cries of passengers who, in vain, searched for some place of safety on board the doomed ship. Closer by, there was the sound of weeping. Women on board the lifeboat were thinking of their husbands. The fate of those on board the *Titanic* seemed inevitable. Yet, there was always a faint glimmer of hope... What were they all thinking during these final moments? And what of Holmes?

'What hit me?' I asked.

'I am afraid I did, with the handle of my gun,' said Miss Storm-Fleming. 'You were being stubborn.'

'Our apologies for the sea water, Doctor Watson, but it was all we had.' Miss Norton was mopping the water from my face with her handkerchief.

'Miss Storm-Fleming, I do believe that was overstepping the mark...' She interrupted my rebuke with a stern look.

I looked at the sadness in the eyes of my fellow passengers and said no more.

I noticed that I was wearing a life jacket. So were my companions. Miss Norton said that Mr Wilde had provided them before the boat was lowered. Apparently, there had been some difficulty getting the boat in the water. The angle of the ship had been so steep that the lifeboat continually banged along the outer hull. The passengers in the boat had to push against the hull to provide clear descent into the water.

Our small Englehardt Collapsible was nearly full, but those of us inside were only a handful compared to the 2,200 that had been on the *Titanic*. Overall, the four Englehardts could carry a total of nearly 200 people. The ship's sixteen standard lifeboats, larger than the Englehardts, had a total capacity of nearly 1,000. Even if all twenty lifeboats were filled – which they were not – almost half of the passengers would be left without a boat. Their fate would depend on a ship arriving in time. But, given the speed at which the *Titanic* was sinking, that prospect was looking bleak.

'Any signs of a rescue ship?' I asked.

'No,' Miss Storm-Fleming replied, 'although we have been watching that light out there.' She pointed to a white light miles off in the darkness. 'It must be a ship, but it has not moved. Surely it has picked up our wireless messages, or seen our distress rockets. But it remains stationary.'

I suddenly remembered something. 'Oh, the little girl who was injured. I must see to her.'

'She is well,' said Miss Norton. 'We used the first aid kit. Why not rest for a while, and examine her later?'

'Is everyone else unhurt?' As I looked about the boat, I saw the familiar face of Bruce Ismay some distance away, illuminated by the light of a candle held by one of the passengers. He was seated behind an oar, helping to row.

'Ismay is on board?' I said.

'Yes,' said Miss Storm-Fleming. 'He jumped into the boat just as it was being lowered. I cannot say I really blame him. There was space on board and all the other passengers had left the area. The crew called for women and children, but no one was around.'

'But still, the owner of the line...'

'I know captains are supposed to go down with their ships, but I am not sure about owners,' Miss Storm-Fleming continued. 'I suspect he will face a lot of questions once we get back. Our lifeboat is filled with mostly women and children, although there are a few of the crew on board to make sure we get to a rescue ship.'

'Why are we rowing?' I asked.

'They are afraid that if the *Titanic* goes down, the suction will take down any craft that is nearby,' explained Miss Norton. 'So they want to be well away.'

Suddenly, pain raced through my head and I was forced to sit back. I thought of Holmes and what must be transpiring on board the ship. Had my friend encountered Moriarty? Was he alive? Would I ever know his fate?

'Look!' a woman shouted. We all turned immediately towards the *Titanic*.

The stern of the ship was rising into the air, slowly, like the second-hand of a clock. As its arc steepened, we heard dreadful crashing sounds caused by the ship's furnishings and cargo tumbling towards the sinking bow.

There were screams in the distance. Screams from the people who were gathered at the stern, holding on to any part of the superstructure they could find. Screams from those who had already jumped or fallen into the freezing waters of the North Atlantic. On deck, passengers were climbing up the sloping decks on their way to the rising stern. Perhaps the stern would not sink, at least not for a while. Perhaps the air remaining within the hull would hold it above the water until help arrived.

I looked at my watch. It was 2.18 – more than two and a half hours since the *Titanic* hit the iceberg. My companions in the lifeboat, for the most part, were staring intently at this drama. Their eyes were wide open, some glistening with tears. A notable exception was Mr J Bruce Ismay, who was leaning over his oar, his face buried in his hands.

Out across the water the brilliantly lit ship suddenly glowed red. The lights blinked, then blinked again. Moments later, all that could be seen was the ship's dark hull, as it eclipsed the bright stars of the night sky.

I watched as the *Titanic* continued its upward arc. The sounds of screaming heightened. In the darkness, I could only imagine what it must be like for those remaining on deck. The effort needed to hold on to rails and other fixed points grew with each passing moment. Gradually, many would lose their grip and go tumbling down the deck. If they remained conscious, they would soon suffer the stinging pain of the cold sea.

It would be even worse for those still trapped below. Visions of the steerage passengers came to mind – families huddled together in the darkness against the forward wall of their quarters. Uncertainty must be the greatest fear of all. And what of my friends, the Svenssons, whom I had met on my journey through steerage with Futrelle? Did they make it safely to a lifeboat? And what of Futrelle? Was he clinging to a rail, or was he already in the water, with a life jacket keeping him afloat?

The *Titanic* was now nearly vertical in the water. For a long time it just stood there, its stern pointing towards the sky. Then it began its gradual descent, down towards its dark and peaceful new home. As it made its way down, there was a loud bubbling sound as air escaped from the hull.

When the first of the ship's tall funnels hit the water line, it snapped off like a twig, sending a cloud of soot and steam into the air. It appeared to glide through the water for a moment before it sank. One by one, the other funnels followed suit.

Suddenly, there was a mighty shattering sound below the surface of the water. Some cried that the *Titanic* was breaking up, but I could not tell for sure. An enormous bubble of air rose from the water as the stern remained poised for one final moment, and then disappeared.

'She has gone,' said Miss Norton. She could barely find the breath to speak. All those people... Mr Holmes... Oh, my God!'

Miss Storm-Fleming's head rested on her arms. I could hear her sobbing. I lifted my elbow over the edge of the boat and placed my free hand on her shoulder.

I held back my tears: they would come later, at the proper time.

I looked over at Ismay. He was bowed down over his oar. I could only imagine what he must be thinking.

Minutes passed as we quietly contemplated what had happened. The only sounds were a frothing noise from the sea and a chorus of weeping in the lifeboat.

But the cause of our grief had not yet ended. The worst of it was about to begin.

Back where the mighty ship had just sunk, we heard the cries of hundreds of souls. They had survived the sinking and were out there in their life jackets, floating in the still water amongst the ship's debris.

There were both cries for help and screams of pain. The temperature of the water was below freezing. They would not last long.

My two companions were staring out into the darkness. Soon, Miss Storm-Fleming turned to me. She had the look of someone who desperately wanted to jump over the side to help, but knew that would be futile.

'Doctor Watson, is there nothing we can do?'

I put my right hand over the side and into the water. At first, it merely felt cold. I left it there. It did not take long before I felt a stinging sensation. I lifted my hand out of the water and warmed it under my arm.

'You there!' I motioned to the crewman in charge of the boat. 'We must row back and help. We can fit a few more in here.'

My statement sparked a wave of debate up and down the boat. The man pondered the request.

'Very dangerous, sir. True, we might save a few. On the other hand, we might find ourselves surrounded. In the state those folks are right now, they'd all try to climb on board at once. If that happened, this little canvas boat would sink like a rock.'

Private debate continued throughout the boat.

'Perhaps we should wait a while...' one woman shouted, '...until things have quietened down a little.'

Miss Storm-Fleming jumped to her feet, but I put my hand on her shoulder and held her down.

'By then they will be nearly dead!' she cried. 'Is that what you mean?'

Our boat never did go back for survivors. I would later find out that there was very little effort by any of the lifeboats to pull people from the water.

The one notable exception was Fifth Officer Lowe in Lifeboat No. 14. He divided his fifty-five passengers among four other boats and took on board a few of the experienced crew. They mounted a valiant rescue effort, but to little avail. Most of those in the water had already succumbed to the cold temperatures.

After a while, the cries in the distance ended. We were left to silent contemplation and prayer. This was interrupted, from time to time, by talk of being rescued. That light off in the distance never did come to our aid. But we were confident, hopeful even, that help would soon be on its way.

As time passed I found myself growing drowsy and disorientated. Chills ran through my body. Despite my lightheadedness, I recognized the early signs of hypothermia. The cold sea air and the ordeal of the past several days were taking their toll. At some point, I fell fast asleep.

I awoke as light began to fill the sky. My head was resting in Miss Norton's lap, and I was covered with a blanket. There was considerable conversation taking place among the passengers. Some thought they saw the outline of a ship in the distance.

Miss Storm-Fleming, who had been looking across the sea with the others, turned to me and felt my forehead.

'What time is it?' I asked.

'Four o'clock.'

'Is there a ship?'

'We still do not know. There is something out there in the distance.'

I rose to a sitting position and looked out across the sea. For a moment, in the pinkish light of dawn, it appeared that we were surrounded by sailing boats. But, as my eyes cleared, I could see that these images were just a continuing reminder of our ordeal. The white objects were icebergs. Most were small, but they were scattered all over the sea. Not far from the side of our boat I saw a deckchair floating.

'You must rest now, Doctor Watson. For a while we thought we were going to lose you,' said Miss Storm-Fleming.

I closed my eyes, feeling old and useless. I then slept for two more hours.

'Doctor Watson, wake up, it is time to go. The rescue ship is here.' Miss Norton was lifting up my head.

We were pulling up alongside a small liner, the *Carpathia*. Below the single funnel of the Cunard ship, I could see passengers lining the rail. Some, judging by the blankets draped over their shoulders, were survivors of the *Titanic*, looking for relatives in approaching lifeboats.

I attempted to climb the ladder that had been cast down from the deck, but found I was still too weak. A member of the crew threw me a rope, which was looped at the end. I put this under my arms and began to climb, as he pulled me from above.

We were offered blankets and coffee by one of the *Carpathia*'s passengers, which we accepted, gratefully. The mood on board was, as one might expect, very sombre. Some passengers were sitting in chairs, staring blankly at the deck. Others were walking about, searching for loved ones.

We saw Officer Lowe, who was strolling about trying to console survivors of the disaster. After speaking to a woman in a deckchair, he walked over to where we were standing.

'Doctor, I am very pleased to see you here. Can I help you with anything?'

'No, no, thank you,' I replied. 'I was just wondering if you, perhaps, had seen Commodore Winter?'

'No, I am afraid to say I have not.'

'Mr Futrelle?'

'No, nor him either and, if I'm not mistaken, most of the boats have pulled up alongside... Forgive me, Doctor, but you do not look well. Why do you not go below? The *Carpathia*'s passengers have given up their cabins for the survivors. They are all being very kind and helpful.'

'We will soon, Mr Lowe. Thank you.'

I was feeling unsteady on my feet and somewhat dizzy. With the assistance of my two companions, I contacted a member of the *Carpathia*'s crew, who took me below to a cabin. Again, I slept.

When I awoke, hours later, Miss Storm-Fleming was sitting by my bedside and we were alone in the small, modest cabin.

'Doctor Watson, you will be pleased to know that the ship's doctor said you should recover fully. All you need is rest.'

'Holmes?'

She gripped my hand. 'Still no sign. And there is no sign either of Futrelle, the captain – or that scoundrel, Moriarty.'

She had been talking to the other passengers and crew and told me what she had learned. The captain had apparently gone down with the ship. There was a report that he had been on the bridge when it went down, while someone else said they had seen him swimming in the water. One rumour had it that he had swum to a lifeboat carrying a baby and then left without attempting to save himself. The young wireless operator, Mr Bride, had survived, but his colleague, Mr

Phillips, had not. They had both heroically stayed at their posts until the very end, when the captain relieved them of their duties.

One of the strangest stories was of Mr Andrews, the ship's builder, who apparently decided to see the end in the ship's smoking room. Someone reported seeing him standing there, without a life jacket, staring at the painting of *Plymouth Harbour*. His old debating partner, William Thomas Stead, was there too, sitting quietly with a book.

Some of the ship's officers, including Lightoller, Boxhall and Pitman, who had been put in charge of individual lifeboats, had survived. Others, like Mr Murdoch, were among the dead.

There had been many acts of heroism during the night – some of which, undoubtedly, will never be known. But one that must not be overlooked was that of Arthur Rostron, captain of the *Carpathia*, who guided his ship through a field of icebergs to come to the *Titanic*'s rescue. While his ship had been too far away to arrive before the sinking, her crew acted valiantly to rescue survivors. Another ship, the *Californian*, had apparently been much closer, but had shut down its wireless equipment minutes before the first disaster call went out. Some of the crew had seen the rockets being fired, but did not recognize them as a disaster signal.

In all, just over 700 of the *Titanic*'s 2,200 passengers and crew had survived. By far, the heaviest losses were among the steerage passengers and the crew. All thirty-six of the ship's engineers, who kept the engines and lights going until the very end, had apparently died.

And what of Holmes? Mr Lightoller told Miss Storm-Fleming that he had seen him struggling, hand to hand, with Moriarty just before the ship went down. But he could not say what happened to him after that.

'They say we will reach New York by Thursday,' said Miss Storm-Fleming.

I did not answer at once but lay there, staring at the ceiling.

'I was just thinking about Holmes...and about all those people on deck. Some just refused to believe that the ship would sink, right to the very end. Hundreds more might have been saved if they had taken the danger seriously. Did they really think that the *Titanic* was unsinkable?'

'I suppose we have become arrogant, somehow believing that we had overcome the forces of nature once and for all. We have forgotten humility. I think, if anything, the *Titanic* is a reminder for us to face the future with more humility. But, if you want to talk about legacies, let us consider the one left by Mr Holmes.'

'What do you mean?'

'Mr Holmes certainly believed in the power of reason, but there was far more to him than that. His character and unswerving devotion to justice were unmatched. And the clarity of his values gave him the courage to recognize the villains of the world. I say courage, because once he recognized an injustice, he felt duty bound to challenge it. And he did this with an energy and confidence that set an example to everyone else.'

'Indeed, he did, Miss Storm-Fleming.'

'Doctor Watson, you too have shown those qualities. In fact, they live on in your books. There is your legacy to future generations.'

There was a knock at the door and Miss Norton walked in. 'Why do you not come up on deck with me and get some fresh air?'

'Well, Doctor Watson?' said Miss Storm-Fleming. 'Are you ready for a turn on the deck?'

'Miss Norton, Miss Storm-Fleming, fresh air is just what is required.' I rose from the bed and smiled at my companions. 'We must be fit. There is still much to be done.'

Chapter Thirty

SUNDAY 21 APRIL 1912

It was reassuring to feel solid earth beneath my feet. The sky was blue and the sun had just risen over Chesapeake Bay. I was walking along the bank of the Severn River, which was dotted sparsely with oak and maple trees. I paused to listen to the chorus of chirping birds and the water splashing over the rocks. There is nothing quite like the serenity of a fresh spring morning.

I was being treated to this welcome respite by American intelligence officials. An acknowledgement of my role in the delivery of the submarine plans, they had offered me free use of a guest cottage at the US Naval Academy at Annapolis. I accepted gratefully.

My two companions of the last two weeks were also enjoying the hospitality of the US Navy and staying at guest cottages near mine.

Try as I might, I could not remove the haunting memories of the *Titanic*'s sinking and the loss of my dear friend from my mind. But here, alone with my thoughts, I was just beginning to comprehend fully the enormity of what had happened.

I walked on, poking at shrubs with my walking stick as I moved at a brisk pace. The air was becoming warmer and I considered stopping to remove my overcoat. The fresh air and exercise were making me hungry, and I was beginning to think about breakfast. I turned to see how far I had walked from the academy.

Behind me, I could see only the river and the vast solitude of the fields. I had apparently lost track of time and walked further than I had planned.

Then, in the distance, I saw another hiker. The man had just emerged from behind a ridge, and was walking along the river bank, following the same path I had just travelled. He was a tall, gaunt figure wearing a long grey travelling coat and close-fitting cloth cap. There was something familiar about the man – his gait, the look of his clothing – but I was too far away to obtain a good view.

As the man came closer I began to get a clearer look. I was stunned suddenly by the thought that someone might be playing a cruel joke on me. The man was the very image of my departed friend, Sherlock Holmes. He was even wearing the same type of outdoor clothing that he had worn during many of our investigations.

I decided to head back towards the naval academy. We would cross paths and I would soon get to the bottom of this mystery. As I began to move in his direction, the man suddenly stopped and raised his walking stick high into the air.

'Greetings, Watson!' he shouted. He then hurried forward at a faster pace, taking long strides all the way.

My head became dizzy with anticipation as I made my own way along the bank. Only concentration kept my legs moving. I saw that my hopes were not unfounded for I could see that my friend was very much alive.

When we reached each other I grabbed him by the shoulders and stared in disbelief, wondering if this could somehow be a twin.

Holmes had a satisfied smile on his face. He loved his little surprises.

'Yes, my dear Watson, it is me. And I must say, it is very good to see you, old fellow. Very good, indeed.'

'But how...?'

'Well, Miss Norton and Miss Storm-Fleming remarked on that very same question last night. It was their conclusion that I am indestructible. I found that most flattering, although...'

'Where have you been and why did you delay your return?' There was a note of anger and disappointment in my voice. 'It appears that everyone – except your best and oldest friend – has been aware that you are still alive.'

'My apologies, but I am not quite as thoughtless as I may seem. It is true that Miss Storm-Fleming has known for some time, but I only told Miss Norton last night. I knew that you have a habit of retiring early, so I decided to wait until this morning.'

'But it has been a week, Holmes. Where have you been?'

'Well, I am afraid that our friends in American intelligence, while very generous with their hospitality, have been rather secretive. They thought it was best for my mission that even my closest friends thought I was dead. It was not until yesterday that Miss Storm-Fleming and I were able to convince them otherwise.'

I calmed down and even managed a smile.

'Wherever did you get that outfit?' I asked. 'Surely they are not wearing such old-fashioned garb in America these days?'

'Oh, the ulster and deerstalker, they were Miss Storm-Fleming's idea. She used her influence to have them purchased at a shop in Baltimore and delivered here to the academy. She thought it would be...nostalgic for our reunion.'

'Indeed, it is... But Holmes, tell me...we thought you were dead. How did you manage to escape from the *Titanic*? And what about Moriarty?

Lightoller said he saw you struggling with him.'

'Yes, good old Lightoller. I owe him much, including my life.'

'Lightoller saved you?'

'Yes, but let me start at the beginning. As you know, while Miss Norton and I were on the boat deck, a page delivered a note from Moriarty.'

'Miss Norton knew that he asked you to meet him, but she did not know where.'

'The note directed me to go to the roof of the wheelhouse, the uppermost deck area of the ship. At that moment, there was very little activity there. The crew was busily loading passengers into lifeboats on the boat deck, one level below. On my way to meet Moriarty, I was apprehended by a member of the crew, who handed me a life jacket and insisted that I put it on. I must say, if I had not bowed to that sailor's orders, I would not be here today.

'At first, I could not find the man. The deck area above the wheelhouse actually extends back past the second funnel. Yet, while searching this large area, I had a sense that I was being watched. Frustrated by my failed attempt to locate Moriarty, I leaned over a rail and watched the activity below. It was a dreadful sight...men trying to comfort their families before loading them into lifeboats. I never in my life felt greater sadness.

'I was standing next to a lifeboat, similar to the one that you all departed in. I would later be saved by that boat, although I must say it seemed far more precarious than yours.

'As I looked at the deck below, I heard a deep voice from behind. It was Moriarty, standing there in a life jacket, staring at me with grim determination in his eyes. His words showed the utter contempt for human life that he shared with his brother: "Exciting, is it not?" he said. "It is unfortunate that survival is allowed for women and children only, rather than those of us who can make best use of it."

'I exchanged some remarks with him. I learned that the "Hot Russian Honey Bear" was a reference to the submarine plans – part of a prearranged code he had made with his buyer in New York. The "pipe organ in the smoking room" was, of course, the model of the *Titanic* in the reception room. This was their back-up position for exchanging the plans for money. I must say, he was quite upset that I had found his hiding place.

'Soon, overcome by anger, he lunged at me. We struggled about the deck for some time. Out of the corner of my eye I saw Lightoller and some crew cutting through the lashings of the Englehardt and attempting to launch it into the water, which was rising well above the bow. They must have thought we were quite mad to be struggling on the sloping deck as the ship was about to sink. But they made no effort to stop us. They had far more important matters on their minds. Soon, they were able to push the boat off the wheelhouse roof and into the water.

'As I continued to struggle with Moriarty, I felt the bow plunge downwards, then stop. A bulkhead had apparently given way. This caused water to flow over the boat deck, leaving our battleground as one of the last remaining oases. Some passengers began to struggle up to our deck, while others climbed towards the ship's stern.

'As you know, my knowledge of baritsu, the Japanese system of wrestling, has saved me from similar situations in the past. I slipped loose from his grip, and sent him tumbling back towards the sinking bow. Just then the ship began to tilt upwards at an ever-quickening pace. Moriarty fell back over the rail and into the water, amongst a frightened and freezing group of passengers. As the stern continued to rise, I decided that my only chance was to leave the ship. I jumped off the starboard side just as the ship's huge forward funnel broke free and went crashing down into the sea. It slammed into the water just where Moriarty had landed. I heard many screams of terror just before it hit the surface.

'The shock I felt as I hit the water was tremendous. I cannot describe how cold it was. Lightoller later told me that it felt as though a thousand knives had been driven into his body. I believe that is as good a description as any.

'I swam as far from the *Titanic* as possible as the ship slowly descended into the water. When it finally went under, the water was momentarily boiling with air bursting from the hull and debris floating to the surface. It was all I could do to keep my head above water long enough to get my next breath of air. I should note at this point that the struggle with Moriarty and my time in the water had removed the beard and make-up from my face. Commodore Giles Winter had disappeared with the *Titanic*.

'After the sea had settled a little I found myself clinging to the sides of the collapsible lifeboat that had been on top of the wheelhouse. It was floating upside down with a, group of passengers just barely managing to stay on top and was being rocked by some of my fellow swimmers who were trying to get out of the water. Soon Lightoller, who had been hanging on to the side, climbed onto the boat and took charge. He managed to get many of us into standing positions on the boat, all facing in the same direction. As the boat tilted, he ordered us to shift left or right to compensate for the boat's movement. We stayed there, with the cold water lapping over our feet and ankles. As time passed, some succumbed to the elements and fell into the water. But many of us survived and were picked up by the *Carpathia*.

'No one on board the lifeboat had paid any attention to me. They were all too busy trying to stay alive. With the help of Mr Lightoller, I was moved secretly to a private cabin on the *Carpathia* and allowed to stay there until the ship arrived in New York. For the sake of my mission, the secrecy of my arrival had been maintained.

'After a day's recuperation, I asked Lightoller to bring Miss Storm-

Fleming to me. Of course, she was quite surprised to see that I was alive. She went on to arrange my meeting with American intelligence authorities in New York, asking me to stay in hiding until then. That, of course, prevented me from contacting you and letting you know that I was safe and sound. But believe me, old chap, I had no intention of beginning my mission without seeing you first.'

'Well, at least it was not three years, as it was after the Reichenbach Falls. That was a far more dramatic resurrection from the dead.'

'Now, now, Watson, you know that I have apologized for that many times.'

'I know, Holmes.' I smiled and patted him on the shoulder. 'But after this mission, I expect to see you again immediately. And no more dramatic reappearances.'

'Indeed, but I also have a request to make.'

I nodded.

'If, after I return from this mission, you decide to publish an account of it, I would like to choose the title.'

'And what would you like to call it?'

He stroked his chin with his thumb and forefinger, and looked towards the sky.

'I would like you to call it *His Last Bow,* for after this I plan to retire – permanently.'

'You have my word.' We shook hands.

'Well, Watson, to breakfast, but please do not eat too much.'

'And why not, pray?'

'The cook is preparing a special meal for us.'

'A special meal?'

'Yes, we are having woodcock, with all the trimmings.'

'But Holmes, Mrs Hudson used to make that all the time. I have long since grown tired of it.'

'And all this time I thought it was your favourite... Good old Watson, never one to complain.'

'I am sure it will be quite delicious.' We both laughed.

'Shall we return to the academy?' I said.

He nodded and we strolled back along the river bank, quietly enjoying a most spectacular dawn.

Acknowledgements

Special thanks are owed to Martin Breese, who first published this book back in 1996 and used his magic touch to produce a quality publication and ensure its successful introduction to readers.

My deepest appreciation goes to family members and friends who provided help and encouragement when I was writing this book. This includes past and current members of Seattle's great Sherlockian society, *The Sound of the Baskervilles*, with whom I have shared canonical adventures for the past three decades. I would also like to thank Bob Cumbow for his advice and support.

This book would not have been possible without the research of *Titanic* historians, particularly Walter Lord, author of *A Night to Remember* and *The Night Lives On*. A wealth of information on the structure, equipment and interior features of *Titanic* is contained in a 1911 issue of *The Shipbuilder* magazine.

Above all, I owe my thanks to Sir Arthur Conan Doyle, whose Sherlock Holmes stories first captivated me in my childhood and still have a firm hold on my imagination.

William Seil
November 2011

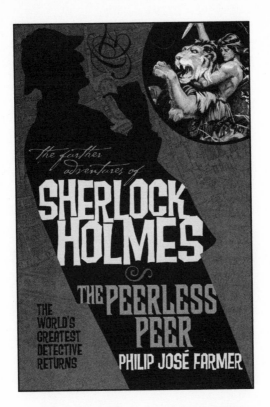

THE FURTHER ADVENTURES
OF SHERLOCK HOLMES

THE PEERLESS PEER

Philip José Farmer

During the Second World War, Mycroft Holmes dispatches his brother, Sherlock, and Dr. Watson to recover a stolen formula. During their perilous journey, they are captured by a German zeppelin. Subsequently forced to abandon ship, the pair parachute into the dark African jungle where they encounter the lord of the jungle himself…

ISBN: 9780857681201

AVAILABLE NOW!

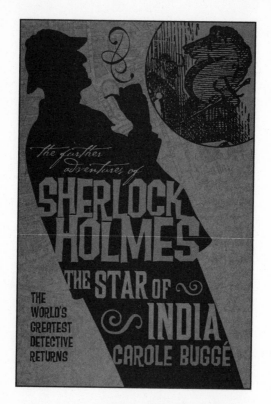

THE FURTHER ADVENTURES
OF SHERLOCK HOLMES

THE STAR OF INDIA

Carole Buggé

Holmes and Watson find themselves caught up in a complex chessboard
of a problem, involving a clandestine love affair and the disappearance of a
priceless sapphire. Professor James Moriarty is back to tease and torment,
leading the duo on a chase through the dark and dangerous back streets of
London and beyond.

ISBN: 9780857681218

AVAILABLE NOW!

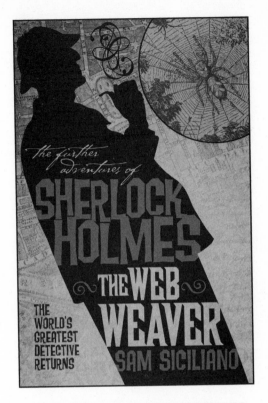

THE FURTHER ADVENTURES
OF SHERLOCK HOLMES

THE WEB WEAVER

Sam Siciliano

A mysterious gypsy places a cruel curse on the guests at a ball. When a series of terrible misfortunes affects those who attended, Mr. Donald Wheelwright engages Sherlock Holmes to find out what really happened that night. Can he save Wheelwright and his beautiful wife Violet from the devastating curse?

ISBN: 9780857686985

AVAILABLE NOW!

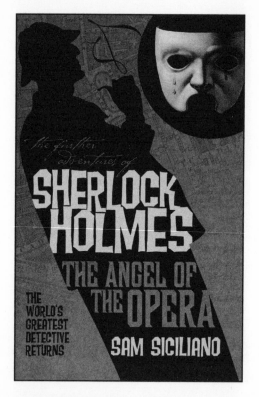

THE FURTHER ADVENTURES
OF SHERLOCK HOLMES
THE ANGEL OF THE OPERA
Sam Siciliano

Paris 1890. Sherlock Holmes is summoned across the English Channel to
the famous Opera House. Once there, he is challenged to discover the true
motivations and secrets of the notorious phantom, who rules its depths with
passion and defiance.
ISBN: 9781848568617

AVAILABLE NOW!

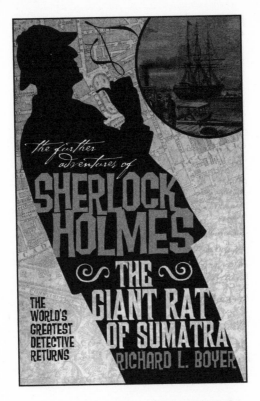

THE FURTHER ADVENTURES
OF SHERLOCK HOLMES

THE GIANT RAT OF SUMATRA

Richard L. Boyer

For many years, Dr. Watson kept the tale of The Giant Rat of Sumatra a secret.
However, before he died, he arranged that the strange story of the giant rat should
be held in the vaults of a London bank until all the protagonists were dead...

ISBN: 9781848568600

AVAILABLE NOW!

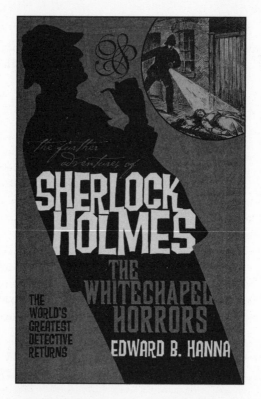

THE FURTHER ADVENTURES
OF SHERLOCK HOLMES

THE WHITECHAPEL HORRORS

Edward B. Hanna

Grotesque murders are being committed on the streets of Whitechapel.
Sherlock Holmes believes he knows the identity of the killer–Jack the
Ripper. But as he delves deeper, Holmes realizes that revealing the
murderer puts much more at stake than just catching a killer…
ISBN: 9781848567498

AVAILABLE NOW!

PROFESSOR MORIARTY: THE HOUND OF THE D'URBERVILLES

Kim Newman

Imagine the twisted evil twins of Holmes and Watson and you have the dangerous duo of Professor James Moriarty—wily, snake-like, fiercely intelligent, terrifyingly unpredictable—and Colonel Sebastian 'Basher' Moran—violent, politically incorrect, debauched. Together they run London crime, owning police and criminals alike.

A one-stop shop for all things illegal, from murder to high-class heists, Moriarty and Moran have a stream of nefarious visitors to their Conduit Street rooms, from the Christian zealots of the American West, to the bloodthirsty Si Fan and *Les Vampires* of Paris, as well as a certain Miss Irene Adler...

"It's witty, often hilarious stuff. The author portrays the scurrilous flipside of Holmes's civil ordered world, pokes fun at 'guest stars' from contemporary novels and ventures into more outré territory than Conan Doyle even dared."
Financial Times

"*The Hound of the d'Ubervilles* is a clever, funny mash-up of a whole range of literary sources including Thomas Hardy, HG Wells, EW Hornung, Maurice Leblanc and most of all, Conan Doyle's Sherlock Holmes stories and novels... It is extravagantly gruesome, gothic and grotesque."
The Independent

SHERLOCK HOLMES
THE BREATH OF GOD

Guy Adams

The nineteenth century is about to draw to a close. In its place will come the twentieth, a century of change, a century of science, a century that will see the superstitions of the past swept away.

There are some who are determined to see that never happens.

A body is found crushed to death in the London snow. There are no footprints anywhere near it. It is almost as if the man was killed by the air itself. This is the first in a series of attacks that sees a handful of London's most prominent occultists murdered. While pursuing the case, Sherlock Holmes and Dr. Watson find themselves traveling to Scotland to meet with the one person they have been told can help: Aleister Crowley.

As dark powers encircle them, Holmes' rationalist beliefs begin to be questioned. The unbelievable and unholy are on their trail as they gather a group of the most accomplished occult minds in the country: Doctor John Silence, the so-called "Psychic Doctor"; supernatural investigator Thomas Carnacki; runic expert and demonologist Julian Karswell...

But will they be enough? As the century draws to a close it seems London is ready to fall and the infernal abyss is growing wide enough to swallow us all.

A brand-new original novel, detailing a thrilling new case for the acclaimed detective Sherlock Holmes.

WWW.TITANBOOKS.COM